PUTTING THE CLUES TOGETHER

Addie added *argument?* to the blackboard, stood back to review, and then drew a line to the list of names above. "These are all Jared's business associates in Greyborne Harbor. The current line of investigation is focusing on the fact that one of them wasn't happy with their business arrangement or the terms of it or something and killed Jared during an altercation . . ."

"To get their contracts back or some other documents he had that were in the briefcase, which matches the point you have about Jared letting the person into the store Monday morning because he knew them."

"Yes," said Addie, "but how does that fit with the misunderstanding about the briefcase having already been paid for in Boston?"

Books by Lauren Elliott

MURDER BY THE BOOK

PROLOGUE TO MURDER

MURDER IN THE FIRST EDITION

PROOF OF MURDER

A PAGE MARKED FOR MURDER

UNDER THE COVER OF MURDER

TO THE TOME OF MURDER

Published by Kensington Publishing Corp.

A Beyond the Page Bookstore Mystery

TO THE TOME OF
MURDER

Lauren Elliott

KENSINGTON
PUBLISHING CORP.

www.kensingtonbooks.com

KENSINGTON BOOKS are published by

Kensington Publishing Corp.
119 West 40th Street
New York, NY 10018

All Kensington titles, imprints, and distributed lines are available at special quantity discounts for bulk purchases for sales promotion, premiums, fund-raising, educational, or institutional use.

Special book excerpts or customized printings can also be created to fit specific needs. For details, write or phone the office of the Kensington Sales Manager: Attn.: Sales Department. Kensington Publishing Corp., 119 West 40th Street, New York, NY 10018. Phone: 1-800-221-2647.

The K logo is a trademark of Kensington Publishing Corp.

First Printing: November 2021
ISBN: 978-1-4967-3512-6

ISBN: 978-1-4967-3516-4 (ebook)

10 9 8 7 6 5 4 3 2 1

Printed in the United States of America

Chapter 1

Addie Greyborne swiped at the condensation on the window and pressed her nose against the cold glass. Her face lit up when Paige Stringer, her assistant manager—who had been following her hand directions—placed the last copy of Louisa May Alcott's *Aunt Jo's Scrap Bag* six-volume set of short stories front and center of the Thanksgiving display. Addie gave her an excited two-thumbs up, clasped the collar of her bulky tunic sweater to halt the biting, damp wind from snaking down her back, and dashed toward the door.

"Brr." She shivered as she bolted into Beyond the Page, her book and curio shop. The door bells tinkled merrily above her. "It's *really* nippy out there."

"It seems awfully early in the year for all this, doesn't it?" said Paige, gazing beyond the bay window they were decorating. "It's still three weeks until Thanksgiving."

"I know. I was stunned when I woke up this morning to see all *that* covering Greyborne Harbor." Addie waved her hand toward the white landscape beyond the door. "And I'm afraid the air smells like we might be in for more snow before the day is done."

She stamped her numbed feet on the doormat and gazed down past her skinny-legged jeans at her little black booties. "I think it's time for the winter boots to come out of the closet, too, because these aren't going to cut it if this is the kind of winter we're in for."

A blast of frigid air swirled around Addie as the door opened behind her, and a Yorkipoo scampered in, dragging a tousled redhead through the door. "Slow down," Serena squealed. "There's your mommy. See, I didn't lie to you. Now, you can relax."

"Where have you two been all this time?" Addie bent down to sweep the excited little fur ball into her arms. She warded off an over-exuberant pink tongue as it lapped at her face. "When you offered to take Pippi for a walk, I had no idea you meant around the *entire* town." She chuckled and pushed the little Yorkipoo's head away from her mouth.

"Well"—Serena unclipped the leash from Pippi's collar and handed it to Addie—"Auntie Serena took our little friend here shopping. Look at her new booties. Aren't they just the dearest?" Serena's weather-mottled face turned a deeper shade of red as she eyed the pink, laced, knee-high leather boots on the little dog's wriggling paws. "I knew they'd be perfect for her." She gave the dog a scratch behind the ear. "After all, we have to keep those little tootsies warm and snuggly, don't we?" she cooed.

"She already had some on, plus she has three more sets

at home," Addie said with a soft laugh, as she fingered the supple leather and slipped them off her little friend's feet. "But I do admit they are nice ones, so thank you." She grinned and admired the laced boots in her free hand as she stepped back into the shop to let Serena pass. "Now, tell me something, Mrs. Ludlow." She eyed her friend warily. "Since your mothering instincts seem to be working on overdrive right now, is there something you want to share with us?"

Serena's freckles stood out against the rosy blush that made an appearance when her emotions got the best of her and she tried to hide her feelings. Addie knew all her friend's *tells* well after the past couple of years. "Is there"—Addie fixed her steadfast gaze on her—"something we should know?"

Serena's face turned from a winter-chilled ruddy to a piqued shade of crimson. "I . . . um . . . am not sure yet?" She bit her lip and cast her glance downward. "Maybe?" she mumbled, wincing.

"Really?" The booties dropped from Addie's hand as she seized Serena's jacket sleeve. "Fantastic! How long? When are you due? Tell us."

Serena shook her head and raised her gaze to meet Addie's. "I'm not sure . . . I've been too chicken to take the test."

"Why? Isn't that something both you and Zach would want to know, now? You know, so you can start planning?"

"Yes, but . . ."

"But what?" Addie studied her muted friend's paling face. "Are you afraid you're not and don't want to get your hopes up to have them crushed?"

"No." Serena twisted her gloves in her hands. "I'm afraid I am, and I don't—"

"I remember that feeling," said Paige, gliding up to Serena's side. "When I was pregnant with Emma, I was terrified to take the test. Torn between dreading I was and what that would mean, you know all the changes it would bring to my life. However, at the same time secretly hoping I was and petrified to discover I wasn't." She placed her arm around Serena's quivering shoulder. "Is that how you're feeling about it?"

Serena nodded.

Paige leaned her curly blond head on Serena's shoulder and whispered, "Take your time. It is what it is, test or no test. Then when you're ready to do it, I'm pretty sure you'll be able to deal with the results, whatever the outcome."

"Thanks." Serena squeezed Paige's hand. "You're right. Test or no test, it is what it is no matter what the result." She slid her jacket off, laid it across a counter stool in front of the antique Victorian bar Addie used as a sales and coffee counter, and gazed back at her friends.

Paige flashed a reassuring smile and Addie shrugged. "Okay, as long as you know we're here for you regardless of the outcome."

"I know and thank you. So?" She glanced past Addie toward the window display. "What are the two of you cooking up over there? Need some help?"

Addie glanced back at the window then at Serena. "It's almost ten. Don't you have to get next door to Serena-TEA?"

"Nope." Serena skirted past Addie to the far side bay window and giggled when the wet soles of her boots made mouse-like squeaks as she crossed the polished, wide-planked wooden flooring. "Anyway," she said glancing down at her boots or *huggy things,* as Addie called them, "ever since I went on my river cruise honeymoon in England last June, and Elli commandeered her grandmother, Vera, as a volunteer to help her out when you guys all got put in that lockdown, I've discovered that my presence really isn't needed during opening hours."

"Yes, but that was six months ago." Paige glanced questioningly at her. "I knew through Elli that her grandmother was still helping out on occasion, but I didn't know it was a permanent thing."

"It wasn't really until recently. But Vera hated being retired," Serena said. "She even tried to work in the Hollingsworth Real Estate office with her daughter Maggie."

"I hear that didn't last long." Addie chuckled.

"No, those two get on like oil and water. Then Elli told me how miserable her grandmother was now that her services weren't required in the tea shop, and I was still trying to set up our new house and deal with Zach being home every night."

"Yeah, but you have to admit," said Addie, "it must be nice that he's working full-time day shifts at Doctor Lim's clinic and doesn't have to pick up all those evening shifts serving at the Grey Gull Inn anymore. You know, since he's finished his internship and is a full-on naturopathic doctor."

"I guess, but who knew having him home every night would be such a change?" Serena said. "Anyway, I was starting to feel overwhelmed with all the changes marriage brought, and I felt pulled in too many directions. So, I asked Vera if she wanted to come back on a paid, part-time basis."

"Well, I'll be," said Paige. "I mean I've seen her in there, but I had no idea she was actually on staff now and wasn't volunteering. Neither she nor Elli said a word about that."

"No, they wouldn't," Serena said. "She still is a volunteer as far as she's concerned as she has refused to accept any pay for her services, but I think I'm wearing her down. I keep pointing out how she's jumped in with both feet and has been a true godsend. Her having been born and raised in England, for most of her early years, at least, has made it so easy for me to convert my shop into more of an English teahouse than I ever thought possible. I tell you, those two, Elli and Vera Hollingsworth, have embraced my new vision and have everything running like a well-oiled machine."

"How does that make you feel? I mean the shop was your dream and your baby . . ." Addie's hand flew to her mouth. "Sorry, I guess baby was a bad analogy, I didn't mean to—"

Serena waved her off. "It's actually been great. It's given me time to get used to having a man under foot *every* night, but I've managed to keep him busy at least. You know, hanging pictures and rearranging all my new ornaments and the antique furniture I came across."

"You mean everything you pilfered from my basement and attic?" Addie laughed.

"I had to make sure everything was perfect so it would do that historic craftsman bungalow that we bought from Gloria justice, didn't I?" she said with a teasing grin. "It appears that your love of everything old has rubbed off on me, finally."

"Good, maybe you won't balk this coming spring about going to any garage sales with me."

"As long as they're not at any haunted houses, it shouldn't be a problem," Serena said with a wry smile.

"Does this mean you're a lady of leisure now," Paige asked, pulling a trolley piled with books closer to the window display.

"Not really. I still go in to make up the special-order tea blends and do up all the packaging and bookkeeping, so it's not like I'm never there. I just am not pressured to be there all the time." She leaned against an end-unit bookcase. A faint smile touched her lips.

"What's the smile for?" asked Addie.

"It's also given me time to learn how to cook *real* meals, not just desserts and pastries for the shop, and I think Zach likes us not eating out all the time," she said with a little snigger. "I know he's gained a couple of pounds recently anyway."

"Does that mean you're entering this?" Paige fished a piece of paper out of a binder on the book trolley and thrust it into her hand.

Serena glanced down at the brightly colored brochure announcing the annual MAKE IT - BAKE IT FOOD MARKET cooking and baking competition and handed it back to Paige. "Yup, why not. I thought I'd throw my hat in and see what happens."

"Good for you," said Addie, pulling a copy of Sarah Josepha Hale's 1827 edition of *Northwood: A Tale of New England* from the cart. "You asked what we're cooking up, and this is it."

Serena glanced at the book and then blankly at Addie.

"This"—Addie pointed to the brochure—"where it says the theme for the competition is to be authentic Civil War Thanksgiving dinner dishes and desserts."

Serena pointed to the book in Addie's hand. "So that is a Civil War recipe book?"

"No, not really. This is more like an entertaining editorial account that addresses the differences in lifestyle between people living in the North and South. However, it does include an entire chapter about a farming family in New Hampshire and their Thanksgiving meal." Addie waved toward the window display. "The point is, the displays are going to feature books and magazine articles from the Civil War period."

"The same period," Paige piped in, "that has been selected by the Essex County Association Chapter of the Massachusetts Historical Society, who, by the way, is sponsoring this year's weekend food festival and selected the theme for all the recipes entered."

Serena gulped. "I didn't realize when I read this that all the dishes entered *had* to be from that era."

Paige nodded.

"Did you guys happen to come across any recipes books then?" Serena looked from Paige to Addie hopefully.

"As a matter of fact . . ." Addie swung around and darted to the counter, tore the brown paper wrapping off a package, and slid out a stack of posters. "These might be of interest to you since it's clear"—she glanced back over her shoulder at Serena and gave her a knowing smile—"that you haven't selected a recipe yet." She spun around and displayed a full-colored sketch of an old-fashioned dinner table setting.

Serena fingered the semi-gloss poster. "Nice, but how will this help me?"

Addie slid the next poster to the front. "Because there are also copies of authentic Civil War recipes from the *Godey's Lady's Book* in here that my friend Barbara sent me from the Boston Library collection."

Serena's eyes filled with confusion as she glanced from the poster to Addie.

Addie grinned and laid out the posters across the counter. "*Godey's Lady's Magazine* or *Godey's Lady's Book,* as it is often referred to, was a Philadelphia-based monthly magazine that was in production from 1830 to 1878. For forty years, the magazine was edited by Sarah Josepha Hale, the same woman who wrote *Northwood,* that book I showed you. She also wrote many of the magazines articles, like this one." Addie pointed to one about Thanksgiving.

"Yes," said Paige, joining them, "but you might know her better as the author credited for writing the nursery rhyme, 'Mary Had a Little Lamb.'"

Serena nodded. "That I *have* heard of, but I don't think I ever thought too much about who wrote it."

"Most people don't," said Addie. "It's just one of those nursery rhymes we all grow up knowing but aren't aware of the history behind them."

"Addie was telling me earlier that there was some scandal about that, too," said Paige.

"Really?" Serena's eyes widened as she glanced over the posters. "There was a scandal over a nursery rhyme?"

Paige nodded. "Yup, it seems it may have been really written by a young boy about his friend Mary Sawyer's lamb that actually did follow her to school one day."

"Yes," said Addie, "but that was never actually proven because by the time Mary Sawyer made the claim, the poem was so well known that most people could recite it by heart. The case never held up in court."

"Interesting." Serena nodded. "But it really doesn't help me come up with an authentic Civil War recipe that's going to knock the socks off the judges and guarantee me the winning prize of five thousand dollars and . . . an article featuring my tea shop in the Christmas edition of the historical society's newsletter, does it?" she said, searching through the stack of posters.

"No it doesn't," Addie said laughingly. "It's just something interesting about the woman behind this incredible magazine. Who also, by the way, relentlessly petitioned Abraham Lincoln to sign an executive order proclaiming Thanksgiving a permanent holiday."

"What about the pilgrims?" exclaimed Serena, her face reflecting the disbelief in her voice. "Wasn't it celebrated before that because of them?"

"Yes, originally," said Addie, "but mainly in the northern states because the South didn't trust anything northerners celebrated and even then, it was all very erratic with a different date being set by each state governor."

"So the South didn't have Thanksgiving?"

"Not so much before the proclamation I don't think," said Addie. "That didn't happen until the country became so decimated by the continuation of the Civil War, that finally Secretary of State William Seward, along with a lot of prompting by Sarah Josepha Hale and the articles she wrote for her *Godey's Lady's Book*, convinced Lincoln that something had to be done to try to reunite a fractured nation."

"Yeah," added Paige, "and I read that it wasn't until October of 1863 that Lincoln proclaimed a national holiday to be observed on the last Thursday of November. You know, in the hope that it would help bring the nation and families together again after the war."

"Wow, she sounds like an amazing woman, and fairly influential given the times." Serena glanced down at the posters. "Can I look through these to see if there's something I can use?"

"Sure, take your time. Paige and I have to finish the window display before we start tacking those up around the shop anyway."

"Great, thanks." Serena grinned and plopped down on a stool before scanning the images. "Some of these are just fashion pictures from that period."

"Yeah, but keep digging. There are recipes in the pile too. Barbara wasn't sure exactly of my vision for the display, so she threw in a little of everything."

Addie scooped up the books on the counter to make room for the sketches, and Serena discarded the ones that weren't relevant. She paused and glanced at her cell phone vibrating on the counter beside the shop landline where she had placed it earlier. *Hudson's Creations on Main* flashed across the screen.

"Is that the dashing Doctor Simon Emerson calling to check up on you?" Paige said, laughing from where she was sorting through books on the trolley by the window display.

"No." Addie chuckled and reached for her phone. "Unfortunately, it's only my cousin."

"Before you answer that," said Paige, "wanna make a bet she's calling to tell you that she broke a nail and can't

make the sweet-potato casserole you assigned as her con-
tribution to our group Thanksgiving dinner?"

"I want a piece of that bet." Serena chuckled.

"Quiet, both of you." Addie shushed them with a wave
of her hand and grabbed the phone. "Hi, Kalea, what's
up? . . . Wait, slow down . . . I can't understand you . . .
what? Who? No, I can't make out what you're saying.
Calm down . . . Where? Never mind I'll be right there."

Chapter 2

Addie flew up the back stairs in the alley behind her cousin's dress shop and pulled on the door handle. It didn't budge. She pounded on the unyielding door with her fist. No answer. She pounded again and felt a distinct thudding of a bass drum through the vibration of the steel door under her hand. She banged harder and winced when pain shot through her arm. It was no use. The thudding music blasting from inside was just too loud.

Her cousin's last cryptic words to her rang clearly in her memory. She hopped back into her red-and-white Mini Cooper, threw it in reverse, raced down the alley, turned onto the front side of Main Street, and came to a skidding halt on the slush-covered roadway in front of the dress shop. She flew out of the car, yanked on the store's front door handle to no avail, and hammered on the glass.

Pressing her face to the window, she desperately sought out signs of life from inside.

Her cousin glanced up from where she sat on the floor by the sales counter, stumbled to her feet, and staggered to the door. When it opened, Addie was hit by a wall of crescendoing symphony music. She threw her hands over her ears, sprinted across the marble floor to the stereo unit behind the u-shaped sales counter, switched it off, and turned back to her cousin, who still stood beside the door. Her face was gray and haggard.

"Kalea, what's going on, and what's with the music?"

Kalea's unseeing eyes met Addie's. She didn't say a word but pointed toward the counter.

Addie took a quick look around the sales desk and shrugged. "But you said something about a murder, or did I hear you wrong? Were you robbed?" She glanced at the closed till.

Kalea shook her head and pointed again.

Confused, Addie stepped around the open end of the counter and focused her gaze in the direction her cousin had indicated and promptly tripped over a purse from the display table lying on the floor. She gingerly stepped over another and then another. She scanned the sales floor area to her left. Handbags from the center display stand weren't the only things littering the floor. Most of the shoes from the wall rack on the far side were also strewn across the floor. She glanced back questioningly at her cousin, and the fear that swelled in Kalea's hazel eyes made Addie's skin prickle.

In her whole life, Addie had never seen her usually flippant, high-spirited cousin in this condition, and it worried her. What was around the end of the counter in the small customer sitting area that had her on edge like this? She tiptoed to the counter, afraid of what might meet her. Addie gasped and danced a step backward. There on the floor was Jared Munroe, Kalea's boyfriend—a broken plastic clothes hanger protruding precariously from his lower chest. Addie grabbed the wall for support but missed and tumbled into a dress rack trolley.

Frenzied, she clawed at the dresses, which tore away from their hangers. Pawing them from her face, she pushed the mound of brightly colored prints off her and wobbled to her feet. Her heart pounded out a staccato beat against her chest wall in pure rebellion to the horror she now couldn't unsee. Kalea, now lying in a heap on the floor by the door, sniveled.

"Kalea." She raced to her side. "What happened?" Addie sat her up and shook her shoulders. "Who did this?"

Kalea's head flopped to the side, and large tears rolled from her eyes and dribbled down her cheeks. "I don't know," she hoarsely whispered.

"Did you see *anything*?"

Kalea didn't answer.

"I said, did you see anything?" Addie shook Kalea's shoulders again. Her cousin's head straightened, and her gaze locked on Addie's.

"No," she replied meekly.

Addie relaxed her grip on Kalea's shoulders, sat back on her haunches, took a series of deep, head-clearing breaths, and studied her cousin's anguished face. "Okay," Addie said, "tell me exactly what you do know."

Kalea's detached gaze traveled back toward the sitting area she had created for spouses, friends, and family members to wait while her ladies tried on outfits.

Addie took both Kalea's hands in hers, forcing her cousin to look back at her. "Start at the beginning, and tell me *exactly* what happened?"

"I don't know," she finally said, stifling a sob. "Jared stayed with me last night upstairs in my apartment. He said he had an early meeting this morning in Salem, so if he was gone when I got up, not to worry." She broke into heartfelt sobs, and her fingers tightened their grip on Addie's.

"Take your time," Addie whispered. "What happened then, after you got up?"

Kalea pushed a tangled mass of auburn hair from her face, wiped her damp cheeks with the back of her hand, and sucked in a noisy breath. "I didn't think twice about it and got ready to come down to work as usual to open at ten. When I got to the foot of the stairs and came around the corner onto the sales floor—" She glanced back at the far end of the counter and shuddered. "That's when, that's when . . ." She pulled her hands away from Addie's. A bandage on her finger snagged on Addie's bracelet, and Kalea tugged her hand away, revealing a gaping wound across its tip.

"Ouch," said Addie, "that looks sore. Are you okay?"

"I guess," Kalea said, gazing at her hand as though she was seeing it for the first time.

"Good." Addie massaged her temples. "So you didn't see anything or anyone, right?"

Kalea shook her head. "I didn't know what to do, so I called you. I just couldn't . . ." Her voice trailed off as her whole body quaked.

Addie squeezed her hand reassuringly.

Okay, think, Addie, think. What to do? Call 911, but check the body first! What if he was still alive and in distress? The dispatcher needs to know if he's injured or . . . dead.

Addie scrambled to the far side of the u-shaped counter, crouched down beside his body, and placed two fingers on his neck under his jawline. Nothing. Her eyes opened just enough to see past her lashes. She focused on his upper chest and avoiding the grisly appearing diaphragm area. No rise or fall. She leaned over. Her cheek hovered just above his gaping mouth. No wisps of air whispered against her skin. Shakily, she rose to her feet, turned away in fear of her stomach rebelling, sucked in a wobbly breath, retrieved her cell phone from her jacket pocket, and dialed 911.

When she clicked off from the dispatcher, a wave of relief surged through her. The police were on their way. They would be able to figure this out, and perhaps when Simon came and conducted his coroner's onsite examination of the scene and the body, he would determine that Addie's hopes were correct, and it *was* an accident. Jared had most likely walked into a clothing rack in the dark and impaled himself. She knew she might be reaching with that theory, but it was the only logical explanation she could come up with. After all, she knew Kalea was having problems with the overseas shipment of bulk clothes hangers she'd purchased. There had been an ongoing issue with everything from the hooks snapping off to the bars breaking and even a few that the shoulder arms snapped under the weight of a heavier garment. In Addie's mind that was the only plausible justification for a piece of the arm becoming embedded in Jared's abdomen.

However, those hopes faded as she surveyed the disheveled state of the sales room. It was clear by the purses, the shoes, and the costume jewelry scattered across the floor that something violent had occurred prior to Jared's body being discovered by her cousin. Addie glanced back over at Kalea sitting on the floor. Her long willowy arms clutched around her knees, and she rocked robotically back and forth.

Addie quietly approached and crouched down in front of her and lifted her chin so her gaze met Addie's. "Kalea," she said softly, "the police are on their way. They're going to have a lot of questions for you. Do you think you're up to answering them now?"

Kalea's vacant gaze locked with hers, but she nodded.

"Good, it's going to be tough on you to relive what happened this morning, so when you've had enough, don't be afraid to tell them you need a break." Addie waited for a response. "Kalea, did you hear me?"

Kalea nodded, sniffling.

"Good, but first," Addie sat back, "I have a question. What was with the loud philharmonic music when I came in? That's so unlike you. That's not what you usually listen to?"

Kalea's gaze dropped. "I needed to drown out the noise in my head after I found Jar—him. I couldn't think because of all the voices screaming in my head about what I was seeing." She met Addie's gaze. "That's his favorite symphony and I thought . . . I thought if I played it . . . he'd wake up." She buried her face in her hands, weeping, and resumed her aimless rocking.

Behind Addie, a snap of cold enveloped her, and she turned to see an officer bursting through the door, crouched low, gun drawn.

"It's okay, Jefferies, we're the only two in here."

"Are you sure?" he whispered.

The fine hairs on the back of Addie's neck prickled. "No." She swallowed hard. "I . . . I didn't check the back room after I found—"

After giving a young officer hand signals directing him to the back, Officer Jefferies made his way toward the sales counter. The other officer circled around the two women on the floor by the door and guardedly made his way toward the cream-colored, swagged-curtained entrance leading to the back storage and dressing rooms. A moment later an "All clear" rang out, and Officer Curtis Brewster, Elli's boyfriend, appeared in the doorway, holstering his gun.

Addie let out a pent-up breath. *How stupid, stupid, stupid of me.* She mentally scolded herself for not thinking of making sure there was no one hiding back there before she did anything else. *What if* rang through her mind over and over.

As Jefferies holstered his firearm, his eyes scanned the sales floor from the open end of the counter, and he glanced at Addie and Kalea. "The chief will be along soon. I think we can leave the questioning to him, so I'm going to just take a look at the . . ." He swallowed and fixed his gaze on Addie's. "The victim. Can you point me in the direction?"

"Over here." Brewster, still standing by the curtained entrance, jerked his head toward the far end of the counter.

Addie nodded at Jefferies in agreement. He flashed her a weak smile and cautiously stepped over and around the merchandise scattered across the floor to where Brewster now stood by the sitting area.

Addie wrapped her arm around her cousin's trembling

shoulders and whispered, "When we're done here, how about I take you upstairs and make us a pot of Serena's Heavenly Delight tea?"

Kalea nodded mutely.

The door flew open. Addie looked up. Her gaze met Police Chief Marc Chandler's expressionless, honey-brown eyes as he glanced from her to Kalea and then watchfully made his way past the merchandise on the sales room floor over to where Jefferies and Brewster were taking photos of the body. Addie placed a comforting hand on her cousin's shoulder and then rose to her feet. Her gaze fixed on the three officers as Jefferies gave their initial findings report to Marc. He waved Addie over, and she sidestepped around the purses and stopped at his side.

"Wanna tell me what happened here?"

She took a deep breath and delved into a babbling account of exactly what occurred when Kalea called her and everything that transpired right up to the point when Jefferies arrived. When she finished, she struggled to catch her breath but still managed to force out her hopeful speculation about the possibility of an accidental impalement.

Marc glanced at the body and then back at Addie. "We'll see what the evidence says. Thank you. You can go back and join your cousin." He glanced over at Kalea. "I'll question her in a while after she's calmed down a little more."

Addie stumbled back to Kalea still huddled by the door. She dropped down beside her as Lieutenant Jerry Fowley entered the store, a black crime-scene investigation bag in hand. Marc gestured for him, Jefferies, and Brewster to rejoin him by the body. After a whispered discussion, Jerry disappeared into the back room, and Brewster strode past Addie, went out the door, and approached a cruiser that pulled up. He said something through the open window and the two officers got out and began stringing bands of yellow crime-scene tape around the perimeter of the dress shop entrance.

Brewster made a call on his police radio and removed another black crime-scene case from the back of the cruiser. He returned to the sales floor, where he was joined by Jefferies. The two officers began taking photos of the merchandise, then placed yellow numbered location markers in a spot as they collected the items, and dropped them into evidence bags.

As the flurry of activity through the door increased, Simon arrived with two paramedics wheeling in a gurney. Addie urged her cousin to inch back against the wall out of the way. Simon flashed her a fleeting nod of gratitude and mouthed, "Are you okay?" She nodded, and he strode over to Marc, and they scanned the scene where the body lay. Simon dropped out of Addie's sight when he crouched down behind the counter.

She glanced at her cousin, whose sobs had renewed, and then locked her gaze on Marc, willing him to look at her in the hopes that her eyes conveyed her feelings about leaving the two women in the center of all this commotion, and that he would do something about it.

Jerry came out of the back room and whispered something to Marc and pointed toward the back. Marc glanced over at Addie before following Jerry to the back-room entrance. Jerry gestured toward a box on the shelf just past the curtained doorway. Marc studied it for an instant and then disappeared down the hall. When he returned a few moments later, he gestured for Addie to come.

She helped Kalea to her feet and supported her as they made their way past the officers bagging evidence.

"You can settle your cousin in the back, but then I want you to wait there in one of the dressing rooms until we're ready to take official statements."

"You can't be serious," Addie snapped and stared at him in disbelief. "You want to separate us?" Addie glanced at Kalea and then at Marc. "Can't you see she's in shock? She needs someone to stay with her right now."

His jaw tightened, but he stepped aside and motioned for her to go into the back room. As she walked past, Addie glanced at the box that he and Jerry appeared to have taken an interest in. It was filled with pieces of broken clothes hangers. She recalled Kalea mentioning to her that she was going to ship them back to the supplier and demand a refund. Addie finally understood why as the box was overflowing with hanger shrapnel.

Kalea wobbled, and Addie clasped her tighter as she aided her cousin past the two curtained dressing rooms. If only she could make it down the narrow hallway, past the small bathroom on their right, and to the closed door that led up to the apartment on the second floor.

Marc must have sensed her destination. He cleared his throat and motioned toward the storage room.

"Really?" She fumed inwardly as she steered Kalea to the back and gently deposited her on a chair at the small table beside the alleyway door. She spun around and glared at Marc. "I think," she dropped her voice to a low hiss, "it might be a whole lot easier on Kalea and would help her calm down if you let her wait upstairs until you're ready to take her statement, don't you?"

Marc pursed his lips into a thin line. "I can only go by what you told me, and I haven't taken her statement yet.

But judging by the state of the sales room, we'll have to search the apartment before I can let anyone up there."

"Surely you can't be thinking that you'll find anything to do with what happened down here, do you?"

Addie didn't miss the slight tic in his jaw—his tell whenever he didn't want to talk about something or knew something he wasn't going to share. She stepped toward him. "Marc, what are you thinking?" She glanced back at Kalea. That detached, robotic look in Kalea's eyes had returned, and she peered back at Marc's solemn expression. "It can't be that she had something to do with what happened here, can it?"

"Addie," he whispered, leaning in so close his warm breath wafted across her cheek. "Let *me* . . . do . . . my . . . job."

At the strangled edge to his voice, her mouth snapped closed, taking away any thoughts she had of a retort.

"Chief," called Jefferies from the curtained back room entrance. "The doc needs to speak with you again."

"I'll be right there," said Marc flatly and turned to leave. He stopped. "And Addie . . . stay put, don't touch anything, and no talking between the two of you." He raked his fingers through his dark-chestnut hair. "The mayor's going to have my head as it is when he hears that I have broken every police procedure there is by allowing you two to remain together at a crime scene." He shot her a biting glance and marched off. "I'll be back soon to take your statements," he called over his shoulder.

Addie turned on her heel in exasperation and slid up to Kalea's side and gently rubbed her back. The gesture was not only to help calm her cousin and give consolation in her grief but also to calm herself. "Don't talk to each other," she huffed, mimicking Marc's voice. "I should separate you." *He couldn't possibly have Kalea on his radar, could he?* She glanced down at her sniffling cousin and shook her head. *No.* There was no way he could even think that she had something to do with the man she loved lying dead on the cold marble floor.

The heavy tread of boots caught her attention. Addie swiveled around and locked her questioning gaze on Marc's darkening eyes.

"Addie, step aside please," he ordered. His voice was cold and flat.

"What? Why?" She searched his face and those of Jerry and Officer Brewster's, who flanked either side of him.

"Kalea, I'd like you to accompany me to the police station."

Kalea glanced at Addie. Sheer terror reflected in her eyes.

"Are you arresting her?" Addie gasped in disbelief.

Marc broke their eye contact and stared down at a sniveling Kalea. "Please, Miss Hudson." He held his hand out to assist her to her feet. "We just have a few questions for you about the events that occurred here this morning."

Kalea nodded begrudgingly and slowly dragged herself to her feet.

"I thought you were going to question us here?" Addie said. "That's what you said, and I thought after I could take her upstairs and get her settled." Addie glanced at Kalea and then at him. "Surely you can see how all this has affected her. It would be the humane thing to do, wouldn't it?"

"This is for the best right now," Marc said firmly,

avoiding Addie's puzzled gaze. "You're free to go now. Someone will be by the bookstore later to take your official statement."

Addie glanced past Jerry and saw two officers, carrying a black crime-scene bag, open the closed door to the upstairs apartment and disappear up the stairs.

"That's it, Miss Hudson. Easy does it. Now, just come along with me," Marc said, steadying a wobbly Kalea, and ushering her toward the sales room. "Jerry," he said from the curtained door, "see that Miss Greyborne gets back to her bookstore now." He mumbled, "And for Pete's sake, Lieutenant, keep her away from the station today."

Chapter 3

"Jerry?" Addie grabbed his jacket sleeve as he started to follow the chief into the sales room. "What happened that's making him drag her into the station?"

Jerry glanced down at her hand on his arm.

"Sorry," she said, smiling weakly as she removed it. "But why can't he question her here like he said he would?" She glanced out the front window as Marc settled Kalea into the back of his cruiser. "You know that's ridiculous, right? He's treating her like she had something to do with Jared's death."

"Addie, let it go for now," said Jerry. He adjusted his police utility belt and strolled into the sales room. "I'll get someone to drive you to your bookstore," he called over his shoulder.

Addie's eyes widened. "But . . . but—" She glanced at Curtis, who stepped in line behind his superior officer.

"Wait! You all saw how upset she was at discovering her boyfriend's body, didn't you? So why is she being treated like a suspect?"

Officer Curtis Brewster paused and shook his head. "Addie, I can't tell you why. Let it go just like the lieutenant said."

"No, I can't. That's my cousin, and I can't believe for one second that she could be a suspect here?" She grabbed Curtis's arm. "Please, tell me. Did something turn up that I don't know about?"

Curtis drew in a deep breath, puffed out his boyish cheeks, glanced into the sales room, and back at Addie. "All I'll say is"—his voice dropped to a murmur— "there's proof that he was murdered."

"So it wasn't an accident?"

"No, this is definitely a murder case . . ."

"And?"

"And there is no sign of a break-in. Plus evidence found on the body suggests—"

Jerry cleared his throat and flashed the young officer a warning glare.

"Suggests what?" Addie pleaded and fixed her gaze on his childlike, round eyes.

Curtis shook his head. "I can't," he said and scooted over to Jefferies, who was still numbering, collecting, and bagging merchandise from the floor.

Addie gagged on the bile rising in the back of her throat as the paramedics wheeled the gurney containing the black body bag out the door and loaded it into the back of the ambulance. Simon, who waited outside for the gurney to be loaded, glanced back through the window and flashed her a meek, helpless half smile and hopped into the ambulance before it pulled away.

The pit of her stomach rolled as she surveyed the disheveled sales room area. None of this could be real, could it? She rubbed her forehead and tried to make sense of what occurred, hoping it was a dream. Jerry laid his hand on her arm, and she jumped. No, it wasn't a dream. This was all too real, and she knew this wasn't a nightmare she could awake from.

"I'll give you a lift back to the shop," he said softly.

"Ah, no. That's okay." She shook her head. "My car's out front."

"Do you think you can drive right now?"

"Yeah, I'll be fine."

"Okay, but you heard the chief. Go back to your bookstore and wait for someone to come by to take your statement."

"Yup, and stay away from the station, right?" She looked up into his softening brown eyes.

"You heard that part too, huh?"

"I'm surprised that's all he said. Usually, I get an earful."

"I think he was trying to be . . ."

"Be what? Nice?"

"Yeah, considering how close to home this one hits for you."

"If he was trying to spare my feelings then why won't he tell me what's going on and why he had to take Kalea down to the station? You all saw the condition she was in. It's inhumane if you ask me. Jerry, what happened to change his mind?"

"Addie, you know I can't discuss an ongoing case."

"Right, but *he* could have given me a hint as to what happened to change his mind about taking our statements here in the back room and"—she waved her hand toward the window—"what just happened."

"Please." He shifted uncomfortably in his boots. "Just go back to your shop and wait. I won't be much longer here, and then I'll come by to take your statement."

"Okay," she said, resigning herself to the fact that he was going to play by the rules. For now. But she mentally crossed her fingers that she could get him to slip a little something her way when he questioned her later.

Addie walked to her car, and her head spun with Curtis's last words. *There's proof that he was murdered, and it wasn't an accident. There were no signs of a break-in and evidence on the body that suggested . . . what? What did it suggest that Kalea may have killed the only man she said she ever truly loved?* On mental autopilot, she drove to the next left turn down Birch and into the alley behind her bookstore and pulled into her parking space. She loosened her white knuckled grip on the steering wheel, shifted the Mini into park and glanced around, not sure how she even got there. Instinctively, she got out, and teetered through the back door into her shop. An all-encompassing numbness settled through her mind and body, and she collapsed on a wooden book crate in the storage room.

The jarring rings of laughter echoed in her ears, and she realized Paige and Serena, not aware of the morning's events, were having a good giggle over something out front. Laughter seemed so foreign to her in this moment, and she knew that when she made her appearance on the bookstore floor, it would become just that to them, too. Although both her friends had issues with her cousin, neither ever wished her harm nor misfortune. And it didn't get much worse than a dead boyfriend and Kalea being questioned as a suspect in his murder. All too soon their laughter would stop, and she hated the thought of that, but it was what it was.

Addie took a moment to gather her thoughts and push the rampage of the morning events into a box in her mind, where it would have to stay until she learned more about what happened in Kalea's dress shop. It was no use going off half-cocked and making up scenarios about all her unanswered questions. She needed the facts first, and then she'd know what to do to help her cousin through this horrific tragedy.

Addie dragged herself to her feet and lumbered through the shop toward the front. Empty bookshelf space and toppled books glared back at her along her path, but the urge to tidy and straighten required more energy than she could muster at the moment. Forging ahead, she followed the happy voices of her two friends to a bookcase by the Thanksgiving display window and peered at them from around the corner.

"Now, just a smidge to the right," instructed Serena, gesturing with her hand.

"Here?" Paige asked.

"No, not there, up a bit. Yes! Now it's perfect," Serena said with a laugh. She was stationed at the foot of the short ladder she held for Paige as she hung one of the *Godey's Lady's Book* posters on the wall above a bookshelf.

Addie admired the work they had already accomplished. The posters on the walls, hung with expert precision around the store, completely incorporated the image she had in mind. Her heart swelled with pride. She really hated to end the jovial scene, but they needed to know what happened, and it was better to hear it from her than on the street.

"Well, that's the last one," said Paige, climbing down to the floor. "I only hope we've displayed them how Addie wanted them done because I'm not a big fan of ladders."

Addie cleared her throat and stepped into full view from around the end of the bookcase.

Her two friends swung around.

"I . . . I didn't hear you come in," stuttered Paige, who eyed her closely. "I take it from the look on your face that Kalea didn't just break a fingernail?"

"What happened? You look like death itself," cried Serena. "Why did you mumble something about murder and then race out of here without another word?"

"Yeah," said Paige, "we didn't know if you were going to murder your cousin or if she had murdered someone else—"

"Like *her* mother, Martha." Serena added with a nervous giggle and jerked her thumb toward Paige. Her gaze scanned Addie's face. "But I guess that wasn't it either, was it?"

"No, and I need to sit down," said Addie and weaved her way toward the counter. All the inner strength she had rallied in the back room faded away now that she was going to have to relive the details of her morning to her friends. Her legs turned to jelly, and she plopped down hard on a stool. Pippi, sleeping in her bed behind the counter, perked up at the sound of Addie's voice. She came skidding around the end of the counter at full-tilt and, after coming to a halt, perched gopher-like on her hind legs beside Addie. Addie scooped her little begging friend into her arms, buried her face in the soft fur, and recapped the morning events to her stunned audience.

When she was done, Addie began to shake. The shock had finally set in, and she began crying. First, the tears were just pin-sized drops, edging from the corners of her eyes, but soon her grief broke into intermittent racking sobs, punctuated by bouts of hiccups. Nothing eased the pain and tears. Not the cup of tea Serena waved under her nose nor the lapping of Pippi's tongue across her damp cheeks.

"Should we call Simon?" whispered Serena, glancing sideways at Paige.

"I don't know. I've never seen her like this?"

"Neither have I," said Serena. The pitch of her voice rose. "What do we do?"

Addie tried to focus her tear-blurred eyes on her friends and waved the white tissue clutched in her hand as a sign of her surrender. "I'm fine," she croaked between strangled sobs and hiccups. "Really, I'm fine. It just all hit me, that's all." She blew her nose into the tissue and then pasted what she hoped was a smile on her face. After scratching her furry friend behind the ears, she set Pippi on the floor and looked up at her friends. "See, I'm just fine."

"You're not fine, and I can see why." Serena stroked Addie's back. "What a horrible mess this is."

"Curtis really told you there were no signs of a break-in and some kind of evidence was found on the body, so Marc dragged Kalea to the station?" asked Paige.

Addie gestured with a bob of her head and plucked a clean tissue from the box Serena handed her.

"Did they handcuff her?" Serena shuddered. "I remember the cold, hard steel snapping closed on my wrists once, and it sure wasn't pleasant."

Addie shook her head and wiped her eyes with the fresh tissue.

"Well, that's one good thing," said Paige.

"Right," Serena said. "Maybe Marc just thought since Kalea was so upset being in the store where she'd discovered . . . you know, he thought she might relax more in a different environment?"

Addie stared up at her. "I wonder? You know I never thought of that." She jumped to her feet. "All this time I was thinking what a heartless cad he was, but maybe it was just the opposite, and he was helping Kalea." She glanced hopefully from Serena to Paige.

Paige bit her lip.

"What, you don't agree?" asked Addie.

Paige shrugged. "We can hope."

But Addie could tell by the look in her china-blue eyes that she wasn't buying what she was saying and was only paying lip service for Addie's benefit.

Addie sank back down on the stool. "Yeah, you're probably right. There's still the matter of no sign of a break-in—even though the shop appears as though it had been trashed—and whatever the evidence was they found on the body. Plus, the fact that Marc didn't want us to talk to each other in the back room and only allowed me to stay with her because Kalea was such a wreck."

"I bet she was," said Serena. "I can't imagine the state I'd be in if I found Zach like that."

"I know, right?" Addie shook her head. "I have no idea what he thought we were going to talk about, anyway. The poor thing couldn't put two coherent words together after what she'd just been through."

Paige slid up to Addie's side. "It'll be okay. After Marc talks to her, he'll see she couldn't have had anything to do with it." She gave Addie's shoulder a reassuring squeeze.

Addie met Paige's gaze and then glanced out the window. "That's the problem," Addie whispered. "After what Curtis said about proof that it was murder, I just don't know for sure now if she did or didn't." She looked back at Paige. "I keep asking myself, if someone broke in and killed Jared and then ransacked the shop. Why didn't Kalea hear any of it when she was right upstairs?"

Chapter 4

Addie glanced down at Pippi. A soft smile crept to her lips. Pippi's little head was resting on the toe of Addie's bootie, and she really hated to disturb her. Addie glanced longingly at the coffee machine at the far end of the counter and carefully tried to slip her foot from under her little friend's head.

"She really seems to sense when something is off with you," said Paige.

"I think she's just spoiled and likes to be carried around, and she can't understand why I'm not holding her right now." Addie edged her foot free and laughed when Pippi leapt to her feet, stretched out, and snuggled her little tricolored body against Addie's leg.

"Don't be so quick to dismiss what Paige said." Serena glanced down at the little dog. "They say animals have a great sixth sense for picking up on people's emotions.

That's why a lot of people have them for emotional support."

"Yeah." Paige nodded. "They say some can even sense when a person is sick before they even know they are."

"Look at you two. Suddenly, you've become dog experts over the past few months."

"Mom has a cat," Page said. "I did some reading about animals and what they can sense in people. I noticed that whenever Emma gets an owie, Cleo goes to her side to make sure she's okay and sits with Emma until she stops crying."

"I've heard Emma wail a time or two when you wouldn't let her have something she wanted," said Addie as she plopped a pod in the coffee maker. "Cleo probably thinks she's a kitten meowing in distress. The sound is eerily similar."

"I agree," Paige chuckled softly. "The sounds she belts out can sometimes be nerve-wracking, but the trick every parent has to learn is to read the various cries." Paige filled the end rack bookcase by the door with books from the cart. "Is she hungry, is she tired, is she really hurt, or just trying to get attention?"

"Geeze," said Serena, glancing down at her belly. "I never thought about stuff like that." She looked at Paige. Panic filled her eyes. "Are there parenting books that teach you all that?"

"Don't worry," Addie said, grinning at her friend over the rim of her steaming cup of coffee. "When the time comes, we have a whole section on baby and childcare."

"I can't wait until one of you has children," Paige said, straightening the books on the shelf. "In about seven years, Emma will be old enough to babysit, and your kids will be like little sisters or brothers to her."

"It won't be me, at least not for a while," said Addie with a shiver. "I'm just getting the hang of having a fur baby, so I know I'm definitely not ready for a real one." She glanced at a very pale Serena seated on a stool at the counter.

"Don't look at me," Serena sputtered. "I'm rethinking the whole thing. Maybe Zach and I will get a puppy and start with that, too."

"Come on, you two, don't be silly." Paige pushed the book trolley to the counter. "Sure, parenting has its challenges, but there are so many rewards. I'll tell you, you live for those. It's like an unseen pat on the back that says *Hey, you got this. See what an amazing little person you're raising.*"

Addie wiped a tear from her cheek. She wasn't certain if it was because of the profound love Paige held in her voice when she talked about her daughter or all the jumbled emotions of the morning resurfacing. She took a sip of her coffee, trying to stem the flow of renewed tears, and gazed out the window. "Shoot!"

"What's wrong?" Serena jumped to her feet and glanced in the direction Addie was looking.

"Jerry's here." Addie swiped at her damp cheeks. "I don't want him to see the blubbering mess I've been. I need him to take me seriously, so I can get to the bottom of what happened with Jared and Kalea." She set her coffee cup on the counter. "Paige, give me a couple of minutes and then send him to the back room." She hurriedly walked to the back as the bells above the door jingled out their cheery greeting announcing his arrival.

*   *   *

Addie stared at her reflection in the washroom mirror and winced. *Fish eyes! I hate bulging fish eyes.* She frantically splashed cold water over her face in hopes the red rims around her puffy eyes would disappear. She rifled through her handbag, pulled out a hairbrush, swept her long hair up, and fastened it into a messy bun on top of her head. She grabbed the emergency mascara she carried in her bag, made a quick touch-up, pinched her pale cheeks, and shrugged. "That appears to be as good as it's going to get right now." She flicked off the light and stepped out into the storeroom.

She grinned and stifled a laugh at how tiny Pippi appeared, nestled in the crook of Jerry's brawny arm.

He glanced down at the ball of fur nuzzling into him, and his face cracked with a smile. The tips of his ears turned fire-engine red. "Yeah, this little one came right up to me, stood on her hind legs like a gopher, and begged me to pick her up." His large hand smoothed the fluffy fur on the back of Pippi's neck. "I guess she knows I'm a softy at heart."

"That could be it, or . . . she senses something is bothering you."

He cast her a questioning glance.

"Paige, Serena, and I were just talking about how animals can pick up on our emotions. Perhaps she senses something is troubling you today and wanted to bring you some comfort?"

"I guess that's not a stretch since I'm here to investigate a murder," he said, glancing down at the little dog snuggled into him.

"Then you admit that what I heard this morning about it being a murder and not an accident is true?"

He glanced at her and pulled himself up to his full six-foot-three height. "That's all I'll admit to. So, if you have any intentions of getting something else out of me, please remember my position—"

"I know. Since you were promoted to lieutenant, you're now Marc's right-hand man and blah, blah, blah means keeping me out of the loop."

"I'm glad we can come to an understanding on that."

"Yes, as soon as you received the promotion, I realized you weren't going to be able to give me any more tidbits of information, right?" She looked at him under a raised brow.

"Exactly."

"Even if that information has something to do with the last remaining blood relative I have in the *entire* world." Addie fidgeted with a stray thread on the sleeve of her sweater. "But I get it. Any investigating I do might some-how put your case in jeopardy, right?" She glanced at him a teasing lilt in her voice. "I can't possibly be of any help to the police when it comes down to putting clues to-gether, can I?"

His eyes narrowed on her face. "Addie, I see what you're trying to do here."

"Moi?" She shrugged, honey dripping from her voice. "Whatever do you mean, Lieutenant? I would never pre-sume to think my snooping around helped solve *any* of the cases the police were investigating."

His smile didn't quite reach his eyes, and she knew she'd have to find another loose-lipped officer in the de-partment to feed her pertinent information in the future.

Obviously, Jerry took his new position seriously, which meant another door had closed for her. It was bad enough when she turned down Marc's marriage proposal nearly two years ago and ultimately chose to be with Simon. The pipeline to information Marc had previously shared with her shut off faster than the actual turning off of the water faucet. Since then they had managed to get back on somewhat of an amicable footing again, but that well of inside information had dried up completely. She'd had to gather what little she could from Jerry—before he received his promotion from sergeant to lieutenant, of course—and now she'd just have to bide her time by using her powers of observation and, of course, eavesdropping—a skill she had honed in previous years. Perhaps a few nudges in rookie Officer Curtis Brewster's direction would glean results.

Jerry stepped toward her and tapped his finger on the yellow-lined writing pad he had placed on the small desk in the back room while she was making herself presentable. "You know the drill."

She nodded, resigning herself to her new reality and settled into the desk chair to begin writing out her recollection of the events of the morning from the time she received the frantic call from her cousin to the moment the police arrived. At one point she hesitated and stared blankly at the page.

"Is everything okay?" Jerry asked, his voice softening.

She blinked back the tears burning like acid behind her eyes. "It's just hard." She swallowed and searched his face for a moment. "To think that Marc has evidence that implicates my cousin as a suspect in the death of the only man I've ever known her to truly love." She sucked in a wobbly breath and returned to the task of finishing her statement.

"Is this the homemade crime board I've heard so much about?" His voice came from the direction of the tarp-covered blackboard attached to the opposite wall.

"Yes," she said without looking up, but out of the corner of her eye, she could see him flip the painter's tarp up and tack it on the right-top nail holding the blackboard to the wall. The clacking sounds of chalk over the board surface distracted her when she went to sign her name on the bottom of the page, and she glanced up to see him step back from the board, reread what he'd written, and set the chalk on the tray.

She quickly scribbled her signature and stood up so she could read what he'd written, but he turned and handed Pippi to her, wiped the chalk dust from his hand on a tissue, mutely gathered up the yellow pad, and headed for the door.

She gaped in astonishment at his actions and approached the board to see what on earth he could have written. Expecting a warning perhaps to stay out of police business, she blinked in astonishment when she read his words. Her heart slammed into her ribs. "Wait. What does this mean?"

Jerry turned back to her, one corner of his mouth twitching. "It means you didn't *hear* it from me."

Chapter 5

Addie read and reread what Jerry had written on her board.

Blood droplets and smears on victim's shirt sleeve obviously not belonging to the victim due to the location and pattern of smudges.

She tried to wrap her head around why this would implicate her cousin in Jared's murder, and then she recalled the bandage on Kalea's finger this morning.

Addie dashed to the front of the store. "Has Jerry left yet," she cried and took a fleeting look around the shop. Through the window, she caught sight of his police cruiser pulling away from the curb. "Dang it!" She tugged her phone out of her sweater kangaroo-pouch and, thumbs flying over the small keypad, typed a text to Simon.

When will you know if Kalea's blood matches the blood on Jared's shirt?

She shoved her phone back into the pouch and glanced up to meet wide-eyed stares from Paige and Serena.

"What?" she said, her gaze darting from one to the other and then fixed her eyes on Serena. "And why are you still here? Shouldn't you be at your shop by now?"

"I wanted to make sure everything was okay after . . . well, you know. So, what happened back there?" Serena asked.

"Yeah," said Paige, "judging by the way you bolted after him and whoever it was you just frantically texted, I'm guessing he told you why Kalea is considered a suspect."

"Did you manage to loosen his tight lips a bit?" Serena chimed in.

"He didn't *tell* me anything, but I did discover why she's a suspect now."

Both her friends looked at her in confusion.

"It's a long story," Addie said, "but we did talk, and I know why he's become so tight-lipped lately. It's not easy on him being Marc's right-hand guy now, and I'm pretty sure he feels really torn, but I did manage to find out what the evidence on Jared's body was that implicated Kalea."

"What is it?"

"There was some smeared blood on his shirt sleeve, and because of where it is, they don't think it's Jared's but his attacker's."

"That should clear your cousin then, shouldn't it?" asked Paige.

"That's the problem. She had a badly cut finger and was wearing a bandage on it when I got there. I didn't think much about it at the time because she's always pricking herself with a pin when she's sewing, but it was enough for them—combined with the state of the store—to take her into the station. I'm guessing they wanted to draw a blood sample or do a DNA test on her or something."

"Oh dear," Paige said. "That sounds like it might be some pretty solid evidence."

"Yeah, I know. I just texted Simon, hoping he'd have results, but I guess he's still either running tests or at the station with Kalea."

"Now that I know you're okay and what's going on, I had better get back to my tea shop. Elli called and said they had some special blend orders, so . . ."

"What's that in your hand?" asked Addie, spying a book.

Serena grinned. "Just the best find in the whole world. Look what Paige unearthed from the box of books your distributor sent."

Addie glanced at the title. "Well, I'll be." She took the cookbook into her hand. "It's a 1995 printing of *Civil War Recipes: Receipts from the Pages of Godey's Lady's Book* complied by editors Lily May Spaulding and John Spaulding."

"Yes, and it has the same recipes as I found on a couple of the posters you have, so they're authentic from the magazine."

"Well done," said Addie. "I must admit this cookbook will be easier to work with on your kitchen counter than one of the huge posters would be."

"You bet," Serena said, waving the book in the air as she started toward the door. "I'm guaranteed to win now!" She clucked as the door closed behind her.

"I didn't know you had ordered those *Godey's Lady's* cookbooks," Addie said, glancing at Paige by the window display.

"Once we found out what the theme of the food festival was this year, I ordered everything available from the distributor's catalogue that had anything to do with the Civil War. Who knew then that one of the books would be a reproduction of the same recipes in the magazine that your friend sent the posters of." Paige chuckled as she thumbed through the books on the cart. "And look, here's a couple more Civil War recipe books I forgot I ordered."

"Those should sell like hotcakes now because I doubt Serena is the only entrant in town scurrying around to find the award-winning recipe." Addie's vibrating cell phone cut her laugh short. She tugged it out and read the message on the screen.

I don't even want to know how you came across that information—head-shaking emoji—meet me at the dress shop in ten.

XXXXXX

Addie shoved her phone back in the pouch and grabbed her jacket. "I have to go and meet Simon. Hopefully, he has some news about the blood sample." She flew out the door and slipped her way on the slush-covered sidewalk to the corner of South Main and Main Street.

Addie repeatedly punched the crossing button and even attempted to navigate the busy intersection before the light turned, but she was forced back when a delivery van made a right turn around the corner mere inches from her. Finally, on WALK, she slipped across the road and down the street to Hudson's Creations on Main, ducked under the yellow crime-scene tape, and breathlessly knocked on the glass door.

Simon looked up from a paper he was reading, strolled toward the door, unlocked it, and stood back as she burst through. "That was a fast ten minutes," he said with a soft snicker and locked the door behind her.

She reeled when she glanced over at the two waiting area chairs that had been moved from beside where the body had been to in front of the sales counter. "What's going on? Why is Kalea here?" She searched Simon's face.

"Marc's hoping that being back here will tweak something in her memory that can give them a lead on another suspect."

"But you saw the state she was in this morning after finding Jared's body. Being back in here so soon will destroy her right now." She started toward the chairs where Marc and Kalea were seated.

"Stop." Simon clasped her coat sleeve. "She's okay. I gave her a mild sedative at the station to calm her down, and the initial shock has worn off. She's doing much better and being very cooperative."

"But—"

"I would never have approved this if I didn't think she would be able to cope with it now." A soft smile, just enough to highlight the dimples in his cheeks, twitched at the corners of his lips. "Trust me, okay?"

"Okay, you are the doctor."

"Don't worry. Marc's just about finished, and then you can go to her."

Addie broke her gaze from Simon's lingering sea-blue eyes to her cousin. Kalea's head drooped, and her fingers fidgeted with the tissues clutched in her hands. Addie glanced back at Simon. "Does this mean he's going to officially charge her with Jared's murder?"

"It's hard to say what will eventually happen because there are still too many questions, but right now the good thing is that preliminarily report shows that not all the blood on his shirt was an exact match to hers."

"What do you mean by not *all* the blood? Does that mean some of it was?"

He studied her face. "How you even know about the evidence discovered on his shirt is beyond me." His voice lowered to a husky murmur, "But after all this time, there really isn't anything about you that surprises me anymore."

"I have my sources," she said as she glanced back over to Marc and Kalea. "But you didn't answer me." She turned and stared him straight in the eye. "What blood matches Kalea's?"

He puffed out a breath and dragged his hand through his thick black hair. "There were two blood patterns on his sleeve. One was a smear on the backside of his lower sleeve, and the others were droplets inside the cuff. The blood inside the cuff is a one-hundred percent match to Kalea's."

"There has to be a logical explanation for that, right?" Her voice lowered to a frantic whisper.

"I'm sure there is."

"Yeah." She stared down at the floor and replayed through her mind everything she had seen and what Kalea had told her. "I know." She snapped her fingers. "That cut she has on her finger! Jared must have helped her apply the bandage and some of her blood dripped down inside his cuff. That could have happened, right? Something as innocent as that could explain a couple of droplets on his shirt."

"That's a possibility, I suppose," Simon said, shifting uncomfortably. "But you do know Marc will have to look at all the evidence before he can make a call like that."

"You sound more like him every day." She shook her head. A sense of betrayal lingered in the air. She took a quick look over at Kalea and Marc. "Is that why he brought her back here to re-question her?" She scowled at Simon not able to hide her disdain for the whole scene, because her cousin must have repeated the story ten times at least by now. It made her stomach churn, and she was afraid she was going to be sick. "Is he hoping she'll slip up on a detail or accidentally confess?"

"No, it's because there are still too many unanswered questions. Just before you came in, he had her walk him through all her movements this morning and, given the state of the shop, conduct an inventory check to see what was missing."

"It sounds like he's at least open to the idea that Jared might have caught his would-be murderer in the act of robbing the store and not immediately jumping to the conclusion that Kalea is guilty. I guess that is a good thing."

"Rest assured, Marc is considering all the angles. But now . . ."

"Now what?"

"She says the only thing missing is Jared's vintage brief-case." Simon shrugged his shoulders. "We don't know what to think."

"Nothing else was missing?"

He shook his head.

"Jared always carried a vintage briefcase with him. He said it was his late father's, so it had special meaning for him."

"Well, apparently it's gone now."

Addie's gaze scanned the disheveled state of the sales floor, and a thought struck her. "Do you think something

Jared had in his briefcase was the real target of his murderer and the tossing of the shop was to make it appear as though a robbery had taken place?"

"Interesting point."

"It is a theory to start with anyway, and one that makes a whole lot more sense than Kalea killing Jared." She cast her gaze downward. "To me, anyway."

"Could it have been the actual briefcase itself? Was it worth a lot of money?"

"I guess it depends on what the killer thought of as a lot of money. I believe it was a nineteen-thirties vintage case, so in my off-the-record estimate, it might have been worth four to six hundred dollars, not really enough to kill someone for though in my mind."

"To the average person it wouldn't seem so, but if someone was desperate enough, that's a lot of money."

"The average person, thank goodness, wouldn't kill someone."

"Yeah, there's nothing average about murder, is there?"

She shook her head and considered the purses she saw on the floor by her feet. "I heard one of the officers say this morning that there was no evidence of a break-in."

"I heard the same thing."

"Then how did someone get in and do all this?" She waved her hand around the room. "It doesn't make sense."

"No, it doesn't." Marc's voice rumbled from over her shoulder. "Only one of the many reasons why Kalea was taken into custody this morning."

Addie spun around and fixed her gaze on his. "Hi," she said with a flushed smile. "I'm not interfering, honest. I only made an observation."

"Addie was just saying that she thinks Jared's brief-case was only worth about four to six hundred dollars. That tells me," said Simon, "the murderer wasn't after it specifically, so there had to be another motive."

"Like maybe"—Addie kept her tone hopeful—"that the killer wanted something inside the briefcase."

Simon's gaze wavered between Addie and then Marc. "Maybe."

"You know," Addie glanced up at Marc, "another thought is that someone went to a lot of trouble to make it look like a robbery or scuffle had occurred here. Could it be someone was trying to set Kalea up for the murder?"

Marc drew himself up to his full six-foot-two height and braced his shoulders. "Did she mention anything to you this morning about the argument they had last night?"

"No." Addie's heart fell. "Was it in public? Could someone else have witnessed it and took advantage of that so the logical conclusion for the police would be to do exactly what you did and arrest her?"

He shook his head. "According to her statement, it was here, in the apartment, and it occurred later in the evening when all the shops were closed. There wouldn't have been any witnesses, not even someone passing on the street below."

"I guess that takes us back to the theory that it was the briefcase or something inside it." Addie scowled.

"That's the thing," said Marc. "Kalea said it wasn't the usual case Jared carried."

"What do you mean?"

"She told me that when they were in Boston yesterday, the handle on the one he had broke. Apparently, it fell onto the road and was driven over by a delivery truck.

She and Jared went to a pawnshop and found a similar one and bought it to replace his."

"Maybe," said Simon, "the killer didn't know it wasn't the actual nineteen-thirty case?"

"And the new one was worth more money," Addie said wistfully. "But that's not likely as any from that era would be worth about the same. Besides, how would the killer have known it was a different case?"

"Exactly," said Simon turning to Marc. "So I guess we're back to it being something in his briefcase the killer was after."

"Or," added Addie excitedly, "Kalea was set up because the blood smear on his shirt that didn't match Kalea's proves that someone else *was* here."

Marc raked his fingers through his hair. "Look, all this theorization might be fun for you, but I have to work on the evidence we do have."

"To me that other blood that doesn't match hers *is* evidence that someone else was here."

"Possibly," said Marc, "or he might have rubbed up against something in Boston and picked it up there for all we know."

"Now who's theorizing?" she snapped.

His gaze narrowed to meet hers. "I can only investigate clear evidence and right now all that evidence—"

"Clears my cousin, doesn't it? Seeing that only a couple of blood droplets inside his cuff was hers, and she has an injured finger. He might have helped bandage it, and that's how her blood got on his shirt. I know she might be a lot of things, but she's not a killer."

"What is it you said that your father always said?" asked Marc.

"Anyone," she said begrudgingly, "can be capable of murder given the opportunity."

"Exactly," he agreed, "but not just the opportunity. There also has to be the means, which was something common to what is found in the store, a clothes hanger. Clearly the intruder—if there is one—didn't come armed with a weapon. Plus, Kalea's statement about their argument, which, by the way, is the only thing close to a *definitive* motive we have at this time. And don't forget the fact that there is *no* evidence of a break-in occurring. Therefore, everything else you have just suggested is pure speculation at this point. I need proof. Hard, cold, undisputable proof to give to the DA."

Addie blinked back the tears stinging at her eyes. "Unless Jared knew the person, and that's why he let them in."

Marc slowly blew out a long, deep, exasperated breath.

"I know this is hard, Addie," Simon said, "but Marc's right. Everything we have right now is pure conjecture. We have to let the police work through all the circumstantial evidence. Hopefully, something else pops up that won't tie the murder to Kalea."

"I know, it's just that . . ." She sniffed and glanced over at her cousin staring despondently at the wall behind the sales counter. "Are you finished for now? Can I take her upstairs and settle her?"

Marc shook his head. "I'm sorry, but I can't release the scene yet," he said, his voice softening, perhaps hinting at an apology for his previous tone. "Is it possible for her to stay with you until I can?"

"That would be better for her anyway," said Simon. "It might be too soon for her to stay here. It's going to take some time until she'll be able to face the apartment and"— he glanced around the store—"being back here to work."

"You're right," agreed Addie. "I just thought maybe if she was surrounded by her own things, she'd be more comfortable, but all those things have memories attached to Jared. Yes." She met Marc's impelling gaze. "I can take her in."

"Good, okay. I'll release her into your custody while we try to figure out what happened here today, and when . . . and *if* she's no longer considered the prime suspect."

"But . . . but—"

Marc's cheek twitched. She was pushing it. Snapping her mouth closed, she simply nodded.

"Good, then she's free to leave for now."

"My car's at the bookstore, and I'm not sure she's in any condition to walk the two blocks back to get it."

"I'm done here for now," Simon stepped in quickly before Marc could respond. "I can drop you off at the store."

"Thanks," she said, squeezing his hand. "I'll go tell her the plan."

Addie opened the door to Simon's F-150 and hopped out into a slushy puddle in the alley behind her shop. Ignoring the cold moisture seeping through her shoes, she latched onto the small prescription bottle containing two tiny blue pills that Simon had given her.

Simon joined her on the passenger side. "You can give her one of these when you get home. It will help her sleep, and I think that's what she needs more than anything now. There's one more for the morning in case she needs it to take the edge off. Any more than that, I'll have to assess her first, got it?"

Addie brushed her lips across his warm cheek and whispered, "Thanks."

Simon and Addie assisted Kalea from the back seat of the truck into Addie's Mini. After kissing Addie on the top of the head, Simon jumped back in his pickup, waved, and gave a short honk as he pulled away. Addie dashed into the bookstore to let Paige know what was going on, rounded up Pippi, and the three headed toward her three-story Victorian mansion on the hill. After wrangling both Kalea and Pippi into the house and administering one pill and a glass of water to her patient, Addie deposited her emotionally shattered cousin into the comfort of a bed—the same bed Kalea had slept in for the first several months she had stayed with Addie when she came to live in Greyborne Harbor.

Pippi followed them into the bright blue guest room, her little nails *clickety-clacking* across the wooden floors. Upon reaching the carpet beside the large four-poster bed, Pippi made a flying leap up onto the bed and nestled in beside Kalea, snuggling her little head under the woman's chin.

Addie recalled what Serena and Paige had said earlier about animals sensing emotions and smiled. She started to close the door when she heard her cousin quietly crying and peeked through the crack in the door to check on Kalea.

Her cousin wept into the top of Pippi's little head. "Oh, Pippi, what a mess," she sobbed. "What have I done?"

Chapter 6

Addie stared down at the countertop, unseeingly trailing her fingers over the polished wooden surface. Throughout her restless night, Kalea's words had echoed through her mind and haunted her fitful, uneasy dreams. What had her cousin meant? *What have I done?*

Addie had hoped she could ask her for the answers this morning, but when she could finally pull her sleep-deprived, weary body from her bed to check if Kalea was awake, Pippi twitched her bushy eyebrows at her and rested her head on Kalea's rising and falling chest.

"It's weird, isn't it?" said Paige, wrenching Addie from her thoughts.

Addie glanced up and stared blankly at her assistant.

"Earth to Addie." Paige laughed and waved a hand in front of her face.

Addie blinked and then shrugged. "Sorry, what did you say?"

"I said, it's weird, isn't it?"

"Um, what's weird?"

"Not having the little fur ball underfoot today."

Addie glanced over at the empty dog bed she kept at the shop.

"It feels empty or something in here," Paige said. "Don't you agree?"

"Yeah. I never thought I'd get used to the clicking of her nails against the wooden floorboards like I had to get used to the squeak of the wheels on your book cart," she said with a soft chuckle.

"I'm . . . I'm sorry," Paige said, her voice wavering. "I could oil them if you like?"

"No." Addie waved her hand. "It's become a comforting sound, and one I miss when you're not here." She gave her assistant a weak smile. "Um . . . remember when I came in this morning and told you why Pippi wasn't with me?"

"Yes," said Paige, hesitantly studying Addie's face. "We talked about how the theory of animals sensing what a person is feeling played out right in front of your eyes last night with Pippi's reaction to Kalea."

"Yeah . . . well . . . there was something I didn't tell you . . ." Addie's eyes locked on Paige's uneasy gaze. "After I got Kalea settled in bed for the night, I was leaving her room, and as I was closing the door, I heard her say to Pippi . . ." Addie swallowed hard.

"What did she say?"

"She said—"

The tinkling of the overhead doorbells made them

both jerk and glance at the woman standing in the door-way.

"You that old-book lady?" the woman asked roughly. She eyed Addie from under her brows made bushier by the tight-fitting wool cap pulled down low on her fore-head.

"Yes . . . yes, I suppose I am the old-book lady." Addie approached the woman with her hand extended in greet-ing. "I'm Addie Greyborne. What can I help you with today?"

The woman looked at Addie's outstretched hand and then at her own grimy one. She wiped her hand across the chest of her oversized, grubby, camouflage-brown winter jacket and hesitantly shook Addie's spotless one. "Glad to meet ya', miss. They call me Picker." Her tawny-brown eyes showed the hint of a sparkle. "I hear on the street that ya buy old stuff."

"Books mostly." Addie nodded and studied the woman's weather-burned, ruddy face. "Although . . . Picker?" The woman nodded. "I do also sell knickknacks, so some-times I'm in the market for those, too. Do you have some-thing to sell?"

The woman swiped the back of her hand across her dripping nose and sniffed. "Yeah, but not sure it's a nick . . . whatever ya called it."

"Why don't you come in and let me take a look, and if it's not something I'd be interested in purchasing, then I can at least tell who in town might be?" Addie's palms itched in anticipation. She couldn't wait to see what this unusual visitor to her store had to sell.

The woman glanced back out the door. The tortured look on her face told Addie she was thinking about mak-ing a run for it.

"Would you like a cup of fresh coffee?" Paige called cheerfully from beside the coffeemaker.

The woman glanced at Paige, back at the door, back at Paige and then at the coffeemaker. She stamped the slushy snow from her oversized boots onto the mat and followed Addie over to the counter.

"Cream and sugar?" Paige asked as she filled a cardboard cup.

"Black." The woman snorted and wiped her nose on her hand again.

Addie plucked a couple of tissues from the box on the counter and handed them to the woman. She nodded her gratitude, blew her nose, and then handed them back to Addie.

"You can keep those." Addie waved them off with a thin smile. "We have lots here, but thanks, anyway."

The woman nodded and stuffed them into her jacket pocket then took the cup of fresh-brewed coffee from Paige and took a sip. A wide toothy grin that showed years of neglect and decay came across her ruddy face.

"Best dang cup of coffee I've had in a long time," she said and took another sip.

Addie smiled at the look of peace that came across the skittish woman's face and made an observation that had earlier eluded her. The woman only used her right hand and arm. Since her jacket was so bulky, Addie couldn't tell whether this was because she had just the one arm or if she held her left arm behind her back concealing something in her unseen hand. Uneasiness crept through Addie as the woman continued to take deep pleasure in her coffee but made no effort to reveal what it was she wanted Addie to appraise.

After she drained the cup dry, she plunked it down

on the counter, drew one of the soiled tissues from her pocket, dabbed at her nose, shoved the tissue back in her pocket, and gave Addie her big toothy grin. "Ready to do some business, dearie?"

"Um, yes . . . please." Addie waved toward the counter. "Show us what you have." She squirmed in her knee-high leather boots, not sure what to expect next from this most unusual woman.

Without any fanfare the woman whipped her left hand around from behind her back and dropped a brown leather briefcase on the counter.

Paige and Addie gaped speechless at it, then at each other, and then back at the vintage case.

"Nice, innit?" the woman asked, glancing at Addie.

When Addie could find her voice, she managed to murmur. "Yes, yes, very nice."

"Is it something you'd buy?"

Addie didn't know what to say. This had to be Jared's missing briefcase. She looked into the woman's brown eyes and saw that fleeting look of uncertainty that might mean she was ready to bolt again. Addie knew she had to act quickly. "Yes, it's definitely something we'd be interested in." She locked gazes with Paige. "Right?"

"Oh, yes, perfect for our shop," Paige said with a shaky smile.

Relief swept through Addie that Paige had picked up her cue—no questions asked.

"Good." The woman beamed. "What's it worth to you then?"

"Um . . ." Addie needed to come up with something good so as not to scare the woman off, but she also needed to know where the woman got the case. "I'm sorry. What did you say your name was again?"

"They call me Picker, that's it," she snapped and shuffled in her oversized boots. "How much?"

"Well . . . Picker, for me to make a proper assessment of its value in order to be able to pay you what it's worth, it would really help if I knew the provenance of it."

"Province? I don't know nothing about no provinces. That's something they got up there in Canada, isn't it? It might be Canadian." She shrugged. "I don't know. Does that make it worth more money?" She eyed Addie.

"I don't know if it does or not." Addie fingered the aged leather. "What I mean is that the provenance of an item is the history of its ownership. It helps in authenticating the object for a fair appraisal."

A look of panic flashed in the woman's eyes.

"It's a way for me to know," Addie said quickly, "that I'm giving you exactly what the case is worth and would prove it is actually as old as it appears. If you just tell me where you got it, then I can make you a fair deal." Addie hoped the lilt in her voice would convince the woman of her sincerity as she searched her fear-filled eyes.

"Naw, we'll just say it's mine, and I want to sell it. How much?"

"It would really help me make sure I'm not short-changing you if I knew where you got it?"

"Ya sound like you're accusing me of stealing it."

"No, not at all." This was the last thing Addie needed the woman to think, and it was clear that she was ready to hightail it out of there and then Addie would lose the case for sure. "I just want to make sure I'm paying you what it's worth. But if you can't or won't tell me where you got it from then all I can give you is an un-appraised guesstimate, and I don't want to cheat you out of any money."

"Nope, it don't matter where I got it and sounds like to me you're thinking I stole it and are ready to call the cops." The woman snatched the case off the counter and took off with it.

"Oh no!" Addie darted after her out onto the busy sidewalk. She scanned left and right and then glimpsed the woman disappearing into the park across the road. "Darn it!"

"What happened?" cried Old Bill Unger as he marched toward Addie from the sidewalk in front of Martha's Bakery. He grasped a snow shovel in his hand. "Was Picker causing you trouble? Tell me, *Just* Addie, and I'll have a word with her if she was."

"No, no, Bill, don't worry. It wasn't like that," Addie said, glancing at the park again. "Do you know her very well?"

He shrugged. "As well as I know anyone, I guess. Why?" He eyed her warily. "Ya sure she weren't causing trouble in there?" He jerked his head toward the bookstore.

"No, no trouble, but it's important that I find her again." Addie met Bill's confused gaze and smiled reassuringly. "Honest, I just need to talk to her."

Addie knew, given Bill's background of living on the streets much like she assumed Picker did, that it was a tight-knit community that had little trust for people outside their circle. Even though he had left that life behind when he took his old, high school friend, Martha Stringer, up on her offer for him to live in her garage and be her full-time assistant in the bakery, his tie to that community was still strong. He might be willing to confront Picker if he felt she had wronged Addie, but getting him to reveal any information about her or where Addie could find her might be another story.

"She has something that I'd like to buy from her. But she left before we could make a deal on it, and I'd really like to make that happen."

Bill studied Addie's face. The weathered creases around his pale-blue eyes deepened. "That don't sound like Picker. She's always up to making a deal. That's how she lives."

"Do you happen to know where she lives?" Addie asked hopefully and prayed her question wouldn't open up a sense of duty to protect one his own and have him end the conversation.

Bill cupped his hand around the top of the shovel handle and leaned his chin on it and pinned his eyes on hers. "Did she steal this thing you want to buy?"

"No, well . . . I don't really know, but—"

"Cause Picker ain't no thief."

"I'm not accusing her. I only asked her where she got it so I could make her a fair deal on the price because it might be worth a lot of money, and I didn't want to cheat her."

"Ya sure that's all?"

"Yes," Addie said, fighting to keep her voice even. After all, she had no way of proving right now that the briefcase was the one Jared had, and if it was, how Picker might have gotten her hands on it. She'd have to get Kalea to identify it before anything else could be done and then let Marc know for his investigation. "I just need to know where I can find her so I can buy it and pay her what she's owed. I didn't mean to scare her off by my questions."

Bill stood upright and fixed his gaze on her. Finally, he slowly nodded. "Okay, I trust what you say, *Just* Addie. I know you'd mean no harm to come to her."

"Never."

"Good. Well . . . she has a shack out on Ol' Man Gibson's property there on Smugglers Road. You know the place?"

"Yes, his family used to run the mill out there, didn't they?"

"Yup, been closed for years, but he lets her live in the old mill workers' cottage in exchange for some of the more valuable things she finds in her picking."

"Thank you." Addie beamed, threw her arms around him, and kissed his ruddy cheek. "You have no idea what this means to me."

His gloved hand shot to his cheek and a sheepish smile spread across his chapped lips. "All I'll say is this, whatever it is, must be a real find for you to want to buy it so bad."

"You have no idea."

"Just hope Ol' Man Gibson don't get his hands on it first."

A wave of panic surged through her. "Would he?"

"That's the deal they have. If it's worth a lot of money, might buy Picker rent for a year."

"Oh, no. I have to find her before that happens. Thanks again, Bill, you have no idea how much you've helped me." She spun around and started back inside the bookstore.

"Freda."

"What?" She stopped and glanced back at him.

"Freda. I heard once that's her real name, if it helps."

"It might, thanks." She flashed him a grateful smile and opened the door.

"And *Just* Addie . . ."

"Yes?"

"Don't be coming out in this weather again with no coat on, hey?" He glowered at her, his tone unusually stern as he put his head down and resumed shoveling the walkway in front of the bakery.

Chapter 7

Addie shook her head at Bill's stern, fatherly warning masked in his usual *Just* Addie teasing. She shivered as she opened the door and rubbed her hands up and down her arms to fend off the chill threatening to seep into her bones. Apparently, he was right on. It definitely wasn't the weather to be running around outside with no jacket. Instant relief wrapped around her with the warmth of her shop and aroma of old leather chairs and books. She glanced out the door window and smiled. Bill looked up from his shoveling, gave her a crooked grin, put his head back down, and resumed clearing the walk in front of Martha's Bakery. She chuckled softly to herself while she stamped the snow off her boots.

"What are you laughing at?" Paige asked, standing on tiptoes to see what Addie was looking at outside. "Bill?

I've known him for a long time and never thought of him as much of a comedian. I think my mom would attest to that, too."

"Actually, he has quite a good sense of humor, deep down, and he gets a kick out of teasing me for something I once said to him."

"Do tell. I'd love to know how to crack a smile on the grizzled old face once in a while."

"Well, he used to call me *Miss* Addie, and I told him not to be so formal because that greeting implied that I was older than him and is used as a sign of respect for an elder or insinuated that I was above him in my station. Basically a carryover from the old-world class system."

"Yeah, I know. He calls me Miss Paige."

"See what I mean? I think that because of his years on the streets, he sees us as being above him or something. Anyway, I told him to just call me Addie. Now, when he wants to tease me or he's in a joking mood, he calls me *Just* Addie."

Paige laughed and glanced out the window at Bill. "He is a character that's for sure, but under that rough exterior, he has a heart of pure gold. Just look at him shoveling our sidewalk now."

"Yes, he has that for sure, and I'm so glad he's found a home and a job and is off the streets. Your mother truly is an angel to have taken him under her wing."

Paige choked on a breath. "Have you met my mother?" She sputtered. "An angel? Hardly!" She snorted out something like a laugh that made Addie giggle in response.

The overhead door bells tinkled out a greeting, and Addie turned to meet the Cheshire-type smiles of the two sisters who ran the Greyborne Point Bed & Breakfast down by the marina. "Time to get serious," she whispered to Paige as she shored herself up and plastered on her bookseller's smile.

"Good morning, Bev and Bin, are you looking for something particular today we can help you with or are you just browsing?"

The taller of the two dark-haired women waved her hand toward the bay window. "We are on the hunt for a Civil War recipe and saw your display—"

"And just knew you'd have something here that would be perfect for the competition," chirped in the shorter sister.

"Ah, you're entering the *Make it - Bake it Food Market* competition."

"Yes, us along with half the merchants in town, I'm afraid," said the taller, full-figured sister. "I know it's going to be tough to come up with a unique dish, but we thought you might have something in here that is authentic and will impress those uppity-ups from the historical society."

"Bev!" The more petite woman elbowed her sister in the side. "Be nice."

Sensing these two close sisters were on the verge of starting their own civil war, Addie quickly waved her hand. "I have the perfect selection of cookbooks right over here," she said, starting toward the sisters.

"No, that's fine," said the shorter woman. "Just point us in the right direction, and we'll browse through them."

"You mean more like argue over which one we should get," said the taller woman, glowering down at her sister.

"It's not my fault you can't make decisions," snapped the slighter woman.

"Okay," said Addie, trying not to laugh at the two sisters, who could never agree on anything. Addie wondered how they managed to run one of the most successful B&Bs in town. "I'll leave you to browse through the selection of Civil War recipe books that we have. They are all displayed on the end racks behind the window display."

"Thank you." Bin smiled, and Bev nodded curtly. "Now if I can only get this one to agree to something, we should be out of your hair soon."

"Don't worry about us," said Addie, "that's what we're here for, and if you have any questions, just ask." She turned around toward Paige, gave an involuntary eye roll, and stifled her urge to laugh as the two sisters continued bickering.

"It sure has been a weird morning so far, hasn't it?" said Paige with a little laugh and then dropped her voice. "Like, please explain to me why you were so desperate to buy that woman's briefcase. It's not something we usually deal in."

Addie eyed the two sisters over her shoulder to make sure they were out of earshot. "Because it could be a link to whoever murdered Jared, so thanks for not asking any questions and just going along with me on it."

"The murder? How?"

"Kalea said the only thing missing from her shop yesterday was Jared's vintage briefcase."

"I see. When you were talking to Bill, did he tell you where to find Picker?"

"He told me where she lives and gave me her real first name. I'm going to call Marc because I think he might have more luck getting information out of her than I did."

"I somehow don't think a blue uniform will loosen those tight lips of hers."

"No?"

"Nope, I get the feeling it's going to take persuasion and a whole lot of charm."

"I see that now. I guess I did sound a little desperate for information, and that's what scared her away."

"Yeah, I think so too. You did come off as though you were interrogating her."

"Simon does say that I'm like a dog with a bone once I set my mind on something, but all I could think about was where she got it. Then when she wasn't being forthcoming about it, I thought maybe she was the one who killed Jared for it, and that's why she wouldn't say anything."

"Do you think she would have broken into Kalea's shop to rob it and kill Jared just for that briefcase?"

"I don't know what to think. My mind's all twisted up trying to figure out what happened yesterday morning, and it's complicated by the fact the evidence the police do have leads straight to my cousin. Somehow, I have to get my hands on that case, so I can at least show it to Kalea to see if, in fact, it is Jared's case. It could lead us to the killer, or it might contain something to tell us why the killer took it in the first place." Addie gazed unseeingly out the window, regret eating at her gut. "I should have just kept my mouth shut, paid Picker for it, then none of this would have happened."

The raised voices of the two sisters drifted over from the far side of the shop, and Paige giggled. "They really do love each other you know."

"I know," said Addie, eyeing them exchanging verbal barbs. "But how they manage to run that B&B together and make it one of the most sought after ones in town is beyond me."

"Because they run it with pure love," Paige said,

glancing out the window. "Speaking of which . . ." She dropped her gaze, and a grin crossed her pixie-like face. "Here comes your love."

The door bells tinkled, and Addie swung around. Her gaze waded into the pools of Simon's sea-blue eyes. "Hi!" She waved, unable to stop the smile that simply seeing him brought to her face.

Simon took a quick look between a blushing Paige to an equally heat-flushed Addie. "What am I missing?"

"Yoo-hoo! Hello, Doctor Emerson," Bev, the taller sister, cooed, and she gave him a little finger wave from where she and Bin stood beside the cookbook display.

Simon pivoted and glanced at the two other flushed-checked women, who clearly were as excited to see Simon as Addie was. "Hello, ladies." He nodded in greeting. "It's nice to see you both again . . . so soon."

"I'd completely forgotten that you often came in here," said Bin, the shorter woman, as she stepped forward. She cradled two books close to her heart. "Fancy us running into you like this after just leaving your hospital walk-in clinic."

"Yes, fancy that," said Simon with a forced laugh. "That's small towns for you though, isn't it?" Simon glanced helplessly at Addie. "Well, you ladies enjoy your shopping, and I'll see you next month again at the clinic, right?"

"Well, we are thinking of entering the cooking contest, and we just can't decide on what recipe to make, and we were wondering if you could help us."

"I'm sure Addie or Paige could help you decide which cookbook would suit your needs best. I'm afraid I really am not an expert in that area."

"That's not what we heard." Bev edged Bin behind her. "We heard you're like a magician in the kitchen."

"That's right." Bin elbowed her sister and stepped around her. "We were wondering if we made up some of the dishes from these books if you would come for dinner one evening this week and test them. Then you could tell us which one we should enter in the competition." She batted her short eyelashes. Her gaze never left Simon's face.

Addie's hand shot to her mouth to conceal the laugh bubbling up from her chest.

"Well . . ." said Simon, obviously searching for an answer. "I am flattered to hear that glowing words regarding my meager attempts in the kitchen have reached your ears. Unfortunately, I'm on call in emergency all week, and it would be impossible to accept your generous offer of a dinner invitation."

Hope slipped from both women's faces.

Bin flashed her sister a deflated glance. "I suppose we could decide on a dish ourselves."

"I suppose so." Bev fidgeted with two books she held in her hands. "Okay, you buy those two books you have, and I'll buy these two, and we'll have a friendly competition between us and see which dish our guests prefer."

Simon clapped his hands. "Perfect! See I knew you could work something out between you. You don't need my opinion at all."

"Although, it would have been nice," said Bin, following him with her dark-brown eyes as she fished her wallet out of her handbag.

"Yes," murmured Bev, her voice trailing off dreamily as she placed her two purchases on the counter for Paige to ring up. Her gaze never left Simon. "It would have been a dream come true to have such a guest as yourself at our dinner table. Are you sure you can't make it?"

"I am sorry, ladies, but such is the life of a doctor. Just ask Addie. She has a horrible time keeping up with my erratic schedule."

Bin's eyes flashed on Addie and narrowed. "Yes, I suppose you would know, wouldn't you?"

Addie shrugged. "I guess that's one of the drawbacks of being friends with the town's most popular doctor." She pasted an innocent smile on her face while Paige rang up their purchases and placed them in two separate bags.

When the sisters got to the door, Bin set her searching gaze on Simon. "Should something change in your schedule, you will let us know, won't you?"

"Of course, you'll be the first to hear."

A look of relief crossed the petite woman's face, and she grinned back at him as the bells tinkled out their departure.

"Friends?" Simon looked questioningly at Addie. "Is that how you see our relationship?"

"You saw their faces, Doctor Dreamy. Do you think I'd want to crush whatever fantasy those two have regarding you?"

"Come here." He laughed softly and pulled her into his arms, tilted her chin up, and placed a delicate kiss on her lips. "That's exactly why I love you so much. You would deny your feelings for me to spare the feelings of the Thomas sisters."

"How do you know I was denying my feelings? Maybe that's how I think of us."

"I came by to see how you were holding up, but if that's how you feel, then I'll be off now . . ." He started to pull away.

"What? You can't go yet." Addie clasped his coat sleeve. "You just got here." She put on her best little-girl pouty face and glanced up at him through her thick, dark lashes.

"Come here." He pulled back into his arms. "You know I can't resist that spoiled-brat play you make on me."

"Spoiled brat, is it? I thought I was being endearing?"

"No," he said, tapping her nose with his fingertip. "Spoiled brat."

"He's not wrong, you know." Paige chuckled and used the counter between them as a shield.

"Pfft. To both of you." She peeked sideways at him then her assistant, feigning a mask of righteous indignation.

"All teasing aside." Simon's face grew somber. "I actually stopped in to ask you how Kalea was doing today."

"I'm not sure. She was still sleeping when I left this morning," Addie said, taking a fleeting look at the antique clock on the wall behind the sales counter. "I plan on popping home during lunch to check on her, though."

"It's almost that time now. I can go with you and examine her and then give her a couple more sedatives if she still needs them."

"Sounds good but give me a few minutes. I have something I have to do first." She picked up her cell phone from the counter beside the register. "A woman was in here earlier, and I think she has Jared's missing briefcase, and I have to let Marc know." She entered her password on the phone, bringing it to life. "Marc must know this Picker woman, and he'll be able to track her down faster than I can."

Simon covered the screen with his hand. "Wait. Freda Horst was in here this morning trying to sell Jared's missing briefcase?"

Addie lowered her phone and glanced up at him. "You know her?"

"You said Picker, right?"

"Yeah, but Bill told me her real name was Freda."

"That's her, Freda Horst. She sometimes comes into the free clinic I run at the homeless shelter. She always has infected cuts on her hands and arms from going through the bins in town, looking for salvageable items people throw away."

Paige spoke with a sly lilt to her voice. "I did say that it was going to take persuasion and a whole lot of charm for her to tell you where she got the briefcase, and who better than . . ." She jerked her head toward Simon.

"You're right. Care to take a little drive before we go check on Kalea, Doctor Dreamy?"

"I suppose I could." He eyed Addie skeptically.

"Addie scared her off with all her questions about where she got it," said Paige, avoiding eye contact with Addie.

"So Addie was like a dog with a—"

"Yes, I was, and maybe one day, I'll learn that the direct approach doesn't work on some people."

"Then you wouldn't be you." He tapped her nose teasingly. "Maybe just this time a little tact and persuasion of a less direct nature was called for."

She nodded in agreement.

"Okay, I'll go with you, since I really should go out

and check on Freda anyway. The last time she was in, she had a rather bad gash on her arm. I gave her some medication, but the wound should be checked again, and she didn't come into the clinic last week."

"And you'll use all that Doctor Dreamy charm to try to persuade her to sell me the briefcase so we can ask Kalea if it's Jared's. Maybe one mystery will be solved."

"I'm not sure any magical charms you think I have will work on Picker, but I'll give it a shot." His face screwed up in a grimace. "That was probably a bad choice of words. I hear she's got a shotgun out there, and she's not afraid to use it."

Addie recoiled in horror.

He chuckled softly and winked at Paige mischievously.

Chapter 8

"I bet those are big sellers at Halloween," Addie said with a nervous giggle and pointed to a series of weather-beaten headstones and grave markers that she'd spotted through the side window of Simon's Ford F-150. "Or . . ." She gulped. "Where Picker has buried the bodies of her other victims." She glanced sideways at Simon. "You're sure she couldn't be Jared's killer?"

Simon shifted the pickup into park, pinned her with a fixed stare, and shook his head. "As I've told you a dozen times already on the drive out here . . . *no*." He thrust open the driver's-side door. "I can't see her killing anyone. Stop looking at everyone as a suspect."

"But you said—"

He slammed the door shut.

"Yikes!" she said, flinching with the thud. "Obviously, I've pushed too hard—*again*—the old dog with a bone thing. When will I just learn to let go?" she muttered as she opened her door and hopped down onto the rough graveled driveway. "Okay, I'm going to trust that sixth sense you have about people but stay close just in case it's gone haywire today. If that was Jared's briefcase, the big question still is how did she get her hands on it."

"I'm sure there's a good explanation, and, besides, you don't know for sure that it is his, do you?"

"No." She shook her head and opened her mouth to protest but snapped it shut just as abruptly. The look in his eyes as he scanned the yard told her it was probably a good idea to change the subject and let this one go. For some reason Simon felt endeared to Picker, and it was clear that her constant questioning of the woman's character had challenged his patience with Addie.

"So this is an old grist mill, is it?" she said, forcing her voice to take on a cheerful lilt as she gazed at the crumbling stone building and the waterwheel that appeared to be hanging to its side by its last bolt. "It really is an idyllic setting, isn't it? If you ignore the eclectic collection of her pickings scattered around the yard."

"It is a bit of an eyesore, maybe, but it's how she keeps a roof over her head."

"True," she said, sensing by his brusque tone that his irritation with her was not subsiding.

"From what she's told me, she comes from a long line of pickers, so it's kind of in her blood."

"So she's carrying on the family business then?" she said with a short laugh and smiled awkwardly in the hope her attempt to lighten the situation would defuse the tension between them, but all she got was a shoulder shrug. "You know," she added thoughtfully, eyeing his rigid stance, "with all the trees and the creek, and that old stone mill building, even the clapboard cabin there, it shows a lot of history. I wonder why the historical society never stepped in to preserve it."

"I know, right?" Simon said, his curt tone loosening up as he skirted past a mound of rain barrels stacked pyramid style on the edge of the gravel drive in front of the truck and slid up beside her. "It really is sad to see it wasting away like this. Especially since Freda mentioned once during a clinic visit that the grist mill played a big part in Greyborne Harbor's early history."

"Why was it allowed to go to ruin then?"

"She's not that forthcoming in revealing information, as you know," he said with a crooked grin and a soft chuckle.

And with that little laugh and his dimply cheeked smile returning, Addie knew the old Simon was back and noticeably relieved at the change of topic, too.

"From what I can gather from the tidbits she has shared with me, the owner of the property, Walter Gibson's family, bought it a couple of hundred years ago. When the mill closed because of the change in the local economy, the family running it then wasn't particularly interested in the area anymore and built that big house on the ridge and left this to ruin."

"I guess back then people weren't into historic preservation."

"Not like they are now, and Walter must feel the same as his family did since he's just left it rotting away, which is why he lets Freda live here in exchange for some of the better items she picks."

"Good for her, but it's sad that an important piece of local history is wasting away." Addie shook her head and glanced over the picturesque setting and envisioned what the area could look like if it was shown some TLC.

A loud crash came from the direction of the old stone mill building, and Simon grabbed Addie's arm. "Come on," he cried, and they dashed toward the weathered red double doors. "Freda, are you in here?" Simon hollered and poked his head inside one of the open doors. "Freda, it's me, Doctor Emerson, are you okay?"

"Hi, Doc," echoed a disembodied voice from somewhere in the dimly lit mill interior.

"Where are you?" Simon squinted into the murky light as they entered the large warehouse heaped high with more of Picker's found treasures.

"Up here," she called from the top of a long spindly ladder leaning against an overhead rafter beam. "What brings you by today?" she asked, descending to the flagstone floor. "Out shopping or is this an official visit?" Then she spotted Addie standing behind Simon, and her eyes darkened. "What's *she* doing here?" she all but spat out.

Addie flinched with the venom in the woman's voice and was grateful for Simon's calming presence. Had she tried to confront Picker on her own, there was no doubt she'd be waving that shotgun of hers in Addie's face right about now.

"Freda, this is a very good friend of mine, Addie Greyborne."

"I know who she is," she snapped and glowered at Addie and then at Simon. "What I asked is what is she doing here?"

"Oh, yes, I guess you did meet her at the bookstore earlier, right?"

Freda fixed her cold gaze on Addie.

"I stopped in there to see Addie," he added, quickly glancing from Freda to Addie, "and happened to mention that I was on my way out to the mill to pay you a visit. After all, you didn't come into the clinic last week, and I'm concerned about that cut you have on your arm and wanted to make sure it was healing properly."

She stared at him, her cold eyes thawing when she fixed her gaze on his. "Really? You came all the way out here for *me*?"

"Of course, I worry about you living out here on your own."

Her weather-stoked complexion turned a rosier shade, and Addie suspected that the old Doctor Emerson charm was breaking through this woman's crusty exterior.

"But that still doesn't answer my question, does it, Doc?"

"No, it doesn't, but Addie happened to mention that you were in her shop today and told me about the beautiful vintage briefcase you had and were looking to sell." He drew himself up, appearing more convincing. "And you know me, Freda, and all those patient files I have to lug around. Well, I'm always in the market for something to make it easier. So I thought . . ."

"You wanna buy that old case?"

"If it's still for sale, yes. Yes, I do."

"For you, Doc, it's free."

"No, Freda, I couldn't accept it. From what Addie said, it's exquisitely handcrafted, and I know it's worth a lot of money."

She glanced dismissively at Addie. "Not sure she knows as much as you think she does. If that was true, why did I find it tossed out like trash in a dumpster behind that furniture store on Main Street? Hey, answer me that one, Doc?" She shook her head. "Yeah, I don't think your lady friend here is as smart as you think she is. Nope." She tucked her thumbs into the waistband of her baggy jeans. "You want it? Then it's my gift to you. Consider it payment for this house call."

Addie's heart did a complete flip-flop in her chest. Did this woman just volunteer all the information that Addie had, to no avail, pleaded with her earlier today to tell her? All with absolutely no prompting she divulged it to Doctor Blue-Eyes just like that, really?

Addie tried to focus her thoughts, which were torn between being in awe of the mesmerizing charms Simon apparently had over his patients—the Thomas sisters a clear testament to that, too—and what Picker had just said about how she came into possession of the briefcase. It had to be Jared's. She said she found it in a trash dumpster two stores down from Kalea's dress shop. But why would someone go to all the trouble of stealing it, killing Jared in the process, just to throw it away?

Addie's mind raced with all the possible scenarios that might have occurred in yesterday's early-morning hours right after Jared's murder, but she couldn't make any of it fit with this new information. First, it was clear from the investigation that the store had not been broken into. Second, it was obvious from the merchandise scattered around the sales room that a struggle had taken place. Or at least, someone tried to make it look like it, and that a robbery had been in progress, except only the discarded briefcase—if it was Jared's—was missing. Which meant . . . and she didn't like where her last thought took her. Kalea *did* kill him during a heated argument, and then tossed his briefcase in the trash to mislead authorities into believing

Jared had walked in on a robbery and was killed. *No!* She mentally shook her head at that last one. There would have to be a lot of indisputable evidence against Kalea before she would ever believe it.

She eyed Picker closely as the woman rolled up her red-flannel shirt sleeve, exposing her bandaged arm to Simon. Could they even trust what this woman told them? After all, *if* she had killed him to get her hands on an item that might bring her a fair amount of cash, she wouldn't have admitted it and would have most definitely said something like she just had. *Wouldn't she?* But then why offer it as a gift to Simon if money had been her motive for murder. Nope, it made sense considering her offer to him that she came into possession of it exactly the way she said she did.

"I'm afraid the light in here is too poor for me to do a proper examination," said Simon, peeling back the gauze on her forearm. "Could we go into your kitchen where I can get a better look at it and put on a clean dressing?"

"Sure," Picker said and sniffled. She drew her hand up to her nose, stopped, glanced at Addie, fished a crumpled tissue out of her front jeans pocket, dabbed at her nose, and stuffed the tissue back in. "But she stays outside. I don't need no busybody messing in my business, got it?" She flashed her darkening eyes on Addie.

"Got it." Simon glanced apologetically at Addie. "I'll just get my bag out of the truck and meet you inside, okay?"

"Yup," she said, pushing her sleeve farther up her arm as she strode through the double mill door.

"Sorry," Simon said with a tentative smile, "but if she's not on guard about having you in her home, then I might get farther with her."

"Don't worry. She's already given us more information than I managed to get out of her this morning."

"Good." He grasped her hand and gave it a little squeeze. "She really is more bark than bite. I'll get my bag and be back out as soon as I can."

"Don't worry about me and go do your doctor thing. Fingers crossed she follows through with her offer of giving you the case as payment. We really need to get Kalea to identify it, and, hopefully, something on it or inside it will lead us to Jared's killer."

"So Freda's off your list of suspects now?"

"Let's just say that I'm not as convinced or as concerned about her now as much as I was earlier."

"Even though *if looks could kill*?"

"Yeah, I guess we didn't get off to a good start today, and I pushed her too hard because it's the only lead we have so far."

"*You* push too hard?" He laughed as he headed for the truck to retrieve his bag from the back seat. She could still hear him chuckling as he strolled toward the open cabin door.

Addie rolled the window down, rolled the window up, tapped her fingers on the armrest, stomped her cold feet, turned the truck on, and when she started to sweat with the blast of heat from the vents, she turned it off and rolled the window down again. Her stomach rebelled in that moment by gurgling and moaning and she fished her cell phone out of her jacket pocket and glanced at the screen.

"No wonder. It's half-past one!"

She shoved the phone back in her pocket and rhythmically strummed her fingers on the armrest, staring at the closed cabin door, and mentally willed Simon to come out. What could be taking so long? Was Picker feeding him lunch while Addie wasted away out here in the truck for over an hour? That would be Picker's style, she assumed. Since she was so adamant about Addie not joining them, it would be her way of getting even for Addie being pushy that morning. She seemed like the type that would drag out the visit as long as she could and ply the good doctor with food, lots of food, while Addie starved to death a few feet away.

"Enough. You thought I was pushy this morning in my desperation for answers, just wait and see how pushy I can be when I'm starving to death." Addie opened the door, ready to jump out, when the cabin door opened, and a grinning Simon appeared in the threshold. She slunk back into the cab and closed the door, unable to contain the wide smile creeping across her face. Simon not only carried his medical bag but also the briefcase.

Chapter 9

Addie perched the vintage case on her lap and played her finger over the leather exterior. "It really is exquisite. Just look at the detail and the craftsmanship."

"Are you sure we have to turn this over to Marc," Simon moaned, glancing over at it.

"Come on, you know that first Kalea will have to identify it. If it's not Jared's, I'm pretty sure it belongs to you."

"What if she does say it's his?" Simon said sounding more like a petulant child than a medical examiner.

"Then we take it to Marc, and it will be held in lockup until the investigation is finished."

"I wonder if Kalea would let me have it after they're finished with it?" he said wistfully as he turned down her driveway.

"Maybe, it might bring back too many memories for

her, so there's a good chance. On the other hand, it was the last gift she gave him. She might want to keep it."

"I know I sound silly, but I've always dreamed of owning a handcrafted vintage bag and to come this close only to have to give it up . . ."

"Are you ready?" Addie eyed him before opening the passenger-side door.

"Ready," he said, as they made their way up the wide front porch of Addie's three-story Victorian.

"Chin up, Doc, maybe it's not Jared's, then you can keep it," Addie said with a laugh as she fit the key into her front door lock.

"Is it selfish of me to hope it's not his?"

"Not in the least. It really is a first-rate case. The workmanship that has gone into its construction is something you don't see these days."

"Freda was tickled to be giving it to me. I felt bad and nearly came clean with her about why we were so desperate to get our hands on it. Then I heard your voice whispering in my ear reminding me she could well be a suspect."

"So now you're thinking she *could* have had something to do with killing Jared?"

"Not really, but there is always the possibility, I guess, and we can't disregard anyone at this point, can we?"

"No, so we'd better keep the information about where Freda said she found it just between us for now. Don't even say anything about it to Kalea, okay?"

"Does that mean you're thinking along the same line as Marc and that she is a viable suspect?"

"That's the problem. I'm just not sure at this point." Addie stepped into the large foyer, rubbed her arms up and down her jacket sleeves to ward off the afternoon chill, and froze. "Do you smell that?" She sniffed the air as he hung his jacket up on the coatrack behind the door. "Please tell me you smell burnt toast, too."

"Yes," he said with a chuckle. "Don't worry, you're not having a stroke."

"Thank goodness." She glanced down the long, wide hallway toward the kitchen, pulled off her boots, and hung her jacket up. "Kalea was never much of a cook, so I guess we can add toast to the list of her culinary failures now too."

Pippi poked her hear head out of the kitchen door, let out a yip when she saw Addie, and skittered up the hallway toward her. Pippi's tail wagged, and she danced on her hind legs in greeting, begging to be picked up. Addie scooped her little friend into her arms, kissed her head, and snuggled her close as she followed the acidic scent and trails of wispy smoke to their source in the kitchen.

At the center island stood Kalea, still wearing her pajamas and bathrobe, waving off a cloud of smoke while she fished a piece of blackened bread out of a toaster slot with a knife.

"I hope you unplugged that first?" Panic filled Addie's voice as she dashed toward the island to check the placement of the cord. She breathed a small sigh of relief upon seeing the plug dangling off the counter.

Kalea raised her gaze to Addie's, and Addie could clearly see that sleep had not erased the dark circles etched around her cousin's hollow eyes.

"I'm not a total idiot, you know," Kalea said, her voice strangled as she choked back tears. "Only a partial one it seems. Who the heck can't make toast or soft-boiled eggs?" Her unleashed tears streamed down her cheeks as she jerked her head toward a white-foam-topped saucepan rapidly boiling on the stove. "Or just about anything else! Jared always said we should enroll in the couples' cooking classes at the community center, but I always found a reason not to. Now it's too late and, and . . ." She tossed the knife on the counter and buried her face in her hands, sobbing.

Pippi let out a mournful whimper. Her front paws thrashed wildly in the air as though she were scrambling to get to the sorrow-filled woman. Addie set her on the floor, and Pippi's nails *clickity-clacked* across the red-brick floor as she skittered over to Kalea's side. She nudged her head against Kalea's leg. A weak smile crossed Kalea's lips, and she bent down to pick the little dog up where she promptly snuggled her head under Kalea's chin.

"Kalea," said Simon from the doorway, "I have a couple more sedatives in my bag that I can give you if you think you need them today?"

Kalea shook her head and nestled her chin on the little dog's head. "No, I think this little girl here is all the medicine I need now. Those pills make me so dopey I can't think straight, and I need to figure out what I'm going to do now."

"I'm relieved to hear that," said Simon, coming to Addie's side, "and I think right now we all need some food. So why don't I . . ." He peered into the saucepan and switched off the burner. "Make us all some toasted egg salad sandwiches."

"I'm afraid I ruined the eggs." Kalea began a renewed round of cascading tears.

"They're not ruined," said Simon, his voice calm and reassuring. "By the look of them, they aren't soft boiled now, but for egg salad we need hard boiled, and they'll be just perfect."

Addie glanced past the kitchen door frame and noted Simon had left the briefcase outside the door the hallway. She caught his eye and smiled knowingly. Kalea was too distraught when they had come in to deal with identifying the case. He was right. She needed food first as it might help settle her down.

She gazed over at her cousin cuddled into the three-sided, windowed eating nook off the large kitchen and smiled at her little Pippi nestled into her cousin's chest. Addie wasn't certain how she felt about a dog at the table, but she also knew Pippi was the only thing holding Kalea's frayed nerve endings together at the moment.

Simon ran the eggs under cold water, peeled off the shells, and whipped the eggs into a glorious combination of mayonnaise, Dijon mustard, chopped celery, and green onion with a dash of dried dill and black pepper. He spread the mixture on the lightly toasted bread slices. It wasn't exactly one of his gourmet lunches, but it would do the trick. Her stomach, however, which had been mutinying against her since Freda's an hour ago, found it worthy of a five-star restaurant.

Their late lunch was eaten in silence, and with each mouthful Kalea managed to swallow, color slowly returned to her sallow cheeks. Addie pushed away her empty plate and rose to get the teapot she'd left to brew on the counter, but Kalea waved off the cup offered to her.

"I'm done. This was a good idea, Simon, thank you. I don't recall even eating yesterday at all, so I think this really helped."

"I know it's a tough time," Simon said, his voice even and encouraging, "but you do have to try to take care of yourself, or it will make everything you're dealing with so much worse and harder to cope with."

"I know." A shy smile graced the corners of her lips. "Thank you. You are the kindest man I've ever met." She set her hazel-green eyes on his as she reached across the table and clasped his hand in hers. "I think I'll go lie down for a while now." Her gaze lingered on his face, and her thumb circled small stokes over the back of Simon's hand.

Kalea glanced at Addie and pulled her hand away. "If you'll excuse me." She shifted Pippi from her lap to her arms and started to make motions to leave the table.

Addie caught Simon's eye and jerked her head toward the hallway.

"Kalea, before you go," he said, rising to his feet.

"Yes?" Her dark-circled eyes held a glimmer of hope.

"There is something we need you to look at first."

She shifted in her seat and glanced at Addie questioningly as Simon strode to the kitchen door to retrieve the briefcase. When he turned around, and her eyes settled on what he held in his hands, her face contorted in pain . . . shock . . . fear? Addie wasn't certain, but the sight of the case sent Kalea into a renewed bout of tears.

"Where did you get that?" she sputtered between sobs. "Take it away. I thought I'd never have to see it again."

Addie cradled her cousin's head and stroked the back of her matted auburn head. "Kalea, I know this is hard, but we need you to take a good look at the briefcase and see if it's Jared's."

She shook her head wildly. "I can't, I can't look at it. Where did you find it?"

She gazed up at Addie, and the tortured pain Addie saw made her want to cry, too. Or was the look more of panic at the fact that the case had been found? Addie shook that idea off and stroked her cousin's back. "Please, Kalea, you want to find Jared's killer, don't you?"

Kalea didn't respond.

"Well, don't you?"

Kalea nodded.

"Then if you can identify this case as his, we can take it to the police, and maybe they can find a clue inside it as to why Jared was killed and why this was the only thing stolen."

"It is his."

"But you've barely looked at it," said Addie mystified.

"Is there a silver name plate on the top by the clasp?" Kalea asked without looking at the case Simon still had in his hand.

He glanced down at it. "Yes."

"Are the initials R.W.C. etched into it with scratches across the initials?"

"Yes," said Simon.

"That's the one we picked up in Boston on Sunday. Someone must have tried to erase the initials but made a mess of it. Jared was going to have a new plate put on this week and have his own initials etched into it." Her voice was flat and cold as she uttered the words. "Now, if you'll excuse me. I need to lie down." She cradled Pippi into the crook of her arm and ambled on unsteady legs toward the door. She paused. Her gaze scanned Simon's long lithe frame, finally meeting his eyes. She smiled demurely. "Yes, you are one of the best men I know." She shot a glance back at Addie. "I only hope my cousin appreciates what she has in you," she muttered before making her way down the hall.

Simon looked blankly at Addie.

She shook her head in disgust and all but spat out, "Even in grief she's on the prowl for a man."

"No." He rushed to Addie and placed his hands on her shoulders. "She's grieving, and her emotions are running rampant. She's not in control, and she's transferring the gratitude she has for me as a caregiver to that of—"

"Is transference what she was doing when she was stroking her thumb over the back of your hand?"

"Yes, according to Sigmund Freud, that can be part of it. He said a patient can sometimes transfer what they are experiencing in their grief and mistakenly feel that the comfort they are receiving from their physician is something other than it is. Give her a little bit of time, it will pass."

"I hope you're right because I know my cousin, and combined with some of the evidence, I'm having second thoughts about her innocence." Addie flipped on the switch for the garbage disposal and shoveled eggshells into the mouth of it. The grinding noise blocked out anymore talk of Freud that Simon might want to quote. She knew what she saw, and the look in Kalea's eyes when she saw the briefcase in Simon's hand put Addie's thoughts in a tailspin. Something didn't sit right with Addie about any of this.

Chapter 10

The drive back to Addie's shop was in virtual silence with only a few sidelong glances between her and Simon. She kept replaying her cousin's reactions today over and over in her mind to see if she could see what Simon had in Kalea's behavior toward him. But facts were facts, and Simon didn't know Kalea and her history with men like Addie did, but perhaps he was right.

After all, he did know more about these psychological things than she did. Her cousin's reactions and actions could very well be a case of overwhelming grief and the transference of what she felt for her lost lover onto a healthcare professional, who'd shown her compassion and tenderness during a trying time. Addie herself had been in this very situation once, and the grief that had gnawed at her through those first few months—and years—made her say and do some pretty outlandish things, too.

As they pulled up in front of Beyond the Page, Addie was ready to concede to Simon's explanation of the situation until the words she'd heard Kalea whisper to Pippi came rushing back at her. She stared out the windshield and played that moment over in her head. *What did she mean by "Oh Pippi what a mess. What have I done?"*

"Are you okay?"

Addie jerked and glanced over at Simon. "Yeah, I was just thinking about something."

"If it has to do with anything Kalea said or did today, please don't worry. I do *not* share her misplaced feelings and have had some experience with this situation before."

Addie remembered the Thomas sisters and even Picker's change of tune when interacting with him and smiled. "Yes, I imagine you have."

"Don't worry." He squeezed her hand poised on her lap. "You'll see this is only a temporary phase of Kalea's grieving process. It will pass soon enough."

Addie nodded and hopped down onto the freshly cleared sidewalk and glanced over at Bill, who tipped his hat to her from where he stood in front of Martha's Bakery. His hand gripped a shovel handle.

"Thanks," she mouthed and grinned back at him before retrieving the briefcase from the back seat of Simon's truck.

"Sorry I can't go see Marc with you," Simon said, turning in the driver's seat. "I really need to sleep for a few hours before I start my night shift."

"That's okay. I don't suspect I'll be there long anyway. He really doesn't share much with me anymore, so it'll probably be a matter of me writing out a statement of where we got it and how we were told it came to be there. He'll dismiss me, and my part will be done."

"Tell him if he needs to speak to me about any of it, I'll be in the emergency department at seven tonight, and he can stop by there."

"Will do." She closed the door and turned to give Bill a more genuine thank you for his hard work in keeping their sidewalk cleared and was disappointed to find he was already back in the bakery. "I hope he knows how much we appreciate what he's done for us today with this crazy on again-off again snow," she muttered and gripped the briefcase in her gloved hand and scuffled inside the bookstore, stamping snow residue from her boots as she went.

When she stepped inside, she stopped short. The book-shop was buzzing. Every which way there were browsing customers, but the largest crowd was gathered around the end rack display of Civil War cookbooks Paige had set out yesterday, which, by from what she could see, was nearly depleted now.

In the middle of the crowd was—she blinked, twice—Catherine Lewis. Addie couldn't believe her eyes. Her old friend's usual shoulder-length brown bob was now a smart, chin-length undercut bob showing off the most shimmering shades of silver Addie had ever seen.

Even her clothes were chicer and more put together than normal if that was possible because Catherine always had impeccable taste. However, her current choice of a light, Danube-blue sweater paired with darker azure-blue trousers completely complemented her new hair color and gave her willowy frame a look of total elegance. Addie beamed at the sight of her holding one of the cookbooks open and talking as easily to the group of women surrounding her as though she were giving a book reading of her favorite novel.

Addie glanced over at Paige behind the counter. Customers waited in two lines for their turn to pay. So much for her plan to give Paige a quick update and then dash off to the police station. She hurriedly removed her jacket, dropped it and the briefcase behind the long Victorian sales counter, and bagged purchases as Paige rang the sales in.

When they could finally come up for air, Addie ran the sales totals for the day and whistled. "Wow," was all she said.

"Wow is right," Paige said with a chuckle. "Who knew those cookbooks and the Civil War period novels would be such big hits."

"You did good by ordering them all. Why don't you call the distributor and see if they can overnight deliver anymore for us? Tell them we'd like at least forty-eight more of each of the cookbooks, and while you're at it, see what other period novels they have in stock. Since the cooking contest is a county-wide advertised event, I don't imagine we're the only bookstore experiencing this high demand on them, so tell them we'll take whatever we can."

"They will charge extra for the rush delivery you know."

"I don't care. When we have sales numbers like these after one day, I'm thinking we've struck gold with those books."

"I hope," said Paige, dropping her voice, "that you don't mind my recruiting Catherine to help out in a pinch."

"No, of course not."

"She came in looking for you, and I was swamped. She asked me if I needed some help, and I guess the look on my face told her everything she needed to know because she took her coat off and covered the floor without another word."

"That sounds like her." Addie gazed over at her old friend, who was placing a book in the window display. "She has pitched in before when we needed her and seems to have a knack for sales. I only wish she'd take me up on my offer of coming to work here part time."

"I know. We really need the help. Even for the brief time that Kalea worked here, her second set of hands was a blessing some days."

"You mean the odd day she'd actually showed up to work?" Addie said with a sardonic chuckle.

"Yes, but she was better than nothing, I guess." Paige peered up at Addie. "Speaking of Kalea, how is she doing today?"

Addie shrugged. "It's hard to say. Her emotions are all over the place, and from experience, I know they will be for a long time yet."

"Yeah." Paige dropped her gaze. "I guess you would know that better than anyone."

Addie fought the burning behind her eyes as she recalled her own experience at discovering her fiancé, David, dead in their Boston apartment some years back. "Yup, it takes time," she mumbled and gathered the discarded books from the counter and dropped them onto the re-shelving cart.

Catherine slid up to the counter. "I hope you don't mind that I put that last cookbook in the window. With it being the last one, it looked silly all by itself on that big sales rack."

"It's a perfect solution, and the way they've been selling, I'm sure it won't last long there anyway," said Addie, thumbing through the books on the cart. "It looks like some people came in for something other than Civil War recipe books and novels, and you ladies did a great job in steering them toward the hottest books in stock instead." She laughed.

"That was all Catherine," said Paige, grinning. "She has a sixth sense for knowing what people *really* want."

"Oh pfft." Catherine giggled, and her usual peach complexion turned a cherry red. "I don't know about that, but when I mentioned the cooking contest and how authentic the recipes in the books were, well . . . we couldn't keep them on the shelf. They sold themselves."

"You know," said Addie, eyeing Catherine, "that job offer I made you still applies. We'd love you to come work with us."

"You know that's impossible with my schedule as the event coordinator at the hospital and with all the town committees I sit on. How on earth would I fit a job into my week?"

"That's the beauty of working here." Addie gave Paige a sly smile. "You and Paige could work out a schedule that works for *you*. After all, it would give you a little extra money since most everything else you do is as a volunteer."

"I don't need the money, you know that."

"I know, but it would be a little bit of play money when you go on all those fancy vacations with Jonathan."

Catherine's face drained of all its previous color, and Addie's grin faded.

"What's wrong . . . did you and Jonathan break up?"

Catherine perched on one of the counter stools and interlaced her fingers in front of her. "That's what I came in to talk to you about." She waved her hand in the air. "But my issues aren't important after I heard about the horrible incident at the dress shop yesterday, so now I feel so silly about it all."

"It was horrible, but Kalea is going to be okay. The important thing in this moment is what's happened with you. Why so glum?"

"It's just that Jonathan—"

Addie drew in a sharp breath. "What did the cad do this time?"

"He didn't do anything. That's just the thing. I mean I know the reputation your ex-almost-father-in-law has with women, but he's different with me."

Addie fought her inner eye roll, knowing full well that a leopard can't change its spots, but Catherine was right. He had treated her different from his previous women friends, and Catherine had been so happy with him. "Then what happened?"

"It's what didn't happen." Her hazel-brown eyes reddened with unshed tears. "As you know, I was supposed to meet him for Thanksgiving—"

"At an undisclosed destination, as per usual, right?" said Addie.

"Yeah, the life of a government agent," chimed in Paige. "Poor you never knowing until you basically landed at a destination where you'd be holidaying with him."

"That part of it was actually exciting. It kept me on my toes and took me out of my comfort zone. I never knew when I left for the airport exactly where I'd end up until I got to the ticket counter," Catherine said, twisting her fingers.

"So what happened then?" Addie cupped her chin in her hand and leaned on the counter.

"I got a message from him this morning, telling me

he's been put on an assignment in the South and can't meet me as planned."

"In the South?"

"Yes, that's all he could say, and you know as well as I that could mean anything south of the county line to the South Pole." She glanced up and met Addie's gaze. "That means I have no place to go for Thanksgiving dinner."

"Nonsense!" Addie exclaimed. "You're like a mother to me. You'll come to my house this year like everyone else is."

"I wouldn't want to impose." Her gaze searched Addie's face.

"Catherine, you've known me since I was a baby. You would have married my father if my grandmother hadn't interfered." Addie had a fleeting thought of what her life might have been like if her grandmother hadn't fiercely objected to Addie's father courting Catherine while Addie's mother lay in a long-drawn out coma before she eventually passed away. The idea of how close Catherine came to being her stepmother at one time brought a wistful smile to Addie's lips. "So I won't hear a word about imposition from you. You are part of my family, and you've been dating David's father for long enough for goodness sakes. How many family ties do we have to have until you see that?"

"I guess when you put it like that." Catherine's cheeks took on their usual peach glow, and she grinned. "I'd love to come."

"Great. You can bring one or two of your amazing pies."

Catherine waved her finger in the air. "I was hoping you'd say that because"—she rose and darted toward the window display, returning with the last copy of *Godey's*

Lady's cookbook in her hand—"I saw a recipe in here that I'd love to make for our dinner."

"Then consider the book yours for pitching in and helping Paige out today."

"Really, because I can p—"

"Nope." Addie shook her head. "Paige could you please ring that up and put it under my bill."

"You got it." Paige grinned as her fingers flew across the cash register.

"Then it's settled." Addie glanced up at the antique wall clock behind the counter. "Oh dear, it's almost four. I'd better get to the police station and give this to Marc."

"I see Doctor Blue-Eyes was successful with Picker."

"He sure was. You wouldn't believe the information she gave him about where she found this, but I'll tell you later. I'd better go now."

"Wait," Catherine said, her questioning gaze going from Addie to Paige. "What are you two talking about? Does it have something to do with what happened to Jared yesterday?"

A teasing grin came to Addie's lips. "If you want to stay and help Paige out for another hour until she closes, she could fill you in."

"Of course, I will," Catherine said, rubbing her hands together. "You know how much I love a good mystery."

"Then you're going to love hearing about this one because it has all of us baffled at this point."

Chapter 11

Addie studied the officer behind the reception desk. She didn't look as young and green as most of the other rookies did. In Addie's mind, the woman must be at least mid- to late-thirties, and she wondered if she'd transferred to Greyborne Harbor from a different district. Nevertheless, she had been courteous, not overly friendly, but polite when she told Addie to take a seat and the chief would see her when he could.

As the minutes ticked by, Addie fidgeted with the briefcase handle and debated whether she should try to impress on the officer *again* the importance of what she needed to see Marc about. She was going to miss Jerry always being nearby and her friend Carolyn, Simon's sister, now that she had been promoted to field-training sergeant. She glanced at Marc's closed office door, and her heart ached at the realization of all the changes that had occurred over the course of the past few years. Long gone were the days when she could sweep in here, take a seat at Marc's desk, and discuss a case with him or get tidbits of information from Jerry or Carolyn that would help put a few of the puzzle pieces together.

Addie looked back over at the latest addition to the Greyborne Harbor police force, and realized she was a complete outsider in this new reality. Marc's door flew open. He came out and dropped some papers on the desk in front of the officer, glanced up, and spotted Addie.

"Addie? Are you waiting for me?"

Addie rose to her feet and pinned the officer with a searching gaze.

"Umm . . . sorry . . . chief," the officer stuttered. "I knew you were busy, so I didn't want to interrupt you. I asked Miss Greyborne to wait."

Marc glowered at the officer.

"It's just that Chief Brookes never wanted to be inter-rupted."

"I'm not Chief Brookes, and we do things differently here."

"Yes, sir." She nodded and glanced sheepishly at Addie.

Addie was right after all. The officer was a transfer and from none other than Salem. This should be interest-ing. Addie wondered at Ryley Brookes's motivation by sending the officer to Greyborne Harbor. Was it to spy on Marc? It was no secret that Ryley, even though she had eagerly accepted the position of Chief of Police in Salem, wasn't ready to completely say good-bye to the ties she had to this community—Marc being the number-one tie.

"Come in please, Addie, and I hope you weren't wait-ing too long." He flashed a quick look back at the officer, showing his displeasure, and closed the door behind them. "Have a seat, but I do hope you're not here to plead the case against your cousin because you know I can't discuss an ongoing investigation with you." He sat in his chair behind the large oak desk.

"No, it's this!" She held up the briefcase, grinning. "It's Jared's missing case."

He rose to his feet and stared at it, and then pinned his gaze on hers. "Where in the world did you find that?"

"Funny story," she said, setting the briefcase on his desk. She unbuttoned her red wool coat and slid into one of the two chairs facing him. "Someone came into my shop this morning wanting to sell it."

"Does this someone have a name?" he asked, his gaze still focused on the briefcase.

"Yes, but for now, we'll just say this person says it was found in the trash dumpster behind the furniture store down the street from Kalea's dress shop."

He glanced up at her under a creased brow. "Really? And you believe this mystery person?"

She slowly nodded. "Yes, yes I do. I wasn't certain at first because that seemed like the probable thing even someone guilty of killing Jared might say. Let's just say that due to a few other things that transpired, I am less questioning about the legitimacy of this person's statement than I initially was."

He sat down and fixed his gaze on her. "You know you are going to have to tell me who this person is, and through further questioning, I will determine whether or not this person's statement of how they came to be in possession of this is valid or not."

"I know," she said reluctantly, "but I hate being a snitch, and this person won't take well to be questioned about this by the police."

"Addie . . ."

"Okay, here's the whole story . . ." She went onto tell him the events leading up to how she and Simon acquired the briefcase and Kalea verifying that it was, in fact, Jared's. When she finished, she sat back in the chair and studied Marc's face and watched for the telltale tic of his jaw showing his displeasure with her amateur-sleuthing endeavors. Instead, he shrugged his shoulders.

"Freda Horst, you say?"

She nodded.

"Well . . ." He sat back and tapped his pen on a pad of paper. "I've never known Picker to be a thief let alone a murderer. Yes, I'm inclined to believe her version of how she came across this"—he motioned with the pen toward the briefcase—"so I'll hold off talking to her today."

Relief swept through Addie.

"But I will have to take a run out there tomorrow and ask her about it."

Addie's gut tightened.

"Did you open it?"

"No, and I've only worn gloves since we acquired it."

"What about before that?"

"In my shop, I did touch the leather shell, and I can't say how much Picker handled it, or Simon, although I know he was careful and was wearing gloves, too, for the most part. If you run our prints and Picker's against any others you find on there, it might still be something to go on," she said hopefully.

"Yes, but Kalea said Jared picked this up Sunday at a pawnshop in Boston, right?"

"Yes."

"Then chances are there's going to be a lot of prints we aren't going to be able to identify anyway." He sat back and studied the case. "What do you think it's worth? Enough to kill someone for?"

"Not unless the killer was desperate for money. My thought still is that there was something inside it, maybe some business papers Jared had that the thief was after."

"Okay." He tapped the pen and then clicked on the intercom. "Jerry, are you in your office?"

"Yes, sir," Jerry's voice crackled over the small speaker.

"Can you come up to my office and bring a crime-scene case."

"Be right there."

After Jerry arrived with the kit, Marc sat back and stared at the briefcase. He weaved his pen through his fingers, but he didn't say a word as Jerry brushed the outside of the case for fingerprints. That job done, Marc motioned for Jerry to open the case. They collectively sucked in a deep breath as Jerry unclipped the two fasteners and lifted the lid. Addie edged to the front of her chair and peered inside. The dark-red silk-lined briefcase was empty, as they all suspected it would be, but Addie still felt disappointed. There appeared to be no clues, no scraps of paper, and no residue of an object that might have been enclosed in the case. Nothing that would exonerate her cousin in Jared's murder.

She sat back in her chair and trailed her fingers over the smooth wooden armrests and then shot forward, glancing into the case as Jerry dusted the inside for prints. Based on a hunch, she studied every detail of the lining, looking for spaces in the corners, a sign that it had been tampered with—anything—but saw nothing. It didn't make sense. Her hunch had been so strong. There had to be something different about this briefcase that she wasn't seeing right now.

She slid back into her chair and stared at the case. The sinking feeling that her cousin was going to be charged with murder was growing in her gut, and any hope she had that it would prove her cousin's innocence faded. She sighed and glanced at the clock on the wall behind Marc's desk. *Five thirty, already?* She leapt to her feet.

"It seems we really got nowhere with this, but at least you have it, and I have to go. I'm meeting Serena at the community hall at seven but still need to get home and check on Kalea and Pippi."

Marc walked her out with assurances that if something were to turn up on the case analysis, he would let her know. *Yeah, right?* She crossed the waiting room and opened the glass door to head outside. Behind her, she heard him say, "In the future, Officer Adams, you will tell me when someone is waiting to see me, and *I* will be the one to decide when I can see them. Do I make myself clear?"

The door closed, and Addie couldn't hear the officer's reply, but by the sharp tone of Marc's voice, she guessed it would have been "yes sir." Addie pulled the collar of her jacket tighter to help ward off the brisk winds that had whipped up since she went inside. She gingerly made her way to her car in the police station parking lot and noted that with the sun going down, the slush had started to freeze. She inwardly cringed at the thought of trying to make it up the hill to her house.

When she had finally bumped and slipped her way through the frozen slush ruts on the street and crept to a near standstill to turn into her driveway, she came to a hard stop at the top of the drive. *Why is Simon's truck here?*

Panic surged through her as she pressed hard on the accelerator. After fishtailing down the drive, her Mini skidded to a stop, and Addie raced up the steps to the front door. *What happened? Was Kalea all right?* Worst-case scenarios raced through her mind as she flung the door open. She stopped abruptly at the giddy sounds of her cousin's laughter coming from the living room. Addie peeked through the double-wide doorway to see Kalea reclined on Addie's antique sofa. Her hand rested on Simon's arm as he sat on the edge of the deep, overstuffed couch beside her. Tears of laughter streamed down his cheeks. Addie's panic turned to shock and apprehension of the scene she'd walked in on.

Chapter 12

Since both appeared to be locked in their own world—
one she wasn't a part of—and oblivious to Addie
looming in the doorway, she cleared her throat. Pippi
perked her ears, let out a yip, leapt from the sofa, and
scooted across the oriental area rug to Addie's side. The
flurry of the little dog's activity brought a defeated sigh
from Kalea, and a flushed-cheeked glance from Simon.

He lurched to his feet. "Addie! I, I was . . . just checking on Kalea," he stammered, "and—"

"It looks like your patient's doing just fine, if you ask
me," Addie said coolly as she scooped Pippi up and snuggled her close.

"She was having a bad afternoon," he said as he sailed
toward her and took her hand in his. "She asked me to
bring her another sedative."

Addie glanced past him to her cousin, lying half prone,

propped up on cushions with a catlike smugness in her eyes, and wearing—if Addie wasn't mistaken—Addie's pink silk dressing gown.

"The sedative appears to have worked." Addie pulled her hand away and cradled Pippi closer.

"Actually," Kalea cooed and fixed her unyielding gaze on Addie's, "I didn't end up needing it."

Addie glanced questioningly from her to Simon.

"It seems his company turned out be exactly what the doctor ordered." She giggled. "Simon here was *so* kind and gentle. It took him no time at all to take my mind off my grief." She dabbed at—from what Addie could tell were—dry eyes with a tissue. "I feel so much better now. He really is a miracle worker."

"Yes, he is, isn't he?" Addie turned on her heel. "Well, I'll leave the good doctor to care for his . . . *patient*." Before heading to the foyer, she flashed a glance of distaste at her cousin, who still held the look of an insolent cat about her.

"I have to be leaving now anyway," said Simon, skirting past Addie to the coatrack.

"Oh, don't leave on my account, please." Addie paused. "Finish *caring* for your patient."

"I'm on shift in an hour. I'll call you later," he said, leaning toward her, his lips searching out her cheek.

She recoiled and opened the door. "I won't be home this evening. I'm meeting Serena at seven."

"I can still call later, can't I?"

"I don't think I'll be home until past ten."

"I see." He swallowed hard as he buttoned his jacket. He paused at the door she held open. "Addie, are we okay?"

She hesitated and glanced toward the living room and then back at him. "I don't know, are we?"

"Yes." He leaned toward her and cupped her face in his hands. "It was a house call to a distressed patient who's just suffered a great loss, that's all."

She dropped her gaze and focused on the toes of the wet boots she still wore.

"I mean it, Addie." He tilted her chin up, forcing her to look at him. "There is nothing for you to worry about. It was strictly a professional courtesy for a patient and *your* relative."

Addie recalled Kalea's words to Pippi and then her behavior toward Simon, not only then but also earlier in the day. She didn't doubt his intentions but definitely her cousin's. Something didn't sit right with Addie, and she wasn't buying the grieving girlfriend bit. She knew her evening with Serena would be a mess with thoughts of this awkward incident unless she got to the bottom of it. Soon. However, first she had to get *Doctor Dreamy* out the door. Obviously, he was too great a distraction for her poor—*grieving*—cousin. She wanted to gag.

"We'll talk tomorrow." She all but pushed him out onto the step before closing the door. She leaned her forehead on the cool mahogany wood. Tears burned behind her eyes. "Get it together, girl," she whispered, pulled herself upright, and stared at the open pocket doors that led into her living room. She wheezed in a deep breath and marched over to Kalea, hovering beside her.

"I have to go out for the evening. I was worried about leaving you on your own again, but"—she glanced at her cousin, who had now covered herself with a throw blanket from the back of the sofa—"I can see you're doing just fine, so I'll grab something to eat, change, and go as I planned. We can talk about all this later."

Kalea nodded and tucked the blanket under her chin.

Addie whirled around and started toward the door. Pippi wiggled in her arms and barked, her little paws scratching at the air as she struggled to get back to Kalea. Addie sighed and set her down. She scampered back to the sofa, took a flying leap, and snuggled in next to Kalea's side, a place she had not left for the past two days.

Addie shook her head. It was bad enough she felt betrayed by Simon but now by her own dog, too? She started up the stairs to her bedroom, but just as her foot hovered above the first step, she heard soft whimpers, not Pippi's, but her cousin's. Gripping the carved mahogany banister, her knuckles whitened and burned. It appeared that later was now. She swiveled on the step and went back into the living room. After all, Kalea was family, and family looked after family no matter what. *Right?*

Kalea lifted her blotchy face, revealing tear-blurred eyes. "It wasn't what you think."

"I hope not."

"It's just that Simon is so kind and so caring, he makes me feel . . ."

Addie waited for Kalea to finish her sentence, but she didn't.

"How did you ever get through this?" Kalea asked, her voice distant and hollow.

Maybe Addie had had been wrong and was only remembering the college girl her cousin used to be and the person she was when she first came to live in Greyborne Harbor. She hadn't been seeing her as the smart, talented, businesswoman she had become through the last year, who had also just lost the love of her life.

Addie settled on the coffee table beside Kalea, dropped her head, and stared at an imaginary spot on the carpet. "To be honest, it was tough for a long time. I always felt like I was driving through the fog with my headlights on high beam. You know how that is? When you can only focus as far as you can see in front of you. Everything around you is a distorted blur and nothing makes sense."

"Exactly and sometimes I feel like I'm drowning, you know?"

"Yes, and when you come up for air, you take in another mouthful, and then one day it happens less and less, and one day you can breathe again."

"That's what I hoped for when I called Simon. He's always been so nice and kind to me even when I didn't deserve it and you were mad at me about something. He made me feel like everything would be okay and was always so sweet. Besides, I knew he'd make me feel better just being here because I always have so much fun teasing him and—"

"Flirting with him?"

Kalea nodded slowly. "It was a distraction, that's all. Something that made me feel like my old self again." She fixed her haunted gaze on Addie. "Will I ever get past this?"

Addie recalled her own fears of being locked so deeply into a love that was tragically torn away from her and nodded. "It's hard when you loved someone so much you wonder how you'll ever move on from that. You will make stupid mistakes and say stupid things because you can't think clearly, but, eventually, you will come out the other side."

"What if I didn't? You know . . . love him."

Addie's blood froze in her veins, and all she could do was stare blankly at her cousin.

"I mean, I liked him . . . for a while anyway, but . . ."

"But what?" Addie remembered Kalea's words to Pippi.

"But . . . we had an argument the night before he . . . died." Kalea gulped and shifted on her pillows. "And . . ."

"And what?"

"And we said some pretty nasty things to each other. It's no secret that when my shop started to become successful, he saw Greyborne Harbor as a good business investment. He began financing some of the other business in town that needed money to help take them to the next level or expand."

Addie nodded. "I heard he was financing a few others but didn't know there were problems."

"Oh, there were, believe me. He was cold and ruthless when it came to business. I could always manage to soften him up and—"

"Twist him around your little finger?"

"I guess, yes. But not everyone else he financed could do that, and he was starting to become unsympathetic in his dealings and making a lot of enemies around town."

Addie wasn't aware of any of this. Sure, she had heard a few rumors and grumblings, but she never imagined it was this bad. She sat forward and rested her elbows on her knees. "Marc mentioned you told him you and Jared had an argument, but that's all he said. Did you tell him it was about his business dealings and how he acted?"

Kalea shook her head. "I didn't go into details. It hurt so much, and I knew what he'd think of me if I told him everything."

A shiver ran through Addie, and she leaned closer to

Kalea. "I think you'd better start from the beginning and tell me exactly what happened on Sunday."

Kalea's bottom lip trembled. She nodded, wiped the back of her hand over her tear-streaked cheeks, and drew in a deep breath. "That day we went to Boston because Jared had a business lunch with a corporate CEO he was working with to fund some big development on the water-front there."

"But it was Sunday."

"I know, but the guy is pretty busy, and that was the only day he could meet. Since my store is closed on Sundays, I tagged along and shopped while they had their luncheon meeting. Later, when Jared texted me to say he was done, I told him where I was, which was just down the street. He said he would meet me on the corner. I was standing there, and he started across right when the light changed, but he had to run the last steps because the traffic started to move. Just then, the handle on his briefcase broke, and a truck whizzed by, barely missing him, but it didn't miss his father's antique briefcase."

"That's too bad. I know how much that case meant to him."

"Yes, and he was devastated. Angry. I've never seen him like that before." Kalea shivered. "I didn't know what to do, so I suggested we go to the antique store on Marine Drive to see if they had something he might like."

"So you bought the case that was stolen in Greyborne Harbor?"

"No, he was standing there with a crushed case, all his documents hanging out of the edges, and he shouted at me—right there in the middle of the street—that he needed something now. So I told him about a pawnshop I'd seen earlier and said maybe they would have something there he could buy until he found one like his father's. That seemed to calm him a little until we couldn't see any in the shop, and he started up again. I suggested *again* that we check the one here in town. Well, the young clerk behind the counter—I guess he'd been listening to our conversation—probably couldn't help but overhear because Jared was in such a snarky mood and getting really loud as he stomped around the store, searching. In any case, the clerk came over to me and asked if I was from Greyborne Harbor. When I said yes, he asked if we were looking for something particular. I told him about the briefcase, and he said his boss told him that it was in the back. When he returned, he had a beautiful, hand-crafted vintage case. It was perfect, and Jared loved it."

"The guy just happened to have one in the back?"

"I know, weird, right?" Kalea waved her hand. "Anyway, I wasn't interested in the haggling over money part. I was just happy that Jared found what he wanted. Maybe he'd calm down, and the ride home would be a bit more tolerable. While I waited, I headed over to the rack of vintage dresses on the far side of the store. A few minutes later, Jared was ready to leave, and we started back to Greyborne Harbor. That's when he said something odd."

"What?"

"He thanked me for the early birthday gift." Kalea looked at Addie. "His birthday isn't until just before Christmas, so I had no idea what he was talking about. I thought maybe he meant me going to Boston with him, so I shrugged it off and just smiled."

"And he didn't say anything else?"

"Not until later. I was cutting out a dress pattern, and he came up behind me, wrapped his arms around me, and thanked me again for the gift. He said it was so similar to his dad's that he was shocked and that meant so much to him. He asked me how I knew he would need it when I bought it while I was shopping before he met me."

"What do you mean?"

"I was as lost as you are now. I didn't have a clue what he was talking about, and when I said that to him, he laughed and told me that when he went over to the counter to pay, the boy gestured toward me, and said, 'She took care of everything already.'"

"That doesn't make sense." Addie shifted on the coffee table. "He thought you bought it for him while you were shopping earlier?"

"Yes, but how could I have known then that his other one would get run over by a truck an hour later?"

"Exactly." Addie scowled and tried to follow along with her cousin's story.

"I told him that and said it must be a mistake and that we should take it back to tell the kid we never paid for it."

"Well, yeah, that would be the right thing to do. Obviously, the young man made a mistake, and one that might cost him his job."

"That's what I said to Jared, but he got mad. He said if the kid screwed up then it was his fault, and we got lucky because that case probably cost a lot of money. A win-win he called it."

"You're kidding, right? He felt no remorse over the fact that the clerk might get fired over it?"

"Nope, so we argued for the rest of the evening. No matter what I said, he wouldn't listen to me. He just didn't care. He got what he wanted, and that was good enough for him."

Addie shook her head. "I had no idea he was like that."

"It wasn't the first time I'd seen him with the *me first*

attitude and no regard for how his actions might affect anybody else. So needless to say, I didn't sleep well that night because I decided I was going to break up with him."

"Did you tell him that night?"

"No, I wanted to wait until we had both calmed down and slept on it. He was supposed to come back after his meeting in Salem because he had a difficult, as he said, client here to deal with later that day."

"Did he say who it was?"

"No, and you know when I think back, a few people he'd had dealings with warned me about going into business with him, but I was so cocky I thought I had him where I wanted him and ignored the warnings." She locked her gaze on Addie's. "But I came to find they were right, and he really didn't have a moral compass." She shook her head. "That poor boy. I imagine his boss will take the cost of the case out of his salary, and he will probably lose his job anyway." She sniffled. "And Jared didn't care."

"What about what I heard you tell Pippi?"

Kalea dabbed her eyes and glanced blankly at Addie. "When?"

"When I put you to bed after you were released from the police station, you said, 'Oh, Pippi, what a mess. What have I done?'"

Kalea looked her straight in the eyes. "I felt guilty."

"Why?"

"Because . . . I had wished Sunday night when I went to bed that he would just die."

Chapter 13

The tale Kalea had recited to Addie haunted her all the way down the hill toward the town center. As she passed the police station on Main Street, she noticed Marc's office light was still on. Her foot wavered between the accelerator and the brake. Should she or shouldn't she tell him right now what her cousin had just said? After all, it might be a lead in the case and point the finger at someone else. Provided, of course, he could track down everyone—apparently quite a few people— Jared was having business dealings with.

She slowed to crawl when she approached the turn into the visitor parking lot at the police station, but a horn honked behind her and jolted her from her thoughts. She glanced at the clock. Darn, she was already half an hour late meeting Serena at the community hall. Her tummy let out an agonized moan. Plus, she forgot to eat. No wonder she was in a brain fog and couldn't make a decision. Even one of those stale bran muffins in her fridge would have been good right about then. She grumbled and waved an apology in her rearview mirror and stepped on the gas.

Marc would have to wait until later. His sister and her best friend needed her wingman tonight. For all of Serena's bubbly energy and her easy-going nature, her shyness around a group of virtual strangers must have her paralyzed with fear.

Addie whipped into the community hall parking lot, found an empty space at the rear close to the alley, and hopped out. As she made her way around to the main doors, she admired the stone and clapboard structure. It was hard to believe that it—like the church across the street—had stood on this very spot for well over two-hundred years, and still to this day, the buildings were used regularly by Greyborne Harbor's residents.

She flung open the heavy pine door and stepped into a large entrance, littered with coats. From the stairs leading up to the main hall, voices punctuated by spikes of laughter reached her ears.

It sounded liked like a good crowd tonight, and she crossed her fingers that Serena wouldn't be quivering in a corner as she waited for Addie. She hung up her coat on a peg hook and made her way up the four rough-hewn pine-beam steps into the large hall. She scanned the room in search for her redheaded friend and was taken aback by the work the restoration committee had completed the past year. The wide-planked oak floors gleamed under the overhead lights, and wooden beams and pillars offset the Tudor-styled whitewashed walls. This is what the space must have looked like when it was built by her ancestors as a place to hold their town meetings and to use as a community gathering place.

Her stomach tightened when she realized every business owner within fifty miles must be here. Competition for the grand prize was going to be steep, and she hoped Serena would be up to it and hadn't already bolted. She was nowhere to be seen. Addie's stomach rumbled when she caught a whiff of fresh-brewed coffee. Where there was coffee, there might also be food, and she followed her nose through the crowd, only pausing long enough to say a hurried hello to the Thomas sisters, Betty-Lou from the Candy Barrel down on Marine Drive, and Mario from her favorite restaurant.

Her focus narrowed in on the long table across the back wall, and heaved a sigh of relief when she stumbled up to the table. She hungrily scanned the assortment of fresh-baked products, the large sandwich tray, and immediately set about loading up a Styrofoam plate with generous portions of each offering.

She popped the first petite, crustless sandwich wedge in her mouth, closed her eyes, and savored the moment. Her stomach gurgled in gratitude.

"Addie! I'm so glad you're finally here. You aren't going to believe this, but—"

Serena yanked on Addie's arm, and Addie's plate flipped out of her hand and landed upside down on the white linen tablecloth.

"Oops, sorry."

Addie turned slowly and fixed a cool gaze on a certain petite redhead.

"My bad. I'll clean that up." Serena grabbed napkins and swept the jumble of sandwich pieces back onto Addie's plate. She swabbed at the stain left on the tablecloth, gave up, and moved a tray over to cover it, and presented Addie with her plate of food.

The look on Serena's face took on the same characteristics of a cat sharing its latest kill. Addie glanced down at the shambled mess on her plate and grinned. It probably didn't reach her eyes, but Addie didn't care. She was going for sardonic anyway. "Gee, thanks," she said as she stepped over to the trash can and tossed it in. "Now, tell me"—she turned back to her friend—"What's got you so excited this evening? I expected to find you hiding in the corner when I finally got here."

"What me? No." Serena glanced around. "I know most of the people here, but you have to come and listen to Gwendolyn Buchannan. She's over there, giving a talk."

"Who is she?" asked Addie, standing on tiptoes to try and catch a glimpse of this person, who had Serena so excited she'd literally torn Addie's dinner from her hands.

"She's the chairwoman of the Essex County Historical Association committee and an expert on everything Civil War."

"Oh," said Addie somewhat deflated, not quite understanding her friend's enthusiasm.

"She's giving a mini-lecture on the role of women during the war, including some interesting cooking tips and how to adapt them to our modern technology."

"That sounds like something *you'd* definitely be interested in. Me? My only interest right now is the food arranged on this table that is already prepared with our modern technology and waiting to be devoured. So, if you don't mind, you can find me right here when the talk is over."

"Then I suppose you also have no interest in hearing what she has to say about the literature of the time?"

"Books? She's talking books, too?" Addie craned her neck to get a glimpse of this mysterious woman. "Why didn't you lead with that? Come on." She gave a tug on Serena's sweater sleeve and snatched a sandwich wedge off the top of the tray as they passed. She shoved it in her mouth and even managed to chew and swallow it by the time they got to the edge of the large group of people circled around the woman, whom Serena dubbed, the *grande dame* of the society.

From where they stood, Addie could only catch fleeting glimpses of the woman who had her friend all in a dither, but from what she could see, she was rather impressed with her regal stature. The woman was dressed in a mid-calf, two-piece, champagne-colored skirt suit. A single strand of pearls hung from her neck, and her white hair was tightly curled and worn up. Addie thought it resembled a crown perched on her head. Addie stifled a giggle. All the woman needed was a lorgnette to appear every bit a dowager queen looking down her Romanesque nose as she addressed her loyal subjects.

Addie cupped a hand behind her ear in hopes of amplifying the woman's muffled voice. But it was no use. From where she stood, Addie could not hear even a quarter of what the woman was saying, especially when the background noise drowned out every second word. She went to nudge Serena and tell her she was going back to the refreshment table. Her elbow hit air. Serena was no longer at her side, but front and center, hanging on every word the dowager queen uttered. As Addie turned to make her way back to the only thing she could focus on now, a small voice beside her caught her attention.

"Excuse me. Are you the woman who owns Beyond the Page Books and Curios?"

"Why, yes, I'm Addie Greyborne." She reached out her hand to accept the fragile-appearing woman's slender one.

The woman took Addie's hand in both hers and pumped it harder than her appearance would indicate. Her alabaster skin tone showed a slight blush of the cheeks. "I am thrilled to finally meet you. I'm Ivy Walker, the owner of Time Travels, the vintage and antique shop down on Marine Drive."

"Really?" Addie beamed. "I *love* that shop."

"You've been there?"

"Yes, a few times. It's funny, though, I always thought the owner was a man."

"That's my brother, Nick. We co-own the shop."

Addie recalled when Kalea came to work for her. "That's nice because from my own experience, families and business don't always mix."

"I know. When our parents passed on, and we were left to run it, we decided the only way to make it work, and not kill each other, was for him to look after the day-to-day running of the store, and I would do all the traveling. We have some regular customers that are interested in adding to their collections, and I try to hunt down items on their wish lists."

"You must put on a lot of miles between all the garage and estate sales and auctions."

"I do. It's tough keeping up with the demand for new inventory. Who knew so many people in the county had a love for all things old?" She let out a soft laugh. "But I suppose with your antique and rare bookstore, you already know that."

"Yes, it seems the farther we go into the future the more people crave a connection with the past." Addie waved her hand in the air. "Just look at the turnout for this event and all the people who are itching to produce an authentic Civil War dish."

Ivy grinned, and her electric-blue eyes lit up, illustrating a starker contrast to her raven hair. She nudged Addie's arm. "If you ask me, I think that has more to do with the five-thousand-dollar grand prize and the magazine spread."

"You're probably right," Addie said with a soft laugh.

"But that's what I wanted to talk to you about."

"I'm not entering." Addie put her hand up in a stop motion. "I can't cook to save myself from starvation. Just ask my neighbors. The fire department had to come one night when I made a pot of spaghetti."

"No," Ivy said, "I meant that there's a lot of talk tonight about the *Godey's Lady's Book* and the recipes they published. I was wondering if you happen to have any of the original bound volumes."

"I wish," said Addie. "I'd love to get my hands on even one of the originals."

"That's too bad because I have a regular client who collects all things Sarah Josepha Hale, you know, the long-time editor and contributing writer of the magazine."

"Yes, I'm familiar with her work. She wrote 'Mary Had a Little Lamb,' too, right?"

"You wouldn't happen to have a copy of that would you?" Ivy's eyes held a glimmer of hope.

"Sadly, no," said Addie, "and the only *Godey's Lady's Book* articles I have right now are newer editions and print copies of the originals that a friend from the Boston Library sent me."

"That's too bad, but when I saw you, I thought, hopefully, that you might have come across something in your own travels."

"Not yet, but if I do, now I know you're interested, you'll be my first call."

"That would be fantastic. Maybe between the two of us, we can find something that will help me score points with my client."

"That's what running a successful business is about, isn't it? Keeping our customers happy."

"Yes, and I think I have a few things in the store right now that might make you happy."

"Books?"

"Sorry, I don't have any first editions right now, but I do have a large collection of vintage bookmarks and bookends that I recently purchased from an estate sale. You should come in and have a look. Who knows, perhaps they're something you might consider selling in your bookstore."

"I'm always on the lookout for new items to add for my customers, so yes, I will drop in. When's a good time?"

"Anytime really. I'm back out on the road tomorrow, but I'll tell Nick to finish uncrating them and to keep the collection in the back room until you have a chance to see what's there and decide if you're interested or not."

"That would be fantastic. Tell him I'll try and get in tomorrow around lunchtime."

"Perfect!" She took Addie's hand in hers. "I'm so glad I met you. I have a feeling we have a lot in common."

"I think you're right." Addie grinned down at her. "It's not every day I meet someone who has the same love of all things old as I do."

Ivy disappeared into the crowd, and Addie, still smiling at the thought of meeting a kindred spirit, realized the dowager queen's talk was over. The crowd that had gathered to hear the president of the historical association speak dispersed, and Serena had the queen of the evening all to herself.

Serena spotted her and waved Addie over to them. Fighting against the current of people, Addie zigzagged her way upstream through the throng heading downstream and slid up to her friend's side.

"Addie, I'd like you to meet Gwendolyn Buchannan." Serena grinned widely. "Mrs. Buchannan, this is my friend Addie Greyborne, the woman I was telling you about who owns the used and rare bookstore here in town."

The woman stared down her hawkish nose and nodded. "Miss Greyborne, are you any relation to Anita Greyborne of *the* Greyborne family and town founders?"

"Why, yes, she was my great-aunt."

"Ah, I should have known. You have your aunt's eyes. I must say, it's lovely to meet you, my dear." The woman extended a hand that was more like a road map of intersecting blue veins and crevices, but she made no move to take Addie's. Instead, she simply left it dangling. Addie wondered if she was supposed to kiss her ruby ring or the back of the woman's hand, but neither image appealed to her, so Addie simply shook Queen Gwendolyn's fingertips and let the whole awkward moment go.

"Miss Greyborne, the reason I was anxious to meet you is because your friend here tells me you have a vast collection of *Godey's Lady's Book* articles." At Addie's nod, she gave an imperious smile. "Tell me, are they the bound leather editions?"

"Unfortunately, no. They are print copies of the originals the Boston Library has in their collection."

"That is unfortunate. I guess I was misled." She glowered down her nose at Serena. "As we all know, copies are a dime a dozen, aren't they?"

Addie glanced at Serena, and her friend shrugged sheepishly.

"Here." The woman produced an elegant business card from her clutch purse. "Since you deal in rare books, I would appreciate you letting me know should you come across anything that a distant relative of mine might have published."

Addie glanced down at the gold embossed card and back into the woman's faded-blue eyes. "A relative?"

"Yes, Sarah Josepha Hale."

With a curt nod of her head, Gwendolyn turned her back abruptly, an obvious signal that Addie and Serena had been dismissed. She began chatting to another woman wearing a historical society name badge.

"Addie," Serena whispered, "honest, I never told her you had originals, I only told her you had some articles and posters, and that's where I got the pie recipe I planned on making for the competition."

"Don't worry about it. I have the feeling that Mrs. Buchannan is used to getting whatever she wants, when she wants, and was disappointed I couldn't give it to her."

Chapter 14

"Slow down, there's one right there." Addie pointed excitedly out the window.

"Perfect." Serena brought her Wrangler to a skidding halt and maneuvered it into the parallel parking spot. "I was starting to think we'd have to park at the other end of Marine Drive and walk all the way back."

"Who knew it would be so busy down here at lunch time, right?" Addie said, opening the passenger door.

"We are in the heart of restaurant row on the boardwalk, so I guess we should have known better."

"You're right." Addie stood beside Serena's SUV and gazed out past the boardwalk and seawall to the harbor in front of them.

The sun was showing its face—for the first day in a week—and the scenery was breathtaking. The sunlight glistened like a cascade of diamonds off the crests of the rolling waves as they spilled over the rocks on the beach. As far as she could see, the horizon was dotted with the occasional fishing boat still moored in the harbor, despite the approaching winter months. Through the thin mist, she managed to make out a few of the many smaller islands off the mainland. To her right, was the cruise ship pier, the visitor's center, the lighthouse, and the Greyborne Point B&B, all within easy walking distance.

"You know I really should have opened my bookstore down here on the harbor edge."

"No!" cried Serena, joining her on the sidewalk. "If you had, we'd never have met."

"I'm pretty sure we would have, eventually, but look at these buildings." Addie scanned the row of colorfully painted clapboard shops running down the drive. "These are the original structures that were first built in the town. Long before my relatives decided to move up the hill and create the current town center and everything else up there." She waved her hand. "The preservation and restoration that has gone into maintaining this area is . . . well, it's awe-inspiring."

"Get your head out of the past, and let's go see these bookmarks you're so excited about."

Addie howled in laughter. "Really? We're about to walk into a shop called Time Travels that sells antiques, and you're telling me to get my head out of the past."

"You know what I mean, and if for one minute, you think I'm going to stand idly by as you close up your shop and move down here . . . Well, my friend, you'd better think again." Serena flung open the wooden, framed-window door and stepped inside.

Addie hesitated on the threshold. It was almost too much to take in. Everywhere she looked, there was a display of times gone by. A reverence seeped through her as though she were entering an historic museum.

"I know this store like the back of my hand," touted Serena gleefully. "I think I covered every square inch when I was looking for the perfect pieces for our house. I'm going to head in that direction to check out the pottery display." She pointed to the far front corner beside the window. "Maybe I'll get lucky and find something from the Civil War era to showcase my contest entry on."

A tall, dark-haired man at the sales counter discussed a Tiffany-styled lamp with a young couple. From the alabaster skin tone and shock of raven hair, Addie assumed he was Ivy's brother, Nick.

Browsing while she waited to ask him about the bookmarks, Addie paused in front of an antique china cabinet near the sales counter. Something on top of it caught her eye. A shabby, black briefcase. And from the looks of it, possibly from the same era as Jared's. After squinting at it, she realized it wasn't anything like his but was actually an old medical bag.

She stood on tiptoes and managed to dance it toward the edge of the shelf. It finally wobbled loose and dropped into her outstretched hands with a thud. The weight took her by surprise, and she nearly dropped it on the wooden-planked floor. However, once secured in her hands, the texture of the leather told her immediately it was genuine calfskin. By the satchel style and solid brass hardware finishing, she was convinced it was from the same 1930s time period as Jared's. She couldn't restrain the smile that spread across her face as she turned the case over, assessing the minor wear and tear. It was well used but also well loved by its previous owner or owners. *This would be the perfect Christmas gift for Simon!*

"You have very good taste," said a low-key, silvery voice over her shoulder.

Addie turned and locked eyes with whom she assumed was Nick. "It's really exquisite, isn't it?" she said. "What era do you make it to be from."

"I appraised it as a 1934 case, and if you look inside, you'll find a few extra bonuses."

Addie's fingers quivered as she opened the top of the case. She grinned. "It's a mini wooden spice rack."

"Not spices though." The man reached around her and pulled the three-tiered rack from the case. "Look at the labels on the bottles. Nowadays we would have to have poison warnings on these, but it's a good example of the medicines they were using in the thirties and why life spans were so much shorter than today."

Addie eyed the small green glass bottles secured on her spice rack and shook her head as she read the labels: Laudanum (Opium), Norodin (Methamphetamine), and Kimball White Pine and Tar Cough Syrup (Chloroform) to name a few in the collection. "It's amazing anyone survived long enough to produce our ancestors," she said with a nervous laugh.

"And that's not all," he said, reaching inside and producing a larger leather case. After he unzipped it, he laid it open on the table beside them and exposed a long metal cone-headed stethoscope, a set of tarnished tweezers and forceps, and two corroded pairs of scissors of different sizes.

Addie gasped when she spotted a small hand drill and something that reminded her of a pizza cutter.

"That is a bone saw," the man said with a soft laugh. "Primitive by our standards today, but at the time, it was considered cutting edge, if you pardon the pun." He waved his hand over the bag and its contents. "As you can see it contains everything a discerning doctor of the day would need."

"All this comes with the case?" asked Addie, her voice quivering with excitement. It was perfect, but when Addie eyed the price tag, she swallowed hard. "Well, thank you for showing it to me. I'll keep it in mind." She began gathering up the small cases and replacing them in the bag.

"Don't let the price put you off. I've been known to negotiate that teeny point if there's something a customer is really interested in."

"That's nice to know, and I will think about it," she said, her hand lingering on the top of the case. "It really would make the perfect gift for a friend of mine."

"I assume your friend is a doctor?"

"Yes," she said with a smile of satisfaction as she fumbled to balance the bag back on the high shelf so it didn't teeter off onto the floor.

"Then perhaps your friend might also be interested in—"

"Actually," she chirped in, "I'm here because I ran into Ivy Walker last night at the community hall, and she told me about a shipment of antique bookmarks and bookends you have just received."

His electric-blue eyes lit up, and any question Addie might have had about this being Nick, Ivy's brother, disappeared. "You must be Addie Greyborne?"

She nodded.

He reached his hand out. "I'm Nick, Ivy's brother."

Addie was taken aback by the force of his grip, a complete contrast to the delicate first impression she had of him. "I'm pleased to meet you," she said, hoping her inner wince didn't come across her face.

"Ivy just told me a few minutes ago that you would be stopping by."

"Is she here?" asked Addie. "I thought she was going out of town today."

"Actually, she had a call from a client who's dropping in to pick up a special order, so she thought she should wait and go tomorrow. She's in the back. I'll go get her."

"That would be great, thanks."

Addie eyed the black medical bag on the top shelf and started to reach up for it, thought better, and dropped her arm. It would be the perfect gift, but with a price tag of just over a thousand dollars . . . well, she and Simon had never exchanged more than small sentimental gifts before. What would that convey to him about where she thought their relationship was heading . . . and was she prepared for that? She shook her head and turned her back on the shelving unit just as Ivy came around a glass case filled with antique tea sets.

"Hi, Addie," cried Ivy. "I'm so glad you could get out of your shop to stop in." She ceremoniously set a large open box on the table beside Addie. "So, what do you think?" She stepped back, her intent gaze fixed on Addie.

Addie glanced into the box and choked out a gasp that caught in her throat. It was filled with delicate, vintage French bookmarks, silver and wooden carved letter opener/bookmarks, and paper doll bookmarks common in the 1930s through the fifties. On the top was even a tin lithograph bookmark for *Cracker Jack* with a picture of a Scottie Dog on it. The additional assortment of engraved and monogrammed sterling silver pieces was spectacular. Addie knew she had to have *all* of these.

"I think my customers will go crazy for these." She squealed and bent over and examined the larger box Nick had placed on the floor. At first glance, the bookends didn't disappoint either. There was a set of highly polished black marble antelope, an Art Deco globe set in polished burl-wood, and a set of bronze galleon-styled book ends, complete with waves that had a copper overlaid finish.

She quickly counted at least fifteen sets in the box, ranging from marble to bronze to carved wood, and each one made her chest constrict a little tighter. "I know for a fact they will go nuts for these, too."

Addie, unable to stop the grin spreading across her face, glanced up at Ivy and noted that Ivy's attention had been diverted.

"If you'll excuse me," Ivy said, her voice distant. "Nick will look after you." With that, she was gone.

Addie straightened up to see what had distracted Ivy from their transaction and was astonished to see Gwendolyn Buchannan sauntering toward the sales counter.

"You'll have to excuse my sister," Nick said apologetically. "One of Ivy's regular customers just came in."

"Gwendolyn Buchannan is a regular, is she?" asked Addie. The grand dame of the historical society clutched her Louis Vuitton handbag close to her tailored, calf-length, beige coat and edged her way through the shop to the sales counter. "She doesn't appear to be much interested in any of the displays?"

"Her house is a museum unto itself," said Nick with a short laugh. "She's a very discerning collector of *other* memorabilia that Ivy hunts down for her, and this is the first time she's ever come into the store. So Ivy is rather excited, as you can tell, by her sudden disappearance.

Please, don't take it personally. It's just a big deal for her today."

"If she's never been here before, how do they communicate?"

"Generally, they conduct all their transactions by telephone and email then she sends in her chauffeur, James to pick up her purchases."

"I wasn't aware that running errands was part of a chauffeur's job description."

"He's been with her a long time. Years from what he's said and he appears devoted to her," Nick said with a hollow laugh. "He'd have to be as he's mentioned that she's always sending him off somewhere to take care of her personal matters. Actually, I was surprised when she told Ivy she would drop in herself today."

"So they have never met before today?"

He shook his head.

"I don't understand," said Addie, "how do you know what Gwendolyn's house is like then?"

"I've been there once or twice when James couldn't come in. Part of the business arrangement Ivy and I have is that I do all the deliveries clients require."

"I see."

All of this information was interesting to Addie and something to store away in her mental file cabinet. It had to mean something, didn't it? But it got her thinking what Gwendolyn had mentioned to Addie the evening before their little misunderstanding that led to Serena wanting to drop through the floor. She had said she was an avid collector of everything written or published by Sarah Josepha Hale and had been under the impression that Addie had a couple of copies of the original bound volumes. Since Gwendolyn had never met Ivy before today, could it actually have been Ivy, she thought Serena was talking about when she mentioned the *Godey's* prints and was confused and thought she meant Addie had the originals because she ran a bookstore? Maybe the misunderstand last night was simply a case of mistaken identity. A notion that seemed to be popping up everywhere Addie looked.

Nick rubbed his hands together. "Well, Addie, do either of the bookmark collection or the bookends interest you?"

"Yes, very much so," said Addie, her focus still on the exchange taking place between Ivy and Gwendolyn, which appeared amicable but not overly friendly on Gwendolyn's part at least. Then Ivy, appearing rather uncomfortable, escorted the older woman around the back of the counter to what Addie assumed was a storeroom or office.

She realized Nick was still talking to her and a hot blush crept up her cheeks. "I'm sorry, you were saying?"

"I said, we are hoping to sell them as a case lot. However, if you only wanted to take a few of each, I'm sure that could also be arranged."

"No," she said, her eyes fixed on the older woman and Ivy as they disappeared through the door. "I'll take them all, thank you." She smiled.

"What about the doctor's bag?" He pointed mischievously to the top shelf.

"You don't give up, do you?" She laughed.

"No, I think as a saleswoman yourself, you know the value of upselling." His dark brows wiggled.

"I certainly do." Still torn, she studied the case. "But I don't think I'll take it today." She needed to sleep on it and maybe ask Serena if she thought it too extravagant a gift.

"Whatever you say. However, may I suggest that you leave me your card, and then if someone else shows interest in it, I can call and let you know. That way if you have changed your mind, you won't lose out."

Addie hiked the box of bookmarks onto her hip and paused in thought. "Yes, let's do that. I have been known to change my mind a time or two, so you never know."

"Great, let's go get these rung up, and I'll help you out to your car with them."

As Addie completed her purchase transaction, Serena wandered by without even a side-glance at her friend. Addie clutched at her sleeve. "Earth to Serena."

"Addie?" She giggled. "I didn't even see you."

"I know, you have that singular focus in your eyes. What's up?"

"I'm trying to picture so many things in either my house or the tea shop and am totally oblivious to everything else."

"I can see that."

"Did you find what you came for?" Serena glanced at the two boxes on the counter.

"Yes, and Nick is going to help me carry them to the car, so can I have the keys?"

"Sure," she said, fishing around in her hobo bag. "I have a stack over there on the end of the counter and should be out in a few minutes anyway."

"Did you find a Civil War–era plate?"

"No, but Nick said he had a couple of crates in the back he still has to unpack from an auction Ivy went to last week, and he'll call me if there's anything suitable in there."

"Fingers crossed."

"Yeah." Serena glanced at Nick, who was waiting for Addie. "You'd better go."

"Okay, if I'm not in the car when you're done in here, I'll be across the street, sitting on the seawall. It's such a beautiful afternoon I want to take in as much as I can before I have to head back to the bookstore."

Serena nodded. "I won't be long. I just want to take a peek at that display of china tea sets. I think they might be perfect for SerenaTEA."

Addie and Nick loaded the two boxes in the back of the Wrangler, and then Nick retreated back inside to help Serena with her treasures. Addie stood on the sidewalk and drew in deep breaths of the briny sea air. She loved this little town, its people, its scenery, everything. It was moments like this when she felt she had finally found her home.

A swirl of warm air from the door opening behind her yanked her from her thoughts, and she glanced around to see Gwendolyn traipsing toward an older-model, black Lincoln parked a few car lengths back. Her driver, James, Addie assumed, complete with full chauffeur's uniform, leapt from the car and ceremoniously opened the rear door for her.

Addie noted a brown wrapped parcel tucked under the woman's arm as she slid into the back seat, and her curiosity was piqued. "Hi, Gwendolyn," she called, smiling apologetically at the driver as she nudged in front of him.

"Miss Greyborne? I must say I never thought I would see you here today. Don't you have your own shop to run?"

"Why, yes . . . I do, but it is lunch time, and I have a very efficient assistant manager and—"

The woman harrumphed as she leaned over to close the door.

Addie grabbed for the frame to hold it open and fixed the most innocent smile she could manage on her face. "I had no idea that you and Ivy were acquainted. Small world, isn't it?"

"Yes, indeed it is."

"I recall last night you mentioned you were an avid collector of anything written or published by Sarah Josepha Hale. Is that what she managed to find you? I only ask because you thought I had some copies but perhaps she got luckier than I have been."

She patted the parcel on her lap. "Yes, Miss Walker happened to come across these two first edition bound volumes of the January to June and July to December 1845 editions of *Godey's Lady's Book*." She looked hard at Addie and grasped the door handle. "Ivy Walker is very good at finding me *exactly* what I want. Unlike some others who have their friends build them up to something they *definitely* are not." The door slammed shut.

Chapter 15

"I'll tell you again, Serena"—Addie hauled the larger box of bookends out of the back of the Wrangler and staggered under its weight—"Gwendolyn Buchannan is not the charming, high-society socialite you think she is."

"I don't know about that. Did you see the cashmere coat she had on? I just wanted to reach over and touch it as she passed by me."

"You got your head out of the clouds long enough to see her but walked right past me?" asked Addie mockingly.

"Well, I see you every day, and besides, as nice as your coat is, it doesn't scream *touch me*."

"You're incorrigible, you know. I just told you how she threw you under the bus for *her* misunderstanding, and that's all you have to say?"

"She just comes from a different world than we do."

Serena balanced a box of bookmarks on her hip and closed the back door.

"Well, I have the feeling that when my grandmother used to say, *You can put lipstick on a pig, but it's still a pig,* she was talking about people like Gwendolyn Buchannan. I think she has a real mean streak in her."

"People like her are different than us. It doesn't mean they are mean," Serena said with a short laugh as she opened the front door to Beyond the Page.

"Look at you using fancy homonyms," chirped Addie stepping inside but stopping short in the doorway. "Martha? What's wrong?"

Martha, standing at the counter, quit wagging her finger in Paige's face. Her stout body vibrated as she thrust her hands on her round hips and glared at Addie.

"I'll tell you like I told that Marc Chandler, who, by the way, had better get his head screwed on right if he thinks that cousin of yours could be a suspect in that Jared fellow's murder, then I'll, I'll . . ." She huffed wiping her perspiration beaded forehead with the corner of her apron.

Addie stared at Martha. Although she'd had her share of run-ins with the woman in the past, she couldn't recall her ever using this sharp of a tone with her before. *And is she actually defending Kalea?* This was new to Addie. Martha didn't seem to like anyone.

"Okay?" Addie gulped and lowered her voice when she realized that customers were watching them. "Did he tell you she was one of the suspects?"

"No, but Joe Walsh from the furniture store said it was clear she is, given the way Chief Chandler put her in the back of his car and drove her off to the station."

"As far as I know, they are still investigating and have a list of—"

"Who else is on that list?" Martha snapped.

"I really don't know, why?" Addie shuffled over to the sales counter and set the box down. "Do you know something about his death?" She removed her jacket and placed it on the counter.

"Do I know something about it?" Martha scoffed and folded her arms across her ample chest. "Let me tell you something." She leaned toward Addie. "Mary-Lou Bidwell was just in the bakery, and she heard from Phyllis Granger, who heard from Franny Delong, that there are at least three other names that should be on a list of people who wanted him dead."

"Really? Who?"

"Hal Washburn from the hardware store, for one."

"Who else?"

"The Thomas sisters."

Addie's eyes widened.

"And Clay Diggens from down at the wharf."

"What makes you think they could have had something to do with the murder?"

"Because of what people have heard and . . ." She gave Addie a head-to-toe scan. "You're not the only one in town who can put clues together from things people say when they come into my shop." She leaned closer to Addie and dropped her voice to a harsh whisper. "I know your cousin *used* to love that man, but he wasn't all roses and champagne. At least not to the people whose businesses he'd invested money in. Ask them yourself if you don't believe me."

She stood upright and shook her finger in Addie's face.

"So you tell that police chief to come see me, and I'll tell him what for." She spun around and smoothed imaginary wrinkles from the front of her white apron as she marched toward the door. "If he thinks Kalea, that sweet girl, could be a murderer, then I have an earful for him." With that, she flung the door open and stomped next door to the bakery.

"You knew that was bound to happen." Serena plopped the box of bookmarks on the counter.

"What? That Martha would make such a scene in my store?" Addie glanced apologetically at a customer, who came around the end of a bookcase.

"No, that it wouldn't take long until everyone had an opinion about who did it. Like she said, you're not the only one in town who tries to put clues together."

"Gossip you mean." Addie sighed.

"It gets worse," Paige said meekly from behind the counter.

"How so?" Addie fixed her gaze on Paige.

"One of your neighbors, Ethel Dawson, was in a few minutes before Mom, and she said that when she was on her way downtown and made a U-turn in the dead end at the top of your driveway . . ."

"Yes?" Addie's gaze didn't falter.

Paige visibly swallowed hard, and her words flooded out in a rush. "She said there were two police cars at your house."

"Oh no!"

"I think you'd better go and see what happened."

"You're right." Addie grabbed her coat and purse from the counter. "Do what you want with all that stuff in the boxes, and in case I'm not back by five, go ahead and lock up then."

"Call us and let us know what happened," hollered Serena as Addie raced toward the back room.

Addie dashed up the double-wide front porch stairs and flung the door open.

From where she stood in the foyer, she heard a male voice ask, "Take your time and tell us exactly what happened after that."

"I already told you." Kalea's voice reached a hysterical pitch. "Nothing, we went to bed."

"Together?"

"Yes, and when I woke up in the morning—"

"That's enough, Marc," barked Addie from the doorway to the living room. "She has the right to have a lawyer present if you're going to keep questioning her, and you know that."

"Addie! What are you doing here?"

"By the look of it, I'm the one protecting my cousin's constitutional rights. What are you doing?"

Marc rose to his feet and marched toward her. "Don't interfere in an ongoing investigation."

"Have you read her her rights?" Addie snapped. "Or are you going to keep berating her and confusing her until she confesses to something she didn't do?"

"Come with me!" He seized her arm and steered her down the wide hallway toward the kitchen. Pippi scampered back and forth in a frenzied dance, urging Addie to pick her up, but Marc's pace and the pressure on her arm wouldn't allow for it.

"There," he spat out when they reached the kitchen, "*now* we can talk. First off, Miranda warnings don't apply until an arrest has actually been made. Any questions up until that point are merely a matter of the natural course of an investigation."

He was right, of course, but she couldn't let him see that she knew it, so she scooped her little friend into her arms and snuggled her close, avoiding his piercing gaze.

"Are you aware," his voice echoed his annoyance, "that Kalea and Jared had an argument the evening before he was killed?"

"Yes, she told you that the first time you questioned her." She met his gaze with an equally unyielding one.

"I know, but she didn't tell us they were breaking up. Did you know that?" He glared at her.

"Yes . . . she told me."

"And you never thought it might be important to the case and that it was a fact you should pass on to me?" His breath was hot against her cheek.

She pulled away and stared at him. "I only discovered that last night, and she told me she was *thinking* about breaking up with him. They never really did before he . . ." She looked up at him. "But how did you find out?"

"People talk, and from what I was told it was a done deal, and you know what that means, don't you?"

She stared blankly at him.

"It means there was a strong motive."

"Wait a minute. What people talked? Their argument took place behind closed doors, and no one else was there."

"Are you sure?"

"Are you? Who is this mystery person who seems to know intimate details of a private conversation?"

"Apparently it wasn't so intimate that it wasn't over-heard."

Addie wracked her brain. Who would have been in earshot of an argument Kalea and Jared had in her apartment after the shops were closed on Sunday evening? Had Kalea lied to her about where they argued? Had it been in public and not behind closed doors?

"Why didn't you bring this information to me as soon as she told you?"

"I was going to." Addie stroked the soft fur on the back of Pippi's neck. "But I had to meet Serena last night, and I was running late as it was and then—"

"Never mind. Is there anything else she told you that I should know about?"

Addie shook her head. "Not that I know of involving Kalea, but I was just told that there are at least three people who had business dealings with Jared. Apparently, he was harassing them." Addie relayed what Martha had said and offered up the names she'd been given. "So you see, there was more than one person in town who might have wanted him dead or was after something he had in his briefcase. Maybe their contract?" She shrugged. "I don't know."

Mark spun around on his boot heel and stomped off.

"Now what?" Addie clutched Pippi tight and darted after Marc, trying to match his pace.

"Jerry!" he bellowed. "Let's go!" He paused at the living room doorway. "Kalea, I had hoped we could get to the bottom of this the easy way, but"—he scowled over his shoulder at Addie—"I suggest you get a lawyer." With that, he flung the door open and walked out. Jerry hurried after him and flashed Addie an uneasy glance as he closed the door behind them.

Addie eased out a heavy breath and grabbed the mahogany door frame for support. She slowly breathed in and out and counted one . . . two . . . three. "Okay, Kalea, we need to talk."

"He's not serious about me getting a lawyer, is he?" Kalea huddled in the far corner of the large sofa, tears forming in the corners of her hazel eyes. "Doesn't that mean I'm going to be charged with Jared's murder?" she wailed.

"I don't know what to think now," Addie said, perching on the coffee table beside Kalea. "Generally, you don't need a lawyer until you *are* charged, and if you lawyer-up before then, it makes you look like you have something to hide. So when he said that, it tells me they arc looking at charging you. To be honest, it doesn't look good right now."

"But you're the one who first said he shouldn't talk to me unless I had a lawyer present." She grabbed a throw cushion from the sofa and heaved it at Addie. "This is all your fault, isn't it?"

Addie flung her arm up to deflect the cushion. "I had to say something to stop him. You're such a mess right now. Who knows what you would have blurted out to shut him up. That was the first thing that came to my mind. But from what he told me in the kitchen, they are building a pretty good case against you, so he had already considered that."

"What case? You know me. There is no way I would have—no—could have killed Jared."

"Not even in a heated argument."

"No! And the argument wasn't that heated, as you called it. We just didn't agree with what he should do about getting the briefcase for free, and he, in his usual way, shut me down and refused to talk about it anymore."

Addie fixed her gaze on Kalea's. "How did you get that cut on your finger?"

Kalea glanced at her hand as though she were seeing it for the first time. "This? It was . . . when we started to argue."

"How did it happen?"

"It was when Jared was taking the papers out of his old briefcase and sorting through them and putting the documents into the new one. That's when he thanked me again for the expensive gift. I was cutting out a pattern on my worktable upstairs, and I looked at him and laughed and said I had no idea what he was talking about. He got up from my desk on the other side of the living room and came up behind me and wrapped his arms around me. I jumped and sliced my finger on the scissors. It made such a mess on the material. I was furious." She shook her head. "Like really mad because the client was coming in the morning for her first fitting."

"Then what? Is that when you started yelling?"

"We never yelled. We put a bandage on it—"

"We?"

"Yes, I couldn't manage with one hand, and Jared felt so guilty about the blood on the fabric, and I was crying . . ."

So Addie had been right in her theory regarding how Kalea's blood might have ended up inside Jared's shirt cuff.

"Anyway, I cleaned up the mess and rinsed the material under cold water, while I was telling him I had no clue where he got the idea that I had paid for the case. That's when he told me about the young fellow telling him I had already paid for it."

"Are you sure there was no yelling or raised voices?"

"No, there wasn't. Jared did have a temper, and boy could he holler, but he never yelled at me when we argued. If anything, he'd go deathly quiet, which was even scarier. He would turn cold and distant, which is exactly what he did when I tried to convince him to go back and pay for the briefcase."

"According to Marc, someone overheard your argument."

She sat upright. "That's impossible. We never really raised our voices."

"Never?"

"Well, I might have a bit, but it was late Sunday night, and all the stores were closed. There is no one around who would have heard anything."

"It seems someone did, at least they told Marc they did, and that you were breaking up with him. Marc just told me that equates to a strong motive for murder if it happened in the heat of an argument."

"I already said, we didn't have that kind of fight, and I only decided that night after we went to bed that I was going to break up with him. I hadn't even told him yet, so all that's a lie."

Addie leaned back on her hands and studied her cousin. "Have you said anything to anyone about all this, besides me? Someone who might have wanted to set you up for the murder and let that little bit of information slip to Marc?"

"No! No one." Her eyes widened, and a strangled squeak escaped her lips.

"What?"

"Martha!"

"Martha? When?"

"Last week. I told her I was thinking of breaking up with Jared."

"Wait a minute. I thought you told me you decided that night."

"I did. That's when I decided for sure, but I've been thinking about it for a while."

Addie couldn't believe what she was hearing. "Why would you tell Martha?"

"Because she's my friend."

"Since when?" Addie shot to her feet and stared down in disbelief at her cousin. "Martha and you are *friends*?"

"Yes." She stood up and met Addie's gaze. "As you know, not too many people in this town like me, and she's become a great customer and a *friend*." Kalea wrapped her arms around herself and paced back and forth in front of the fireplace, Pippi whimpering at her heels. Kalea sniffled and picked Pippi up, cradling the little fur ball in her arms. "But why would she turn on me and tell Marc what I was planning to do?"

Kalea was right. Martha could be prickly and vengeful but to set someone up for murder seemed completely out of character for even Martha. Addie chewed her bottom lip in thought. "Maybe she was, in her Martha-way, trying to help?"

"How does telling Marc we had a huge fight and that I broke up with him help me?"

"Martha doesn't always have the best judgment. Sometimes she acts before she thinks, and that might be the case here. She came into my store today and told me—no yelled at me—about the fact that Marc suspected you of murder. She must have been on a roll because she threw out a couple of other people's names who Jared was involved in business transactions with. If one can believe Martha, they had a stronger motive for murder."

"That's why I told her I was thinking of leaving him. Last week when she came in for a dress fitting, she was telling me she had heard rumblings around town about Jared, and she thought I should know. I told her I already knew what he was like in business and was thinking of breaking up with him anyway, so she didn't have to worry." Kalea stopped and stared at Addie. Her eyes widened. "Martha wouldn't have tried to set me up, would she?"

Addie shook her head. "I doubt it. She's been down this road herself. I'm more inclined to think that she thought if she told Marc you were going to leave him anyway, he'd think why you would bother to kill him. Not understanding that in the eyes of the police that leads to a whole lot of other possible scenarios."

"I hope you're right because I really did think she was my friend." Kalea swiped at the tears seeping down her cheeks. "I have so few of those here."

Addie gazed into the ashes of the unlit fireplace, her thoughts raging. None of this was making any sense. There had to be a piece missing, but she couldn't even fathom what shape it was in this disheveled puzzle box. Then a thought struck her. "You said you and Jared argued over whether he should go back and pay for the briefcase?"

"Yes. He didn't agree and wanted to accept the win without any regard to that poor young fellow who probably lost his job over the mistake. That's the way Jared was, though. He didn't care about people, only the almighty dollar."

"Is there any way that kid knew where you lived or worked?"

"He knew we were from Greyborne Harbor. Why?"

"Because all we're left with for motive is something to do with the briefcase—"

"And the fact that we didn't pay for it." She stared at Addie. "What if that guy did lose his job and came here to get the briefcase to try to get his job back?"

Chapter 16

Addie tore a strip of masking tape off the roll and secured the last corner of a sheet of brown paper to the wall close to the window beside the fireplace.

"Here you go," said Kalea as she set two plates, a steaming mug balanced in the center of each, on the coffee table.

Pippi padded in behind Kalea, yawned, stretched out her back, and trotted over to her bed on the far side of the fireplace. Addie smiled when Pippi perched her little head on top of Baxter, the stuffed bear friend she always slept with. "Did she eat and go outside?"

"Yes, and I made us both a sandwich, too, while I waited for the tea to steep."

Addie eyed the two plates. "Well, I am impressed."

"Don't be. They're only peanut butter-and-banana sandwiches, but I did feel like I should eat something and thought you might be hungry, too."

"Then you're feeling a little better?"

"No, but I'm hungry, finally. So, yes, maybe a bit better." She sat down on the edge of the sofa and glanced at the roll of brown paper lying on the coffee table and then at the wall behind Addie. "What's all this?"

"It's a crime board."

"A what?"

"It helps me keep track of clues and evidence."

"Isn't this something like what the police use in their investigations?" asked Kalea.

"Yes, similar, they generally have photographs of the suspects and match hard evidence against each one." Addie began to scribble down what little she knew already. "However, I don't discard anything. No matter how trivial it appears on the surface because it could mean something to the big picture in the end."

"I see." But from the skeptical look in Kalea's eyes, Addie could tell she really didn't see.

Then Addie recalled when she first came to Greyborne Harbor and the series of unfortunate incidents that happened soon after and how, when she had started working like this, Serena held the same skepticism, but that changed. Soon Simon understood her unusual system and turned out to have a knack for it as well. Then Paige and Catherine showed they, too, had an aptitude for putting clues to suspects and looking for motives and opportunity. She mentally crossed her fingers that Kalea would come around and be the second set of eyes she desperately needed. After all, this was to try to prove *her* innocence and find out who the real killer was.

"I start by writing down everything I know in relation to the events leading up to an incident or murder. I, then, make note of whatever clues I come across that can point me in the direction of who the killer is. The whole thing is like a giant jigsaw puzzle, and when you're first starting off, all the pieces are in a jumbled mess. So this"—she tapped the paper—"helps me to see the bigger completed picture in the end."

She paused and glanced over her shoulder at Kalea. "The only thing is, you can't tell anyone what we're doing, and we don't ever share any of the information on here with Marc until we have evidence and proof."

"Why? Wouldn't what you uncover help him in the end?"

"Yes, but I learned a long time ago that the police will only follow evidence and don't want to hear any speculations or guesses."

"Okay." Kalea sat forward on the edge of the sofa. "If it helps clear me, I'm willing to give it a try."

"Let's focus on the briefcase," said Addie. "You said this young guy in the shop told Jared that you already paid for it, right?"

"Yes, that's what Jared told me later. But I swear I didn't."

"Then let's start with that." Addie scrawled on the paper what Kalea told her. "You also said he asked you if you were from Greyborne Harbor, based on a conversation you and Jared were having, right?"

"I guess. We were browsing and mentioned it a few times. When I said yes, he then said he had what we wanted in the back and came out with the vintage case."

Addie scribbled what Kalea was saying across the

makeshift crime board, trying to stick only to the facts. "Was there anything unusual about the case?"

"No, it was a lot like his father's that the truck ran over. Not quite exact but close enough to make Jared happy, why?"

"It just seems weird, don't you think, that he asked you about Greyborne Harbor then suddenly produced the case."

"I guess so, but maybe when we were first looking, he didn't know what we were after, and when he heard, he was just trying to supply good customer service."

"Maybe, but why mention Greyborne Harbor then?" Addie studied what she'd written. "Could he have thought you were someone else?"

"Sure, I guess, but who?"

"That's what we have to find out." She fixed her gaze on Kalea. "You're certain there was nothing out of the ordinary about the briefcase?"

"Like what? It was just an old briefcase as far as I could tell, but Jared said it was worth a lot of money because of the craftsmanship. That's why I think that young clerk might have lost his job and followed us here to try to get it back. Maybe they had a fight over it because I know Jared loved it, and he wouldn't have parted willingly with it."

"But then why did the kid dump it in the alley? No, that doesn't make sense if he took it back to save his job. He wouldn't have thrown it away."

"It was found in the alley?"

"Yes . . . in the dumpster behind the furniture store."

"Why didn't you tell me that before?"

"Would it have made a difference?"

"No, but—"

"So we're back to the case itself." Addie tapped the tip of the pen on the paper. "There was nothing unusual about it, you say. It wasn't a designer line, like Louis Vuitton, but it was a high-quality leather, though, with silk lining, making it expensive but not priceless." She traced her bottom lip with the end of the pen. "So why?"

"Come to think of it, Jared did mention one thing."

"What?"

"He did say it seemed heavier than the one his father had, even when it was empty."

"Really?" Addie paced in front of the brown paper board and stopped. "I wonder?" She read over the board. "This." She tapped the pen under the line *could have been mistaken identity.* "It sounds to me like someone else was supposed to pick it up. You said the pawnshop owner wasn't there and had just left instructions with the clerk?"

"Yeah, at least that's the impression I got."

"This other person from Greyborne Harbor might have arranged to come later in the day, but when the pawnshop owner left, for whatever reason, he thought he should tell the young guy in case the person did happen to show up early. He probably expected to be back for the prearranged transfer. Does that sound like a possibility?"

"I guess. It was all so weird when I think about it now."

Addie glanced at the clock. "You know what, it's only four thirty, so if I hurry, there is someone I can go to and ask about the briefcases of that period."

"Who? I thought you knew about this old stuff."

"Not an area of my expertise, but I did meet someone today who seems to know a lot about medical bags of that era, anyway. Maybe he can tell me if it was common for them to also have different weights."

"If he can help, then go."

"Will you be okay if I leave you for about an hour?"

"Yes, I have my comfort blanket with me." She grinned at Pippi.

Addie softly laughed and handed Kalea the pen. "If you think of anything else, write it under the corresponding column, and we'll look at it when I get back. If my hunch is right, I think that this might come down to a case of mistaken identity and something that was supposed to have been inside the briefcase."

"But it was empty when we got it."

"I know. That's the missing piece of this puzzle we have to try to figure out. What was in it, and where did it go."

"Maybe the kid took it out and kept it for himself to sell later. I just know everything about the shop seemed pretty seedy to me."

Addie stared at her. "Good theory. See, you do have a knack for this." She grinned and turned to leave.

"Wait!"

"What?" Addie stopped in the living room doorway.

"What about your sandwich?" Kalea rose and took her the plate.

"Thanks, I'll eat as I drive." Addie snatched the two halves up and bit into one of them.

Addie glanced at the clock on her dashboard and breathed a sigh of relief when she spied a parking space right in front of the door. After she'd parked and hopped out, she noticed breadcrumbs on the front of her jacket, but when she paused to brush them off, she spotted Serena's Wrangler two spaces up. "So like her." She chuckled to herself. "I wonder what she spotted earlier that she just *had* to come back for."

With only fifteen minutes to spare, Addie dashed through the front door, spotted her friend, and slid up beside her at the sales counter. "Small world," she said with a short laugh.

"Addie! Your ears must have been burning."

"Why, what did I do?"

"I was just thinking I wish you were here to help me make a decision."

"Then your wish is my command." Addie took a low bow.

"Seriously, how did you know I was here and needed you?"

"I'm psychic," Addie said, tapping her finger on her temple. "Actually, I came in to see Nick." She glanced around the store. "Is he here?"

"Yes, he just went in the back to get another plate for me to look at. While we wait, you can give me your opinion."

"Okay," Addie leaned on the counter, "what do you need?"

"Which of these two plates screams *winner*?"

Addie inspected the two antique plates. "To be honest . . . neither."

"What? It's the closest I've come to the Civil War era yet."

"I know, but look. This one is a hand-forged iron plate. See the engraving on the back by the Regimental Blacksmith. So, it's the real thing, but can you guarantee that by today's standards it's food safe?"

"I see what you mean. Well, what about this cobalt-blue pottery platter. It's got an 1863 stamp on the back, so it's from the war period, too, and I could use it."

"Yes, but the same thing with it. It might look great on a collector's shelf, but what's in the clay or the processing? Do you really want to put food on something that might contain lead and end up poisoning the judges?"

"I never thought of that. Now what am I going to do?"

"You said Nick had something else." She shrugged. "Cross your fingers."

"Addie," said Nick as he came around the corner, "have you come back for the doctor's bag?"

"Sadly, no." She chuckled. "You don't give up do you?"

He approached the sales counter with three china plates adorned with fine painted gold and brown leaves.

"Those are stunning," cried Serena. "May I?" She held her hands out reverently.

"Of course," Nick said, placing them on the counter and handing one to Serena.

Addie leaned over Serena's shoulder and studied the plate. "If I'm not mistaken, those are authentic Civil War–era Palissy pattern ironstone china plates by Edward Walley."

"You'd be correct." Nick grinned. "You know your stuff."

"Not that well, but I did do internships at the Smithsonian and at the British Museum before I went on to be the assistant to the curator at the Boston Library."

"I had no idea," he said, studying her. "I'll definitely be putting you on my list of appraisers for the future."

"Oh no," Addie shook her head, "I let my appraisers

certification slip. Any I do now are purely for my own purposes and can't be used as an authentication."

"That's too bad," he said and glanced at Serena. "So, what do you think?"

"I think these will be perfect, don't you?" She turned to Addie.

"Yes, they are, but do you need all three?"

"I can use them in the tea shop later for serving dainties on, couldn't I?"

"Yes, I suppose, but I imagine they are expensive." Addie glanced at Nick.

"Well . . . we could work out a deal." He grinned at Addie. "Just like the deal I was going to offer you on the medical bag."

"Don't you ever give up? Thanks, but no, I only came in to pick your brain about something."

"No charge for that." He leaned his palms on the counter. "What can I help you with?"

"It can wait until Serena makes a decision."

"Very well then. Serena, what do you think?"

"I think I'll take all three." She glanced sideways at Addie and grinned. "They're perfect, and I won't have to worry about poisoning the judges, will I?"

"Not with the plates anyway," said Addie, "but I can't promise that about what you put on them."

"Addie." Serena laughed. "You are bad, aren't you?"

Addie sidestepped her friend's lame attempt to take a swipe at her.

Nick rang in the purchase and then wrapped and boxed Serena's Civil War treasures.

"Do you want me to wait for you?" asked Serena as she slid the box from the counter.

"No, go ahead, I won't be long. I just have a quick question."

"Okay, I'll call you later, bye. And thanks, Nick, for everything. You have no idea how happy you've made me today."

Nick beamed as Serena left, and he turned back to Addie. "That's why I love my job. It makes my day seeing customers that happy with something they unearth here in the store." He flipped a switch behind the counter, and the neon OPEN light in the window fizzled off. "Okay, business complete. Now, what was it you needed?"

"I know you're closed now, so I won't keep you, but I wanted to ask you about vintage briefcases since you seemed to know so much about the medical bag. I thought you might be the person I should talk to."

"Actually, if you're looking for an expert, you want to talk to Ivy."

"I see. Alright, when will she be back in town?"

"She's here, now, in the back."

"I thought she said she was leaving after her special customer came. When I saw Gwendolyn Buchannan, I assumed that she was it."

"She was, but then the shipment from the auction Ivy was at last weekend was delivered, and she felt bad about leaving me on my own to uncrate it all. I can go get her if you like, and then she can answer your questions."

"That would be perfect, and I really am sorry about keeping you past closing."

"No worries, we have a few more hours of work in the back unpacking and taking inventory on the new stock, anyway. I'll just be a minute."

"Thanks." Addie turned and leaned her back against

the counter. Past the display of vintage hatboxes and bread boxes, the black doctor's bag grabbed her attention. It was as though it were calling out to her. "Of course, now you're going to haunt me, aren't you?" She rolled her eyes and glanced away but shot a quick look back at it. *Stop taunting me*.

"Addie, how nice to see you again," said Ivy as she came around the corner, wiping her hands on a rag before extending one in greeting. "Nick tells me you have a question about vintage briefcases?"

"Yes, if you don't mind."

"Not at all. I'll help if I can, but we don't get too many in here, so I hope I can answer your questions."

"A friend of mine has a briefcase from about the 1930s of very high-quality craftsmanship and silk lined. Another friend has a very similar one, but the weird thing is, both seem to have different weights to them. Is that something that's common with that period?"

Ivy leaned against the counter and shrugged her shoulders. "It can be, but not seeing either case, it's hard to tell. I do know that the weight depends on the wood used to frame the cases. Perhaps one came from a softer wood and one was framed in a hard wood like oak. That would account for the weight difference to some extent."

"Hmm, I never thought of that, but it does make sense since they were made by craftsmen and not on an assembly line."

"Yes, but keep in mind assembly lines back then were men and women working shoulder to shoulder on tables. There was no automation back then."

"That's right, so it could just come down to different manufacturers."

"That's my guess unless . . ."

"Unless what?"

Ivy grabbed a long-handled stick with a hook on the top from the slim wrapping counter behind the main sales counter and sauntered over to the shelf, fished the doctor's bag down, and set it on the counter in front of Addie. "This case, for example, that Nick showed you earlier is very heavy, isn't it?" Ivy said.

"Yes, but it has a bottle rack and instruments inside it, so that makes sense."

"But did he also show you this?" She glanced mischievously at Addie, opened the top, placed her thumbs one each side of the top opening, and pressed. There was a twang and a click, and she lifted the top portion of the bag down to the brass decorative band that circled the perimeter and exposed a three-inch-deep hidden compartment containing a black leather case.

Chapter 17

Addie stretched out her jean-clad legs and tapped her high-topped boot toes together. No matter how many times she had been asked to wait in these hard plastic chairs, they hadn't grown any more comfortable. She glanced at the clock behind the reception desk as the second hand ticked by and turned into minutes—fifteen to be exact. She shifted and stared at Officer Adams, willing her to look up from the paperwork she was obviously using as a distraction from Addie's intense gaze. How could she not have felt the daggers Addie was thrusting in her direction? When the buzzer on the intercom sounded and the officer picked up the telephone receiver, an instant wave of relief crossed her flushed face.

"Miss Greyborne," she said, still avoiding eye contact, "Chief Chandler can see you now."

"Thank you," Addie replied briskly as she swept past the desk into Marc's office.

"Sorry to keep you waiting," Marc said, rising to his feet. "I was on the phone with the DA." He waved toward a chair. "Have a seat."

Addie glanced back over her shoulder as she went to close the door and detected a flicker of the officer's tongue. *Did she just stick her tongue out at me?* She closed—banged—the door closed. "What's with her? She's made it clear I'm not welcome here, and she doesn't like me." Addie glowered at the door, strutted across the office, and settled into one of the wood framed chairs. *Her* chair, as she used to consider it, but . . . that was a long time ago and since then there had been many changes. The new desk officer just being the latest one she was going to have to get used to.

"She's okay. Adams is just having a hard time adjusting to how we do things around here." He folded his hands on the top of his desk. "Like some other person I know."

"What? You mean me? And if you're referring to what happened this afternoon—"

"Addie, you threw me out of your house, and might I remind you that I am the *police!*"

"I did no such thing. I only defended my cousin's rights, and as the police, you should have known better."

"As the police, I will tell you that it's not looking good for your cousin right now, and I hoped we could get to the bottom of it *before* I am forced to arrest her for the murder of Jared Munro."

Oh dear. Addie blew out a soft breath and wiped the palms of her dampening hands across the knees of her jeans.

"Now what was it that you needed to see me about that's so urgent?"

"I have a new theory."

"Of course, you do."

"I'm serious, and I think when you hear it, you're going to be impressed."

He sat back, eyeing her, and clicked the top of the pen on his desk. "Okay, go ahead and impress me."

She leaned forward and pinned her gaze on his skeptical brown eyes. "What if there was something hidden in the briefcase?"

"If that is the motive you're going with—"

"I am."

"And not the one that the evidence points to—"

"It's shaky at best," she scoffed.

"And he wasn't killed during a heated argument with Kalea."

Her brows rose in defiance.

"Then as you know, we already established that possibility of the murderer being after a document or contract or something else Jared had in the case."

"Which makes perfect sense since it was found discarded shortly after in a dumpster, so the killer wasn't after the briefcase itself."

"Yes, so how does this make a new theory?"

"What if there was something hidden, and I mean really hidden, inside the briefcase?"

"Like in a secret compartment?" He leaned forward on his elbows. "We already considered that angle if you recall?"

"Yes, but I have more information now."

"But you were here when Jerry examined it. You looked and didn't find evidence of one."

"I had to have missed something." She shifted forward in her chair and met his puzzled gaze. "Is there any chance you can get it out of lockup, so we can take another look?"

He dropped the pen. She didn't miss the twitch in his jaw.

"I'm serious. Kalea told me after you left today that she recalled Jared telling her the case was heavier than the one like his father used to have."

"So, a different make?"

"Possibly, but it got me thinking, so I went to Time Travels to ask Nick Walker about it because when I was in there earlier with Serena, he showed me another case, one I thought might make a nice gift for . . . anyway. He seemed to know a lot about cases from the 1930s, which I pegged Jared's to be. He didn't know if the weight difference was important or common, but his sister Ivy was there, and apparently, she's an expert or something, and she said that different craftsman and different manufacturers used different wood for their frames. Then she said unless, of course, it also had one of these, and she took the medical bag from the shelf"—Marc's brow twitched—"and pressed something in the inside frame, and the bottom opened up."

"Hmm . . . I remember your aunt's penchant for hidden compartments, and your ability to discover those." He tapped the pen on the desk. "So I guess it wouldn't hurt." He flipped on the intercom. "Jerry, can you bring that briefcase up from lockup."

"Yes, chief," Jerry's voice crackled over the speaker.

* * *

Butterflies fluttered in her chest as Addie eyed the case lying flat on the desk in front of them. She leaned forward and then back, weighing up again what she was considering.

"What are you thinking?" Marc pinned a curious gaze on her.

"Looking at it again and from what Ivy showed me, I can see that the interior doesn't look like it's as deep as the exterior of the case. Does it to you?"

Marc leaned down and eyed the case from desk level then lifted the top and glanced inside and then studied it from desk level again. "You're right. The exterior is deeper than the inside is. That means—"

"There *is* a false bottom!" she cried excitedly. "May I?"

He nodded.

Addie shivered with excitement as she stood up and gazed into the void of the empty briefcase. "Okay, let's see what secrets you have to show us today."

She slipped her hands inside the case, pressed her thumbs around the front of the bottom seam of the case . . . nothing out of the ordinary. She stretched out her fingers and slowly felt her way over to the corners. Her right thumb stung as though it had been scraped on something. She stopped and ran her fingers over the two bottom corners. There was a distinct bulge, nothing noticeable to the eye but definitely obvious to the touch. She pushed in an outward motion simultaneously with her thumbs. There was a click as the bottom decorative brass band opened, revealing a space. Her heart fluttered when she raised the top portion, exposing a two-inch-deep hidden compartment.

Jerry let out a low whistle. "Well, I'll be. Except its

empty," he said, peering inside. "So, it hasn't gotten us any farther along."

"But it has," said Addie, meeting his gaze. "It means there could have been something in this briefcase that the killer was after, *and* the killer *knew* about the false bottom."

Marc and Jerry looked questioningly at her.

"Don't you see?" She glanced from one to the other. "Yes, it could have been Jared's papers or something he had that his murderer wanted. Or else . . . remember Kalea said they had only purchased the briefcase the day before? Maybe there was something hidden in this compartment the killer was after, and Jared had no idea it was in there."

Marc eyed Addie, sat down, and instructed Jerry to run analysis on the compartment. He sat back and studied the case. "That's a good theory, Addie, but unless Jerry can come up with something, that's all it is. For all we know the compartment has been empty for years, so it really doesn't prove anything."

"Kalea also told me the young clerk in the pawnshop asked her if they were from Greyborne Harbor and if they were looking for anything specific. When she told him they were from here and what Jared was after, he said his boss told him it was in the back. He came out with this"—she waved her hand in the direction of the briefcase—"and when Jared went to pay for it, the clerk said she, meaning Kalea, had already taken care of it."

Addie pinned her gaze on Marc's blank one. "That's what they argued about Sunday evening. She didn't pay for it, so they got it for nothing, and she wanted him to go back and explain the misunderstanding to the young store clerk and pay for it, so he wouldn't lose his job because he gave away a thousand-dollar item."

Marc picked up the pen, tapped it on the desk, and locked his thoughtful gaze on Addie. "You're thinking this was a case of mistaken identity and someone else from Greyborne Harbor was supposed to pick up the briefcase?"

"It's a theory, and it makes sense. Obviously, this other person paid in advance for it, and maybe, just maybe, there was something hidden in the bottom of it."

"And they tracked Jared down to Kalea's dress shop and just happened to know he'd be staying there overnight and precisely what time he'd be leaving so they could attack him in the shop that hadn't been broken into. He then let his killer in, who then took whatever it was in the compartment out and tossed the briefcase?" He shook his head and rose to his feet. "I'll keep your speculation in mind as we continue to investigate the *facts* further. Thank you, Addie, now if you don't mind . . ." He gestured toward the door.

Addie, mouth gaped open, glanced from him to Jerry, who only shrugged his shoulders. She swung on her heel, stomped to the door, flung it open, and froze. She looked back at Marc with widened eyes.

"What is it?"

"You tell me," she said, poking her head around the door frame, and stared at the crowd in the waiting room. A rough count of the occupied chairs and those standing told her there were at least ten merchants from the Greyborne Harbor area.

"Officer Adams? What's the meaning of this?" Marc asked over Addie's shoulder.

"Sorry, chief." She glanced to the waiting room and then back at him. "Could we have a word . . . in private?"

Addie stepped back as Adams pushed past her and stood in front of Marc. "I was going to tell you as soon as I finished writing down all their names, but it seems, sir . . ." She straightened her shoulders. "Someone has spread a rumor that *all* of these people are on the suspect list for that Munro killing and"—Marc's jaw tightened—"they've all come in demanding to speak to you, and from what I can gather," her voice dropped to a whisper, "each one of them is pointing the finger at someone else."

"A rumor you say. I wonder who could have started that one?" He glowered at Addie.

"Not me! I haven't said a word to anyone."

"Are you certain?"

"Yes, I swear."

"Then who?"

Martha!

"Any ideas?"

"No." Addie gulped. *I can't believe she'd do this.* Although, she was upset earlier and did mention to Addie that there were some names Marc should add to his list. Was this her way of making certain that would happen?

"Okay, Adams." Marc heaved out a deep breath. "Send them in one at a time, and let's hear what they have to say."

"Yes, sir." Adams swiveled around, glanced dismissively at Addie, returned to the desk, snatched up a note pad, and shouted, "Hal Washburn."

Addie zigzagged her way through the waiting room, skimming the faces in the crowd. She wanted to be able to make notes on her board later because she had no idea

Jared was involved with all of these people's businesses. When she passed the Thomas sisters by the door, she clearly heard a forced throat clearing and glanced over at Bin. There was no mistaking the glare of disdain in Bin's eyes.

Addie knew she should explain that she knew nothing about the rumored list, but when she paused to speak to Bin, Addie realized the entire room had now turned their focus on her, and each one of them had the same expression in their eyes.

Addie smacked her hand against the steering wheel. She had half a mind to stop at Martha's house on her way home and rip a strip off her. How dare she throw oil on the fire Addie had worked for over two years to put out? All those rumors about her that Martha had stoked when Addie first came to town—it had taken Addie a long time to gain respect in the community—and Martha now appeared to be back to her old tricks. Addie was sick with the thought that everything she had worked for could be dashed away in a heartbeat. The disappointment she felt in the moment gripped her as she stared out the windshield, waiting for the defroster to kick in and dispel the thin sheet of ice covering it.

No, she couldn't trust herself to speak rationally to Martha tonight. She was tired and hungry and disappointed that her theory about the briefcase was baseless. After the frost cleared from the windshield, she thrust the gear into reverse, spun the tires on the icy road sheen, shifted into drive, and headed for home.

* * *

She glanced into the living room and smiled at the sight of Kalea and Pippi curled up, asleep on the sofa. Then she noticed Kalea had added to the crime board, and tiptoed her way over to it, garnering nothing more than a twitch of Pippi's brows and a half-hearted wag of her tail, and read what her cousin had written. It was names. She assumed of the people in town that Kalea knew who had business dealings with Jared. The three names Martha had mentioned were written down in addition to at least eight others, all of whom Addie had seen at the police station. But it was the last name on the list that made her catch her breath. *Time Travels - Nick Walker*.

Chapter 18

Addie yawned, arched her back, and stretched out her arm, patting the bed beside her. "Are you ready for breakfast, darlin'?"

When no cold wet nose nudged at her, Addie patted the pillow beside her. But when nothing more than chilly morning air swept past her hand, she shot straight up in her bed and took a quick look around. Then she remembered where her furry friend was. Her heart ached. She missed the warm little body nestled close to her. Had she lost her best friend forever? Fighting the tears that burned in her eyes, she flopped back down and pulled the comforter over her head.

As the soft cotton covering whooshed over her face, it brought with it the tantalizing aroma of cooking bacon. She flipped the comforter back, thrust her feet into her slippers, threw on her thick robe, and padded to the top of the staircase. No, she wasn't dreaming. Kalea was cooking breakfast.

She trotted down the stairs in disbelief and wheeled around the end of the banister with only one thought on her mind. In all the time her cousin had lived with her, she had never made breakfast before. But Addie's grumbling tummy wasn't going to object this time, and she laughed. Ready to give her cousin a good-hearted teasing, she stepped across the kitchen threshold.

"Simon? What are you doing here?"

"I hope you don't mind." He glanced over at her from the stove. "I used the key you gave me to let myself in. I tried to be quiet so as not to wake you or my soundly sleeping patient on the sofa."

"Where's Pippi?" she asked, glancing around, trying to dispel the last of the sleep fog from her brain.

"She's outside, and my guess is as soon as she hears your voice through the door—"

Addie chuckled at the scratching sound and opened the back door to her excited little fur baby, who paused long enough to give Addie's hand a cursory lick and then scooted straight for her food bowl, where she sat and waited for her breakfast. Simon picked up a slice of bacon from a platter.

"Don't you dare," cried Addie, "she has her own food." Addie opened a cupboard and pulled out a plastic bin, focusing her sleep-blurred eyes on the measurement markers on the scoop, and filled Pippi's bowl with kibble. "There." She tsked. "And you, a doctor of all things, feeding my baby that."

"Does that mean you won't be having any yourself?"

"No, it just means I care more about her health than my own." She laughed as she danced a step past him to the platter, swiped a slice of bacon, and chomped a bite from it. "My goodness, you look awful!" She turned his face toward her and eyed the scarlet bulge on his cheek and the black and purple discoloration around his left eye. "What happened to you?"

"A patient struck me." He winced as her fingers touched his cheek.

"I hope he was arrested."

"Yes, he and about five others are still in lockup as far as I know."

"What?"

"Yeah." He pulled away to flip the eggs cooking in the frying pan. "You like them over-easy, right?"

"Forget about the eggs. Tell me what happened."

"Right." He turned the burner off and slid two eggs onto a plate with toast. "Well, I guess there was a scuffle outside the police station last night."

"Last night, what time?"

"About eight, I think. Anyway, it wasn't long after my shift started, and the police brought them all into the emergency department to get patched up."

"And someone hit you for trying to help them?"

"Not exactly. A couple of the brawlers crossed paths in the corridor and went at it again. I tried breaking them up, and well"—he shrugged and set the plate on the island countertop—"You can see how that turned out."

"What were they fighting about?" She edged backward onto a stool.

"I'm not sure how it started at the station, but in the hospital corridor, Bin Thomas saw Ingrid Humphries, Bernie's wife, and started yelling something about *you'll be sorry for this*. Bernie must have heard them arguing because he came flying out of one of the exam rooms and pushed Bin off his wife. Then Hal Washburn, who I was just going to inject with a local anesthetic so I could stitch up his cheek, pushed my hand away, leapt up from the stretcher, and went after Bernie. I jumped in and tried to pull them a part and the rest . . . is what you see now." He winced and prodded gently at his cheek.

"My goodness, all those people were at the police station when I left about six."

He slid bacon onto Addie's plate. "From what I could gather through all the yelling is that all of them were pointing fingers at each other and accusing everyone of being Jared's killer. Apparently, they are all on some police suspect list. At least, that's what I gathered as the events unfolded."

"Really?" She gulped.

He plucked a slice of bacon from her plate. "Yeah, but what I don't get is why in the world Marc would have them all go into the station at the same time. That's not his usual interrogation procedure, is it?"

"No, it's not, and he didn't."

"What do you mean?"

"I mean that someone spread a rumor around that *everyone* who had business dealings with Jared was a murder suspect. From what I can gather, when word spread, they all showed up at the station after their stores closed for the day to convince Marc of their innocence."

"And throw the suspicion on somebody else on the list."

"That's what it sounds like."

"But who would have made public a list like that?" He stopped mid-bite and glanced at her.

"Not me. But I'll give you one guess who." Addie snatched her piece of bacon from his fingertips. "A busybody baker who thinks she's helping Kalea but really is making everything worse."

Addie bristled with each bite as she shoveled food into her mouth. Martha's gossip had driven a wedge in the community. These people were friends, and now they were beating each other up and accusing one another of murder. This had to stop. It wasn't going to bring the real murderer to light and would probably just drive the whole thing further underground.

She pushed her empty plate away, slurped down her last mouthful of coffee, and rose to her feet. "If you don't mind putting the dishes in the sink to soak, I'll do them later." She glanced at the wall clock. "I'm going to leave soon. There's a stop I want to make before I go into the bookstore."

"Don't worry, I'll wash them. I'm too wound up to go home to bed. I'll get them done and maybe make a plate for Kalea. I want to make sure she's eating properly."

Kalea! She had forgotten her cousin was still asleep in the living room. Mixed feelings about leaving them alone rampaged through her mind. Then again, Simon was her doctor, and he had assured Addie he did not share any of Kalea's transference of feelings. Plus, her cousin had admitted she only flirted with him to feel like her old self again. Addie pushed her concerns from her mind and fixed a smile on her face. "Bacon and eggs aren't exactly health foods, doc," she said with a forced laugh.

"No, but right now, I'm just worried about her not eating anything." He filled the sink with water and added a squirt of dish soap.

"I do have a dishwasher, you know."

"I know, but I find the hot water soothing."

"Okay, suit yourself," she said, starting for the door.

"Wait!"

"What?" She glanced back.

"Don't I at least get my good-morning kiss and how about a thank-you kiss and a good-bye kiss before you run away?"

"Sorry. I'm trying to work out what I'm going to say to Martha and not cause another brawl to take place. She has a deadly right hook. Just ask Serena. She was on the receiving end of one of those a few years ago." Addie stood on her toes and planted a soft kiss on his neck below his earlobe. "There's your good-morning kiss." Her lips skimmed over his uninjured cheek and planted another. "And your thank-you-for-breakfast-and-cleaning-up kiss." Then she tilted his head down and placed her lips on his. "And your good-bye kiss," she murmured before pulling away.

"That's it? What about all the sympathy kisses I need. I am injured, you know."

"Those you'll get lots of later, but I really have to run."

"You, be careful." He tweaked her nose with soapy fingers.

"Thanks!" She laughed and wiped her face with the edge of her robe collar. "For that, you aren't going to get the extra kisses." She grinned demurely and sashayed out the kitchen door.

Addie hopped out of her car and glanced up the empty street. The nice thing about coming in before eight was none of the shops except the bakery opened for over another hour. She glanced at Martha's store window and through the murky light saw a figure moving around inside. Good, Martha appeared to have stuck to her usual five A.M. baking routine, so this would give Addie plenty of time to give her assistant's mother a good scolding before Paige got into the bookstore at nine.

Addie rapped on the glass door and shielded her eyes to squint into the dimly lit storefront. Bill's head popped up over the high, glassed-front, sales counter. He waved, sauntered toward the door, and pointed to the clock on the CLOSED sign that indicated they'd be open at eight.

"I need to speak to Martha!" Addie shouted.

Bill unlocked the door. "Morning, Miss Addie. Sorry 'bout that. I thought you were looking to buy something, and even though it's almost opening time, I haven't got the cash set up yet."

"That's okay," she said, stepping inside, and was instantly overcome with the aroma of freshly baked bread. "I could smell that all day. I'm not sure how you manage to stay so trim working here, Bill."

His face, weather-beaten by the years he had spent living on the streets, turned rosy. "Awe, I ain't so trim, Miss Addie, just look at what all Martha's cooking has given me." He laughed and pinched a small spare tire above the beltline of his white baker pants.

"I'd have never noticed if you hadn't pointed it out." She lightly squeezed his arm. "But seriously, Bill, I'm so glad to see you looking well and healthy."

"It's all cause of that wonderful woman back there," he whispered, gesturing with his head toward the kitchen. "I don't think I could have done any of this without her. She has the biggest heart of anyone I know." His eyes widened. "No offense, Miss Addie, she's just . . ." He glanced toward the back with a wistful look. "She's a very special lady."

"Yes, yes, she is." Addie shuffled from one foot to the other. This was going to be harder than she thought. All the way here, she had rehearsed in her head how and what she was going to say to Martha, but now . . . well . . . she wasn't so certain. The image of Simon's face popped back into her mind. Never mind . . . she was certain. "Any chance I can go back and have a word with her?"

"Sure." He ambled over to the counter and pulled a hair covering out of a dispenser box. "But you gotta wear one of these. Can't have no hairs ending up in the baked goods. Not great for business, you know."

"No problem," said Addie, fitting the paper covering over her hair and tucking in her ponytail. "Thanks, I'll let you get back to setting up." She glanced at the door and saw three people outside. "It seems I've kept you long enough."

Addie stood at the doorway of the industrial kitchen, and from her vantage point, she could see Martha pulling a pan out of one of the large wall ovens. Addie waited until she'd set it on the cooling rack. The last thing she needed was to scare the woman and cause her to burn herself—Addie glanced at the oven—or shove Addie in there when she heard why Addie was there.

"Good morning, Martha. I was wondering if we could have a quick word?"

Martha peered at her through one of the cooling-trolley shelves. "Morning, Addie, you're out and about early, aren't you?"

"Yes," Addie said, coming around the end of the rack, "I wanted to speak to you before you got busy."

"Judging by all the voices out front, I'd say you're a little late for that."

"Yes, well, sorry, I won't keep you long." Addie drew in a deep slow breath, glanced down at her hands, and laced them together in front of her. "I suppose you know about the fight that broke out in front of the police station last night."

Martha pulled off her oven mitts, set them on a rack, and nodded. "I had heard something to that effect, why?"

"Rumor has it that people were told the police had a list of everyone in Greyborne Harbor that Jared conducted business with and that all the names on it were suspects in his murder."

"So, what does that have to do with me?"

"I wonder where the rumor could have started, that's all."

"Who knows? I told you yesterday people were talking and putting clues together."

"It just seems that there are all sorts of suspicions and accusations being thrown around the Harbor right now, and it led to trouble."

"You know, as well as I do, that in a town like this you can't really keep people from talking."

"That is true, but it seems that someone keeps adding fuel to that fire, and I just can't imagine that person really wants to hurt Kalea with it, can you?"

"Hurt Kalea? How can making sure the police consider other suspects hurt her? It should help them see that poor girl couldn't have done it, but someone else might have had more of a motive than she did." She folded her plump arms across her chest. Her gaze fixed on Addie. "I guess with you talking in circles right now, you assumed it came from me." Her eyes blazed, and she stepped forward and poked her finger in Addie's face. "Yes, it was me. Because I know what it's like to be accused of murder and how it feels to sit and rot in a jail cell."

"As do I."

"Yes, yes, you would." She lowered her hand. "I just had to let people know their gossip about that poor girl being a killer wasn't the truth and that there were other people in this town who wanted Jared dead."

"I know you had the best intentions, and I agree that someone else might have had a motive." Addie lowered her voice and glanced toward the door. "Except, by telling Marc they argued and she was breaking up with him anyway, it actually throws more suspicion on Kalea because so far all the hard evidence points to her."

"But that's why I'm doing what I'm doing."

"I know, but what's needed is clear-cut proof that will establish her innocence and not have the investigation muddied up with gossip. It's only making the good people in town fight each other."

"Gossip, you call it." Martha harrumphed and glanced away. "I call it giving the police more of that evidence you're prattling on about."

"But people are getting hurt, and real damage can be done if this mob mentality continues." Addie drew in a deep breath. "Let me put it this way. Look at what happened last night. Good people are getting hurt by this, so please let the police investigate."

"You mean *you*, don't you?" Martha snapped. "What? Are you afraid I might solve this before you do and take the wind out of your sails? Besides, one of them is not such a good person, are they, because one of them did kill Jared, right?"

"It's just that—"

"Look, missy. I'll do everything in my power to get that girl off the police's radar. Mark my words. That's what one does for a friend."

"You know, I still have a hard time believing you and Kalea are friends."

"Why, am I so unlikable?"

Addie hesitated to choose her words carefully. Sure, over the last year, she and Martha had left a lot of their personal grievances regarding each other aside, but this conversation hinted that the current situation might reignite those past differences. Martha had proven she was a formidable adversary when she stirred the entire town up about Addie's supposed past and tried to get the town council to revoke her business license. Addie really didn't want this situation to escalate any underlying animosity Martha still might bear. "No, it's not that. It's just that the two of you seem so different."

"Well, she makes me laugh, and besides, Bill likes her, too, and he's a good judge of character. He never liked Jared, not one little bit, and said he didn't trust him. Although," she eyed Addie, "Bill likes you, so maybe he's not such a good judge of character after all."

And there it was. The cactus lady was showing her true colors again. Addie bit her tongue—chomped, more like it. But she wasn't going to be baited, not again. She met Martha's smug gaze and pasted what she hoped was an unfazed look of nonchalance on her face. "You don't say. I didn't know she and Bill even knew each other?"

"Heavens yes, she hasn't told you?"

"Told me what?"

"About our weekly dinners with her and Jared."

"You guys had dinners together?"

"Yes, most Friday or Saturday nights. But by the look on your face, I'd say your cousin hasn't mentioned that."

Addie shook her head.

"Yes, we've become great friends, and we get together on whatever night Logan isn't working his crazy fire-fighter schedule and is able to take Paige out for the evening."

"And Bill eats with you too? I mean, I thought he lived in the garage and pretty much kept to himself."

Martha cheeks flushed, and she dropped her gaze.

"I see," Addie glanced away, hoping her urge to smile was masked by the stunned look on her face from the news of their frequent dinners together. "Tell me . . . during all these evenings you spent with them, did you ever get the impression from Jared that any of his business dealings in town weren't going well?"

"Not from him directly, but people do talk, and I know a lot of people who wished they'd never taken him up on his offers of financing."

"What do you know about Nick Walker who runs Time Travels?"

"Not much." Martha's gaze narrowed as she studied Addie's face. "I met him and his sister a few times but never heard either of their names mentioned as being business associates of Jared's. Why?" By the look in Martha's eyes, Addie knew she'd just added more fuel to the gossip firestorm the woman was creating.

Regret gnawed at Addie's conscience. "No reason. I was only wondering that's all."

Chapter 19

Addie gazed out the side glass panels of the bookstore bay window and shook her head.

"What are you looking at?" asked Paige, sliding up beside her.

"That." Addie gestured toward the bakery. "The nonstop revolving door of people coming and going next door."

Paige peered around Addie's arm. "It's been like that all morning. At first, I thought she was having a huge sale to try to take some of the excitement off the bake sale and contest and remind everyone that she's the real baker in town. But then I realized that everybody was leaving empty-handed."

"That's because gossip is free and requires nothing but a small mind to carry it away in."

"Sad but true. I heard through Elli, who heard through

Curtis, about the problems last night at the station and the hospital."

"Yeah, and Simon became a victim himself."

"Oh no! I hope he's okay."

"Yes, but let's just say Doctor Dreamy isn't as dreamy as he once was and won't be for a few weeks."

"That's not going to sit well with her." Paige pointed to Bin Thomas who paused, glared at Addie through the window, and then scurried off down the street. "Did you see that?" Paige asked, her voice rising.

"Yes, and I'm guessing there are a few women in town that will be disappointed and blame me."

"That's ridiculous. They can't think you had anything to do with him getting punched, can they? Although," Paige said thoughtfully, "you may have some real competition now if they all rush so his side to nurse him back to his old self and protect him from the new featherweight in town."

Addie tried to stifle a laugh and snorted instead. "But seriously, before you got in today, I went and tried to reason with your mother and get her to stop stirring the pot with this, as it has pitted neighbor and friend against each other. Her talking about a so-called list of murder suspects, which the police aren't even investigating, isn't helping Kalea at all and might actually be hurting the investigation." Addie pressed her forehead against the pane. Throngs of people entered and exited the bakery. "It looks to me like it's become the official meeting place for Jared's business contacts so they can try to get the goods on someone else on the list." Her breath fogged the glass, but she didn't move from her sentry post. With her fingers, she swiped clear a peephole and kept her vigilant watch.

"Has she named you for being responsible for the list?"

"What do you mean?"

"Just that my mother has a way of spreading rumors but keeping herself distant from any fallout."

"That's a possibility because judging by the look Bin Thomas gave me last night at the police station and just now, I'd say it's implied."

"Did Mom see your crime board?"

"No, and anything I have on there is for my eyes only. You know that."

"I know that, but does she? Perhaps she thought it was an official list that the police were working from? After all, you said you were at the police station last night. Maybe she thought she was putting two and two together."

"Impossible. I only started it last night because of the rumor about the killer being one of Jared's business associates, and I figured the gossip was already spreading and leading to problems. Besides that, the list is at home, and the only person who's seen it is . . ."

"Is who?"

Addie's tummy tightened, and she groaned. "My cousin."

"Then no problem. I doubt Kalea would have been speaking to her."

"That's the problem." Addie faced Paige. "Were you aware they had dinner together nearly every weekend?"

"My mother and Kalea?"

Addie nodded.

"No way."

"Yes way. Apparently, on the evenings you and Logan went out, Kalea and Jared were dinner guests of your mom's."

"I can't believe that." Paige's face paled. "Did Kalea tell you that?"

"No, your mom."

"I knew she was having company more often, but she never said who. I just assumed it was her friends, Mildred or Ida. I had no idea."

Addie eyed her, searching for the correct words. "Are her and Bill . . . you know, together?"

"I don't think they're together-together. After all, he does work six days a week in the bakery, and with the cold weather coming on, she finally convinced him to move into the house."

Addie's brows twitched.

"Not with her, silly. He's in my sister's old bedroom."

"Yes, well, according to her, Bill attends these dinners, too, and has taken quite a liking to Kalea."

"Really?" Confusion clouded Paige's face. "Although now that you say that and I think about it, I have noticed that Mom's changed her hair and wears a bit of makeup every day. Something she hasn't done for years. Come to think of it, she's also been buying a lot of new dresses lately."

"Are all these new dresses from Hudson's Creations on Main by any chance?"

Paige nodded. "Which really stumped me because as long as I can remember she's never cared a hoot what people thought about how she looked. Suddenly, she sees herself as an aging fashion diva?"

"I think her friendship with Bill, her old high school friend might have bloomed now your dad is permanently out of the picture again, and I know she was taken by Kalea's design abilities at Serena's wedding. So, I'm sure that combination is what had sparked this new version of Martha."

"That could be, but to have it all happening right under my nose and I never even saw it? I mean, Bill I can understand. He's such a sweetheart and is completely devoted to Mom, something Dad never was, so that part I'm happy about." Paige shook her head. "But she and Kalea becoming friends? I just can't see it."

"I wouldn't have thought it either. They are a very unlikely duo, and it's that friendship with Kalea that has your mother doing all this. She's convinced of her innocence, and it appears she's willing to go to any lengths—no matter who gets hurt in the process—to cast doubt on police evidence."

Paige contemplated the goings-on next door. "Which one of them are you focusing on first?"

"None of them."

"What? You're kidding, right?"

"No, I think the briefcase is still the key. For now, I'm sticking to that lead. All this other stuff is just a distraction and could well be an intentional one."

"How?"

"Because it's possible that the real killer said something to your mom, knowing her weakness for gossip, and knew exactly what she'd do with whatever he or she told her."

"For what purpose?"

"To confuse the whole situation and have the police chasing their tails, giving the killer more time to cover his or her tracks or leave town without raising suspicion. Which is why I'm going to focus on who we're not seeing there"—Addie gestured toward the bakery—"and who I didn't see last night at the police station."

"Good morning, ladies," chirped Catherine before the overhead bells could jingle out her arrival. "Is Martha having a sale? I had an impossible time finding a parking spot and had to hike all the way over from the backside on East Main."

"Unfortunately, Mom's holding court."

"I always said she was royalty or something in a past life," said Catherine with a short laugh. "Does that have something to do with what happened last night?"

"As far as we know," said Addie. "Would you like a coffee?"

"That would be wonderful. I'm frozen." She rubbed her hands together. "Say, didn't she cause a similar disturbance and circulate a petition one time to try and force you out of town?"

Addie shoved a pod a little too viciously into the coffee maker. "Yeah, I've been the subject of her tirades and proclamations on more than one occasion."

"It's not something like that again, is it?"

"No, she's trying to force the police to consider suspects other than Kalea for Jared's murder by telling everybody that *everyone* who had business dealings with him is a prime suspect."

"Oh dear. The way people in this town react to something half as ridiculous means that this won't go well, and now I understand the reason behind the kerfuffle last night."

"Here's your coffee."

"Fantastic, thank you." Catherine wrapped her hands around the steaming cup. "Anyway, I hope Marc gets this and her sorted out soon. We can't have people beating the daylights out of each other, can we?"

"No, we can't because it doesn't help the investigation."

"True, true." Catherine took a sip and glanced at Addie over the rim of her cup. "But I'm here on a different matter."

"You've decided to accept the job offer?"

"Hmm . . . sort of. I have an idea, and I came to ask your opinion about it."

"You're confusing me, but okay, what?"

"First off, I've been thinking about entering my pies in the Make it - Bake it competition."

"I think the competition part of the event is only open to members of the business community. However, the weekend bake sale is open to everyone, and I heard there was a small prize for the best-in-sale dish, too. Is that the part you mean?"

"No . . ." She slid onto a counter stool and set her coffee cup on the counter. "That's the sticky part. What if I came to work for you on a temporary basis, and then I could enter the main competition as a member of the business community."

"Catherine, that wouldn't be honest."

"I know, I know, but I could stay on afterward and work *occasionally* if you and Paige were still open to my hectic schedule—you did say before we could work around that." She looked hopefully from one to the other.

"As long as you don't quit on us as soon as the competition is over."

"I promise." She crossed her heart. "I can't promise how much I'll be available."

"We'll take what we can get," cried Addie and seized Catherine in an excited hug.

"Welcome to the team. I'm thrilled you'll finally be joining us," Paige said, beaming.

Catherine peeled Addie off of her. "I could start . . . say . . . next week if that's all right?"

"Yes, sure, whatever works for you."

"Great." She took a sip of her coffee and buttoned up her raven-black wool coat. "Because I was just in Serena-TEA to pick up my weekly stash of teas, and Serena was telling me that Ivy and Nick are unpacking the crates of items Ivy bought at an estate sale last weekend. Serena showed me the plates she scored yesterday, so I'm hoping they have a pie plate in this new stock that I can use to present my entry on."

"You are aware that not all the pottery they have is food safe, aren't you?"

"Yes, Serena mentioned that, but fingers crossed they have unearthed something authentic I can use. Her plates are absolutely stunning, aren't they?" Catherine grinned and tugged on her black leather gloves. "But first, I have to get over to the community hall. I hope it's not too late to enter the competition."

Addie looked thoughtfully at her old friend.

"What's wrong? Do I have my lipstick smudged?" Catherine asked, pulling a small compact from her purse.

"No, you look wonderful. That's not it," Addie said, placing her hand over the small mirrored case. "I was just thinking that I might go with you to Time Travels. There's something I want to check out."

"Lovely. I'll just run over to the community hall to register and be back in a jiffy to pick you up."

"Perfect. See you in a few minutes." Addie waved as her old friend rushed out the door.

Paige stared at Addie. "Did you decide to buy that medical bag you told me about for Simon?"

"Not exactly."

"What are you up to?"

Addie dropped a book from the counter onto the trolley. "Well, I'm going to use Catherine's being there as an excuse to look at the bag again. You know, say I came with her to get her opinion on it, but . . ."

"But what's your real motive?"

Addie's face lit up with a roguish grin. "Remember when I said that I'm focusing on who we're not seeing over there"—Addie jerked her thumb toward the bakery—"and who I didn't see last night at the police station?"

"Yes?" Paige's eyes widened. "You don't mean Ivy Walker?"

"No, her brother Nick. When I got home last night, Kalea was asleep, but she had added his name to the list of the clients Jared worked with in town."

"Nick? Really? You suspect him?" Paige pouted. "That sucks. I always liked him."

"I might be way off. I just don't know yet because I never saw him at the station last night along with all the other named suspects on that list who were trying to clear their name. I need to figure out why."

Chapter 20

"Hi, Nick."

"Hi, Addie, come back for the bag?"

"You never give up do you?" she said with a laugh.

"I figure I'll wear you down, eventually," he replied with a teasing wink.

"I brought reinforcements with me just to keep that from happening." Addie grinned. "Someone whose taste and opinion I value above all else. Nick, I'd like to introduce you to my dear friend, Catherine Lewis."

"Catherine," he said, extending his slender hand, "how wonderful to meet you, although you look familiar. Have we met before?"

"Yes, I run the hospital New Year's Gala and a few of the other Harbor events."

"Ah, yes, that's where our paths have crossed. Are you shopping today, too, or just here for Addie's moral support?" He leaned across the counter toward her and dropped his voice. "Between you and me, I think she's already decided to buy that medical bag and just wants me to have to work for the sale."

"You never know," Catherine said with a short laugh. "But to be honest, I'm the customer this trip."

He stood sharply upright. "Wonderful. What can I help you with?"

"Our friend Serena was in here yesterday, and she bought the most stunning plate set, and I was wondering if you came across any more matching pieces to it."

"You are in luck," he said with a broad grin. "There is a soup urn, a pie plate, and a—"

"Did you just say pie plate?"

"Yes." He glanced at Addie and then back at Catherine. "We discovered those other pieces late last night in the last crate we were unpacking, and I meant to phone Serena today to tell her in case she was interested."

"Forget about Serena," cried Catherine. "I'm here now. A bird in the hand, you know. Can I see the pie plate?"

"Sure, it's right over here in the china cabinet." He gave Addie a mischievous side-glance. "By the doctor's bag."

Addie eyed him skeptically. "If I didn't know better, I'd say you planned the placement of these pieces, knowing I'd be tempted enough by the bag to come back with Serena when she came in to see these new pieces, and then you'd do just this, spring the bag on me again."

"Drat!" he said with a melodramatic drawl and twirled a nonexistent handlebar mustache. "You've figured out my devious plan."

"Okay, you win. I know when I'm in the presence of a shrewd archrival." She pressed the back of her hand to her forehead and swooned. "Take down the bag and let me have another look."

He glanced at Catherine with a sly wink and retrieved the bag.

"For you, madame, my most worthy opponent, and"—he opened a glass door of the china cabinet, gingerly removed the Edward Walley Civil War–era Palissy pie plate, and placed it reverently in Catherine's outstretched hands—"for you."

"It's perfect!" she squealed with delight. "Yes, and look at the date on the back, Addie. I can't believe this."

Addie rested her hand on the medical bag, but her gaze was focused on the item beside the now empty space where Nick had removed the plate. "Is that a matching Edward Walley teapot?"

"Yes, that's the piece I was actually going to phone Serena about. She did buy a few other tea sets yesterday, and I thought she'd—"

"I'll take it!" Addie cried. "It would make the perfect Christmas gift for her, so don't you dare tell her you came across one, please." Addie fixed her gaze on his stunned one.

"No, I won't. Scout's honor," he said with a two-finger salute. "Now, what about the doctor's bag." His brows wiggled good-naturedly.

"Okay, yes. Since I'm spending"—she glanced at the price tag dangling from the teapot handle, softly gasped, and swallowed hard—"so much on my friend, I suppose spending another thousand on the man I love isn't asking too much, right?" She glanced at Catherine, whom she secretly hoped would talk her out of her purchases, but Catherine had wandered away with her treasure and was now browsing a display of Victorian plant pots.

"Shall I ring these up or did you want to look around some more?"

"No! No more browsing for me. My bank account can't handle it."

"So then nothing today for your old friend?" He motioned to Catherine now examining an eighteen-century butter churn.

"Don't push it." Addie laughed and fished her wallet out of her bag. "Enough damage has been done already today."

Addie kept an eye on Catherine's whereabouts in the store. She'd explain all this to her later, but right now she needed to figure out if her hunch about Nick was right or not.

"I forgot to tell you that when I said where I was going today, my cousin Kalea mentioned she knew you. Apparently, you were a client of Jared Munro's or something?" Addie said as Nick rang up the bag and the teapot.

"That fellow who was killed?"

"Yes, you were a client, right, or is my cousin mistaken? He had so many clients in town it is hard to keep track."

"I did know Jared, but I don't ever recall meeting your cousin. What did you say her name was?"

"Kalea Hudson. She owns the dress shop on Main Street."

"You must have misunderstood. My sister knows her, but I've never had the pleasure."

"Really? I'm pretty sure she said she'd met you." Addie shook her head. "Maybe you're right, and I misunderstood. But how does Ivy know her? I don't think my cousin is the type to shop in an antique store. Her taste in design is far too contemporary for that."

"The other way around. Ivy was a customer of Kalea's. As a matter of fact, your cousin made some fancy dress for my sister to wear to Gwendolyn Buchannan's Thanksgiving dinner."

"She did? Hmm, it seems Ivy and Gwendolyn are better friends than I thought."

"Not friends. I think the woman only tolerates Ivy because of the work she does in helping put together her collection. The dinner, from what I understand, isn't your typical family meal. It's more of a who's who soiree."

"In that case, good for Ivy on receiving an invitation. With a prominent guest list like that who knows what business contacts she'll make there."

"That's exactly what Ivy's thinking."

Nick passed Addie's purchase over the counter to her.

"I'm sorry about the earlier misunderstanding. I could have sworn, though, that my cousin said she knew you through Jared. I guess she must have said Ivy was in business with him."

"No, you were right. I take care of all the financial dealings of the store. Ivy does the traveling."

"Then you were a client?"

"Yes, but only in the sense that I had a revolving line of credit with his company. I had few dealings with the man himself."

"Line of credit with him? You mean like personal loans?"

"No, it's through his main office. It's a series of short-term loans to cover the purchases my sister makes at the estate sales and auctions she attends throughout the year. We need cash fast and up front—something the banks don't like to do—and a friend recommended Jared's company a few years ago, and he's been more than accommodating since then. To be honest, now that he's dead, I'm really not sure what we'll do. In the winter, Ivy travels south to sales and auctions in a more temperate climate and . . . let's just say, with Jared's death, we won't have the money at our disposal." He gazed at Catherine as she marched, arms loaded, to the counter. "It's sad. There are so many things Ivy comes across in her travels that we won't be able to acquire in the future. It will really put a damper on our business."

"What about finding a new financier?" asked Addie.

Catherine deposited her armful of unearthed treasure on the counter. "No, I don't want to finance these. I'll pay for them today?"

Addie rolled her eyes. "Honestly, Catherine, you know what they say about walking into the middle of a conversation."

She looked innocently at Addie. "No, what?"

"I'm not sure, but I'm sure *they* say something."

Nick let out a deep belly laugh as he sorted through Catherine's merchandise. "You two need to take your stand-up routine on the road. I'm sure my sister would love the company."

Addie chuckled softly as Nick rang up Catherine's purchases and gazed around the shop. She hoped Nick would be able to secure more line of credit funding because it would be sad to see this shop have to scale down on its merchandise. There were truly some one-of-a-kind items here. Her gaze came to rest on a brown leatherbound book sitting on the narrow wrapping table behind the sales counter. "Is that a bound volume of *Godey's Lady's Book*?"

Nick glanced over his shoulder. "Yes, but I'm afraid it's not for sale. It's for Ivy's special customer, *Gwendolyn Buchannan*," he and Addie said in unison, laughing.

"An inside joke, I assume." Catherine's voice feigned rebuke.

Addie glanced sheepishly at Nick and giggled. "Yes, you might say that."

"Is there anything else I can include in your purchases today, Mrs. Lewis? Perhaps some Christmas gifts for your friends? I know Addie here has managed to find a few for hers."

"It's Miss Lewis, and not today, thank you. I can't even think about Christmas yet. She glanced wistfully over her shoulder. "Although, there is that hand-painted Victorian oval planter that would be perfect on my patio . . . never mind. I need to sleep on it. No, this will be all for today." She handed Nick her credit card.

"The Victorian planter you say?" He dropped his voice and whispered to Addie, "Ho, ho, ho, 'tis the season."

She gave him a subtle nod and a small smile crept to the corners of his lips, and it broke into a grin as he handed Catherine her bag. "It was a pleasure to meet you, Miss Lewis. I do hope to see you again."

"Probably sooner than you think." She eyed the planter collection across the store. "Yes, probably sooner than you think."

"I'll put it in the back," Nick mouthed to Addie behind Catherine's back as she headed toward the door.

Addie smiled and nodded, mentally checking off her Christmas shopping list in her head. Serena, teapot, check. Simon, vintage medical bag, check. Catherine, Victorian planter, check. That only left her with Paige and Kalea . . . and Martha. Well, she'd have to wait and see how that one played out, but all in all, not bad considering it wasn't even Thanksgiving yet.

Chapter 21

Addie pulled the alley door to Beyond the Page open and stopped abruptly. "Hello, Logan," she said, discreetly glancing away from the scene playing out before her.

Paige pulled herself from his arms. A crimson blush glowed across her pixie-like cheeks. "Addie! I, umm . . ."

As Addie slipped her jacket off and hung it on the corner coatrack, she noticed he wasn't dressed in his casual day-off attire. "I take it things are quiet at the station today."

"Addie, you aren't going to believe it, but Logan came to tell me that the fire hall held a raffle for two tickets to the New Year's Eve charity gala, and Logan won! Can you believe it?"

"How wonderful! That is a spectacular evening. You're both going to love it."

"Well, I should get back," Logan said, glancing awkwardly at Addie. "I only wanted to drop in and tell Paige in person." His smile broadened when he looked at Paige as he backed out the storeroom door into the shop.

"Addie, I'm so excited. I've always wanted to go to it, but the tickets are a hundred dollars apiece." She twirled in circles, giggling, and stopped. A look of horror spread across her flushed face. "But what will I wear? I don't have a ball gown. That's what the ladies wear, isn't it?"

Addie nodded.

"I can't afford an evening gown! But maybe Mom's got something I can remake. Yes, that's what I'll do. There's plenty of time. I'm so excited!" She squealed and laughed as she danced and twirled up the aisle to the storefront.

Addie gazed after Paige and snapped her fingers. "You know, Paige, I haven't bought your Christmas present yet."

"You don't have to get me anything, you know that," said Paige breathlessly from behind the sales counter.

"I know, but what would you say if I bought you an evening gown?"

Paige's flush drained from her cheeks.

"Well, how about it?"

"I couldn't accept that. That's way too much."

"Nonsense, I want to do it. I could never run this store without you, and you have also become a dear friend."

"Are you sure?"

"Yes, I'm sure you're a friend, silly."

"I meant, are you sure about the dress because they aren't cheap."

"No, if that's what you want, then consider it my Christmas present to you." Addie studied her assistant's face and noted the flush returning. "I'll ask Kalea to make it if you like?"

"If I like? Of course, I like. Her dresses are New York City quality."

"Good, she still has your measurements from when she made our bridesmaid dresses, so all you'll have to do is go through some fashion magazines and pick out a design you like. Since she's staying with me for a while yet, it will give her something to do."

Paige clapped her hands excitedly. "I already know what dress I want."

"That was fast."

"Yes, I want that one!" She pointed to one of the *Godey's Lady's Book* fashion plate posters on the wall. Her eyes glazed over as she dreamily admired the picture. "Without the bustle, of course."

"Yes, I agree. I think they went out of style a number of years ago," Addie said with a little chuckle. "Okay, if that's the one you want, let's make it happen."

"I can't wait to tell Elli. She'll be *so* jealous."

"Go then and tell her the news." It seemed Paige's excitement was contagious because Addie couldn't hold back a grin. "You might as well take your lunch break now, too."

Addie stared up at the image of the woman on the poster and tried to picture Paige. In true Civil War–era style, the woman wore her hair in an elaborate braid, covered in a beaded net, and her shoulders were accented by the off-the-shoulder cut of the wasp-waist gown that spilled out into a wide, full skirt that brushed the floor. Yes, the style was perfect for Paige, minus the bustle, of course, and Kalea would know the ideal billowy fabric to use. *Paige, evening gown, check*. She beamed as she thought about her dwindling holiday shopping list.

"I'm so glad you got more of these Civil War cookbooks in stock," said a stalky middle-aged woman as she dropped two books on the counter in front of Addie. "I was afraid I'd miss out when I heard you were sold out yesterday."

"Fantastic!" Addie grinned and examined the books. "I didn't know they'd come in yet."

"All I can say is I'm glad your Paige there got them out on the shelves before she got the news about the gala tickets."

"Why is that?" asked Addie.

"Because I fear her head will be in the clouds for the rest of the day, so good luck with her working this afternoon," she said with a soft laugh as she fished her wallet out of her handbag. "Say, you don't happen to have any job openings here right now, do you?"

"No, I'm sorry. Currently, I have all the staff I need."

"That's too bad," the customer said, handing Addie her credit card. "I could use a new dress myself." She winked teasingly.

Addie was still chuckling as the woman left, and she flipped opened her laptop to retrieve the latest invoice sent by her book distributor. As she scrolled through her emails searching for it, one subject line caught her eye. *Important Notice - Beware,* and it was from Barbara, her old friend at the Boston Library.

> *I am sending this alert to all my rare and used booksellers contacts in the New England area. The Boston Library has been recently contacted by the*

FBI Antiquities Division to be on the lookout for anyone who might try to pass along a number of first edition publications that went missing over the past week from Hawthorns Rare Books in Boston. See below the list of titles, publication dates, and any pertinent information. Should you come across any of these titles, please contact the FBI immediately.

Gone With the Wind
Mitchell, Margaret – Valued at US$ 85,000.00
Published by New York Macmillan 1936
Signed by Margaret Mitchell on the flyleaf

The Mysterious Mr. Quin
Christie, Agatha – Valued at US$ 53,078.47
Published by W. Collins & Sons Co Ltd, UK (1930)

Frankenstein
Shelley, Mary – Valued at US$ 35,000.00
Published by Carey, Lea, & Blanchard, Philadelphia (1833)

The Picture of Dorian Gray
Wilde, Oscar – Valued at US$ 35,000.00
Published by London: Ward, Lock, 1891 (1891)

The Wind in The Willows
Grahame, Kenneth – Valued at US$ 19,904.43
Published by Methuen, 1908

Addie scanned through the email list, making a mental note of each title, but when she got to the last three entries, she paused.

Northwood, or, Life North and South: Showing the True Character of Both
Hale, Sarah Josepha – Valued at US$ 650.00
Published by H. Long & Brother, New York (1852)

The Ladies' New Book of Cookery: a Practical System for Private Families in Town and Country; with Directions for Carving, and Arranging the Table for Parties, Etc. Also Preparations of Food for Invalids and for Children.
Hale, Sarah Josepha – Valued at US$ 250.00
Published by Long & Brother, New York (1852)

Broadside on cloth: Mary's Lamb in Sunday Lessons, No. 1
Hale, Sarah Josepha – Valued at US$ 4,500.00
Published by Boston Chemical Printing Company, Boston (1830)

The valued price of the first five classics didn't fit with the valuation of the final three books on the list. However, there was a similarity that didn't escape her. The last three entries were all written by Sarah Josepha Hale. *Most curious.* There was a big market for rare books and antiquities, but thieves were known to target items that would bring them a lot of money, fast. Why would they risk being caught attempting to unload books that brought such a low payoff? *Yes, most curious.* She glanced up to greet whoever had sent her door bells into a tinkling dither and flipped her laptop closed.

"Serena, are you spending another day prowling the streets of Greyborne Harbor, seeking treasures?"

"I wish," said Serena as she set down a take-out cup, slid onto a stool, and dropped two brown paper lunch bags on the counter. "I'm working the floor because Vera is off today. Apparently, *Maggie* has some big client in town looking at properties. She begged Vera to come in and man the phones so she could have all her regular staff search listings, book appointments, and cold-call potential listings for the perfect property."

"Hmm, must be somebody important."

"It sounds like it's somebody rich, if you ask me, the way she's got all hands on deck," she said, opening a bag. "I hope you like ham and cheese? By the time I got into Martha's, that's about all she had left. I can't believe how busy she was when I was in there. It's a good thing she's got Bill on full time to help her out."

"Ham and cheese is fine." Addie retrieved her sandwich from the second bag. "Speaking of good hires, did I tell you that Catherine has finally relented and is going to come and work here part time?"

"No," garbled Serena, chewing on a bite of her sandwich. "That's great, especially since we're heading into the busiest shopping time of the year."

"Yes, the timing couldn't be better."

Serena plucked a paper napkin from her bag. "All I can say is that if Martha stays this busy, she'll have to look at hiring someone else on for the holiday shopping period too."

"I imagine when the murder is solved, she'll be a lot less busy."

"What are you talking about?"

Addie peered over the top of her sandwich at Serena. "You know, when everyone in town isn't going in for their daily dose of gossip."

"What gossip?"

"Where have you been?"

"In my kitchen, trying recipes for the competition or in the back room of SerenaTEA, making up special orders. Why? What did I miss?" She set her sandwich on the napkin and took a sip of the tea she'd brought with her.

Addie proceeded to update Serena on the events of the previous evening at the police station and the hospital, the final name Kalea had added to the crime board, and the visit she'd made to Time Travels again this morning with Catherine. When she finished, she fixed her gaze on her Serena. "So what do you think?"

"The competition has gotten a lot tighter is what I think." She set her carryout cup down with a thump.

"What are you talking about?"

"Catherine is entering the baking competition. She's one of the best cooks in town. She could open her own restaurant." Serena hung her head. "I stand no chance of winning now." She looked up. "That's why you hired her, so she'd qualify to enter, right?"

"No, I didn't set out to sabotage you. It was just good timing for both of us, I guess, but forget about the cooking contest for a minute, please. What do you think about what I just told you about Nick and the other people on the suspect list?"

"Did she find a plate for her presentation?"

"Serena?"

"I mean it. Nick told me he'd keep looking for anything else suitable for me, so if she went and bought something he promised to me, well then, I'd say that everything he told you this morning was a lie."

"What's gotten into you? I've never seen you like this before."

Serena's eyes reddened. "I don't know. I just haven't been feeling myself." She pushed her cup and half-eaten sandwich away. "Maybe I'm getting sick."

"Maybe," Addie said, eyeing her friend thoughtfully. "But seriously, Nick did seem sincere in his concern about Jared's death and how that would affect Time Travels going forward. I can't believe he'd kill him, knowing it would hurt his own business by forcing them to downsize, can you?"

"You did say you had a hunch about him because he was visibly absent from both the altercations at the police station and hospital. Enough so that you followed that hunch and talked to him personally." She shrugged. "If your gut tells you he's not the killer, then you're probably right. I don't know. I like Nick and really can't see him as a cold-blooded killer."

"I know. I'm not sure I can either unless there's something else behind this that I've missed completely."

"I think it means the real killer is someone who was there last night trying to put the heat on someone else."

"That's what I'm thinking now too, which is why when Nick wasn't involved in trying to clear his name or pointing the finger at someone else, I thought it suspicious. But after talking to him this morning, I tend to think it's because he knows he's innocent, so he has no ulterior motive."

"Perhaps busybody Martha wasn't wrong in letting that rumor fly around town," said Serena. "She might actually be on the way to making the murderer eventually show his hand through all her meddling."

"You're right. She might really be helping, and I was just being too stubborn to see it."

"You stubborn?" Serena choked back a laugh.

"Stop it." Addie playfully swatted at her. "I only wish people weren't getting hurt by her tactics. There has to be another way to flush the killer out."

"There is . . ."

"What? Now you're going to throw Marc's words back at me and tell me to let the police do their job?"

"Addie, Addie, Addie, since when have I ever taken my brother's side in any of our investigations?"

Addie gazed at Serena. A warm smile spread across her face. "I'm so glad to see the old Serena is back." She patted her friend's hand. "That's the person I need as my second set of eyes."

"I never left, just been unfocused lately that's all, but . . . since this involves your cousin, count me in from now on." She glanced out the window. "Good. Here comes Paige, now." She gathered up the remains of their lunch and dropped them into the wastebasket. "Let's get the tarp off that board and take a look at what we have."

Chapter 22

Addie stood back and reread what she'd written. "I hope I haven't missed anyone. I should have taken a picture of it last night."

"Since I wasn't there when you wrote up the board at home, I can't help. Sorry," said Serena from her perch on a wooden book crate. "But is that the entire list of who in town Jared was having business dealings with?"

"As far as I know, and Kalea did add these last few." She pointed to the last three names she'd written.

"I had no idea Jared was involved with all these businesses," said Serena, after reading over the board.

Hal Washburn – Loose Screw Hardware Store

Bin and Bev Thomas – Greyborne Point B&B

Clay Diggens – Diggens Bait Shop and Boat Rentals

Bernie and Ingrid Humphries – Replay Used Sporting Goods

Matt Bellows – Ship 'n' Anchor Tavern

Sally Harrison – Sweet Treats Ice Cream and Candy Shop

Charles Wilson – Art Connection on Main

Adam and Evelyn Boyer – Adam and Eve's Garden Market

Tara Wylie – Tresses by Tara

Nick Walker – Time Travels

"I didn't either and Kalea thought there might even be a few more that she didn't know about."

"Phew, where do we start?"

"Since my gut tells me the briefcase is the key to the murder, I guess we need to go back to the beginning and figure out what was in it that someone wanted desperately enough to kill for."

"You mean the beginning when Kalea called you?"

"No, further back than that."

"That morning, or the night before when they had the argument that seems to have spotlighted her as Marc's prime suspect?"

"Before that," said Addie, glancing over at Serena, "to Sunday afternoon when Kalea and Jared were in Boston." She scribbled across the board. *What we know . . .*

"Keep in mind"—Serena rose to her feet and joined Addie at the board—"anything you know about what happened *before* you got to the dress shop Monday morning is only what Kalea has shared with you. So if you are still questioning her innocence, it's all hearsay."

"I know, but for the sake of argument, and this"—she tapped the blackboard—"I'm going to write it as factual accounts unless something pops out and disproves anything she's said."

"Fair enough." Serena shrugged. "I just thought I should mention that since you're going to so much trouble to defend her when you're not really certain about that fact yourself."

"I know it doesn't make sense, especially after everything she's put me through since she came to live here, but as much as I consider *you* my sister, she actually *is* my flesh and blood. I have to make the assumption she's innocent unless we find evidence proving otherwise."

Addie began writing a list on the board of everything she could recall Kalea telling her and the police.

Briefcase found in pawnshop in Boston

Clerk asked if Kalea was from Greyborne Harbor, gave it to Jared for no money, said Kalea had already paid for it. She had not.

Jared told her it seemed heavier than Jared's original one

Morning of murder—no sign of forced entry

Did Jared know his would-be killer and let them in? She circled the question mark.

Murder weapon—clothes hanger from the store

Two different blood specimens on Jared's shirt— one Kalea's, one unknown (perhaps killer was

injured during altercation with Jared?) Another
circled question mark.

*Dress shop staged to appear as though it had been
robbed, but the briefcase was the only thing actually missing from the scene*

*Briefcase later discovered in dumpster two shops
down from dress shop.*

False bottom (hidden compartment) in briefcase

"That last point," said Addie, glancing over at Serena,
"is something Marc and I discovered later after Nick and
Ivy showed me the medical case with the hidden compartment."

"That's cool and kind of adds to the mystery, doesn't it?"

"Maybe," said Addie, "but it, of course, was empty,
and Jerry couldn't find any trace evidence inside it, so it
might be nothing."

"Okay, let's stick to what we do know then," said Serena, reading over the growing list. "Don't forget the argument they had Sunday night." She pointed to Addie's
notation on the side about Sunday evening. "Somebody
reported to the police as having overheard it, apparently."

"You're right, and that is suspicious because if what
Kalea said about it is true, no one would have heard
them."

"Unless Kalea was lying about where it took place, or
maybe it was more heated than she admits."

"I already pressed her on that, and she swears it wasn't."

"Then put a question mark beside it for now."

Addie added *argument?* to the blackboard, stood back
to review and then drew a line to the list of names above.

"These are all Jared's business associates in Greyborne Harbor. The current line of investigation is focusing on the fact that one of them wasn't happy with their business arrangement or the terms of it or something and killed Jared during an altercation . . ."

"To get their contracts back or some other documents he had that were in the briefcase, which matches the point you have about Jared letting the person into the store Monday morning because he knew them."

"Yes," said Addie, "but how does that fit with the misunderstanding about the case having already been paid for in Boston?"

"Knock, knock," said Paige, tapping on the back-room door frame.

"Did you need me out front?" asked Addie, glancing at her from the board.

"No, but . . . Elli just called to see if Serena was coming back in?"

"Shoot! I completely forgot she was on her own today, and we're serving an authentic British afternoon tea soon." Serena leapt up, grabbed her bag and jacket, and hurriedly made her way through the bookshop and out the door.

Addie eyed her friend and then looked at Paige, patting her tummy. "I have a feeling that she may start showing the results of that test she's afraid to take long before actually she takes it."

"Do you think?"

"You tell me. Mood swings, lack of focus, memory lapses, says food tastes off or no appetite at all, feeling squeamish?"

"Been there, done that," Paige said with a short laugh. "You might be right."

"I guess time will tell," said Addie, placing the chalk stick on the board ledge. "I'll come up front now."

"No hurry, it's been quiet." Paige mimicked in a posh British accent, "Tis teatime, you know."

Addie laughed and wiped her chalk-covered hands with a tissue as Paige curtsied and swiveled around to leave. Paige stopped midway through her turn and zeroed in on the two shopping bags Addie had placed earlier by the coatrack. "I didn't notice those when you came in because I was so excited by Logan's news, but I see you went shopping when you were out with Catherine."

"Sort of, I guess. I saw this when I was at Time Travels with Serena and decided to get it today." Addie retrieved the larger bag from the floor. "Do you think Simon will like it?" She slipped the medical case out and presented it to Paige. "It cost more than we generally spend on each other, but the more I thought about it, the more I knew it was the perfect Christmas gift for him."

"Oh, Addie." Paige stroked her fingers over the soft pigskin leather. "It's beautiful. He'll love it."

"You don't think it's too much, do you?"

"No, it's perfect. I mean you guys have been together for a long time now and besides . . ." She grinned up at Addie. "I wouldn't be surprised if he gave you a diamond this year."

"What? No, he wouldn't. We're far from that point in our relationship, aren't we?"

"I'd say your comment about *time will tell* regarding Serena might also apply here." Paige laughed and sashayed out the door. "Don't say I didn't try and warn you," she called back over her shoulder.

"Silly girl," Addie muttered and shook her head as she placed the bag on the desk, admiring it. She opened the top and withdrew the rack of antique medicine bottles and wondered how deadly some of these were since she wasn't familiar with a few of the names on the labels—at least the ones she could read that hadn't been smudged and faded over the years. Then she mirrored Ivy's actions and released the mechanism to open the hidden compartment on the bottom of the bag. She had only seen the small black leather package secured inside—now it was time to explore it.

Addie set the soft leather satchel on her desk and carefully untied the fragile leather fastening. Her fingers itched with excitement. The anticipation bubbling up inside her was exactly how she hoped Simon would react when he explored the medical case Christmas morning.

An involuntary gasp escaped her chest when she flipped the case open. It was filled with an assortment of antique glass hypodermic syringes and a small amber vial. She blinked, twice, and studied the bottle. Was this something she should take to the police for analysis? Why would it have been hidden in the false bottom?

"Hi, Addie."

"Carolyn?" Addie scanned her friend's current attire consisting of a navy Sherpa hooded jacket, combat-style ankle booties, and jeans. "I see you're not on duty right now, or are you undercover?" Addie discreetly closed the envelope-styled top of the satchel and shoved it under the bag and out of sight from Field Sergeant Coleman and Simon's sister.

Carolyn leaned her hip on the door frame. "I was on my way to the library to return the kids' books, and our elderly neighbor, Mrs. Donaldson, asked me to stop in and pick up a Civil War book she ordered from you last week? Paige said you had it back here."

"Yes, I do, it must have come in the shipment this morning." Addie grinned, strode over to a wall shelf, and retrieved a newer edition of Louisa May Alcott's 1863 novel, *Hospital Sketches*. "I was going to phone her later and let her know it was here."

"She's got a bit of a cold right now, so she asked me if I could possibly pick it up for her. Say, what's that?" Carolyn slid over to the desk and eyed the medical bag.

"*That* is my Christmas gift to Simon. What do you think?"

"I think he'll be thrilled." She glanced at Addie then back at the doctor's bag. "Just look at the collection of old medicines. What's this inside?" She pulled out the antiquated, coned-head stethoscope and examined it.

"That's not all . . ." Addie glanced uneasily at Carolyn. With a trembling hand, she slid the small black satchel into view and opened it. "I found them hidden in a secret compartment in the bottom of the bag, and I've been trying to figure out if I should report this to the police or not."

"Hmm." Carolyn pulled herself up into police stance, and her cornflower-blue eyes fixed on Addie's. "Did you purchase this bag intact from a reputable distributor?"

"Yes, from the antique store on Marine Drive, Time Travels."

"And is there a certificate of authentication or provenance accompanying it?"

Addie gulped and nodded, feeling suddenly like a small child who's just been caught stealing a package of gum from the corner store.

"Is this case, as is, and all its contents going to a licensed medical practitioner?" Carolyn's taut face relaxed, and Addie caught a twinkle in her eyes.

"You're playing with me, aren't you? You're a horrible friend to make me feel like I'm a criminal." Addie snorted out a laugh.

"I couldn't help it. The look on your face was priceless." Carolyn howled and then made an effort to compose herself. "Yes, these are antiques, and they should be just fine to be in possession of."

"Boy, you really had me going," Addie said, still laughing as she closed the satchel and replaced it. "But tell me something, *officer,* why would this have been hidden in a secret compartment?"

Carolyn shrugged, eyeing the bag. "I'd say this is probably from the 1920s or 30s, right?"

"It was appraised as being a 1934 vintage."

"Remember, back then doctors made house calls, and opioids were prevalent and legal." She pointed to the bottom of the case. "Perhaps they were in there to keep a light-fingered person in a household from walking away with them."

"I see," Addie said thoughtfully. "Like out of sight, out of mind."

"Exactly!" Carolyn picked up the Louisa May Alcott book and read the back-cover blurb and murmured, "This looks interesting. It's about Alcott's experiences as a Civil War nurse." She glanced at Addie. "This town seems to have gone gaga over everything Civil War since the theme of the baking contest was announced. That's all everyone is talking about." She held the book up. "Thanks. I'll pay Paige on my way out. Chat soon," she said, withdrawing into the bookstore.

Addie shook her head and drew herself up stiffly. She was still tingling from the grilling Officer Coleman had given her about the case, and then she softly laughed.

That was a good one. She began replacing the contents of the medical bag back in place and stopped when she recalled what she'd said about the assortment of syringes and needles. *Out of sight, out of mind.* Another thought struck her.

She quickly packed the medical case back into her shopping bag and darted to the storefront. "Is my laptop at the counter?" she called out to Paige as she twirled past her in the aisle.

"Yes, by the phone."

"Thanks." She made a final sprint for it, flipped it open, and reread Barbara's email. "That's it! It makes sense now!"

"What are you talking about?" asked Paige, coming around the back of the counter and peering over her shoulder. "What makes sense now?"

Addie pointed to the last three books on the list. "This. Do you see something similar about them?"

Paige scanned the email. "Yes, they are valued at a lot less than the previous entries. What does it mean?"

"See any other similarity?"

Paige frowned and studied the screen. "No . . . Oh, wait. They are all by *Sarah Josepha Hale*," Paige exclaimed and Addie joined her in unison.

"And who did I tell you is a collector of her work?"

"That . . . that what's her name?" Paige snapped her fingers. "That woman who's the president of the historical association?"

"Bingo!" squealed Addie. "Gwendolyn Buchannan."

Chapter 23

"I haven't been able to shake the feeling," said Addie, "that the murder was a case of mistaken identity."

"That makes sense," agreed Paige, "since the clerk in the store asked Kalea if she was from Greyborne Harbor and then just handed over the briefcase."

"Exactly! Someone had paid for it prior, and we know it wasn't Jared or Kalea. After all, they didn't even know they'd need a new case until shortly before they went into the pawnshop." Addie reread the email. "Something tells me Gwendolyn Buchannan is behind the theft and the murder."

Paige slid onto a stool. "To be honest, she doesn't sound like the type of person who would get her hands dirty with either job."

"You're right. She must have hired someone. Just look

at this book list. Is it a coincidence that three of the stolen books are Sarah Josepha Hale's works, and one of them is the exact same book I was asked about? I think not." Addie stared at the computer screen. "The timing is just too coincidental. She must have paid someone to steal the books in Boston and then made arrangements to collect them from the pawnshop later." Addie gazed over her laptop at Paige. "Could it have been Gwendolyn the young man mistook Kalea for that day?"

"It's a good theory. Maybe the pawnshop owner is the thief, too."

"I have to find out if Gwendolyn has ever been to that shop."

"How on earth are you going to do that? Follow her everywhere she goes?"

"No." Addie paused. "Well, maybe."

"You can't be serious. If she spotted you, she could have you arrested for stalking her. There has to be another way."

A devious smile crossed Addie's face. "Do you want to enter the baking competition, and then I can go over to the community hall with you and casually ask her if—"

"Nope." Paige shook her head emphatically. "Not a chance. Mom decided to enter after all, and there's no way I want to go into a baking competition against her."

The door bells tinkled out a cheery greeting, and Addie glanced over. "Simon," she said, checking the time on her screen. "Why aren't you sleeping?"

"I got a few hours in," he said, wandering to the coffee maker and dropping in a pod. "Got called in for an emergency."

"Wasn't there anyone else who could handle it?"

"It was a patient of mine."

"I'm sorry. Who was it? Unless telling me breaches confidentiality."

Simon stirred a packet of sugar into his cup and smiled a greeting at a gentleman browsing the nonfiction section at the far end of the aisle. "Picker," he whispered, "was found unconscious on that shale ledge under the cliff by the lighthouse early this afternoon."

"Oh no!" Addie's hand shot to her mouth. "Is she . . ."

"No, she's pretty banged up and in a coma, but she's alive."

"Thank goodness."

"What was she doing on the cliff top?" asked Paige.

"Who knows?" He shrugged. "Maybe she saw something off the edge and tried to climb down to retrieve it. We won't know until she wakes up." He leaned over the counter. His lips grazed Addie's cheek and lingered there. "I just wanted to let you know. I'm heading home to grab a bite and have a shower before I'm back on shift tonight."

She turned and met his lips. "Call me later," she murmured.

"I will, and thanks for the much-needed coffee," he said, raising his cup in a toast before he darted out the door.

"I wonder," Addie said, her voice distant as she watched him get into his truck, "if Picker was attacked because she saw who tossed the briefcase in the dumpster on Monday morning, and that someone is now trying to shut her up?" Addie glanced at the clock. "Would you mind if I left now?" She closed her laptop and slid it into the case. "There's something I want to check out before it gets dark."

"No, go ahead. It's nearly four, so I doubt we'll have a rush before closing."

"Great, thanks." Addie shouldered her laptop bag and made her way down the aisle, pausing to answer a question from the gray-haired gentleman perusing the nonfiction section. When she had him relocated in the history section, where the books he'd been searching for were shelved, she went in the back, grabbed her coat, purse, and shopping bags, and headed out into the alley to her Mini.

Addie turned off the ignition and drummed her fingers on the steering wheel while she scanned her surroundings. She was about midway up Marine Drive. Across from her on the sea-front side of the street was Diggens Bait shop and Boat Rentals. Directly beside her was Tresses by Tara. A few stores up and across the road from the cruise ship pier and tourist center, she could just barely make out the sign for Sweet Treats Ice Cream and Candy Shop. Farther up, she knew was Time Travels, and beyond that across the road from the bandstand park by the lighthouse was Greyborne Point B&B. Only a few blocks behind her was the Ship 'n' Anchor Tavern.

That made six businesses that Jared had financial dealings with. All in the same vicinity and all within an easy walk to the lighthouse where Picker was found earlier. Could the killer have seen Picker head to the lighthouse, recognized her from the alley Monday morning, followed her, and pushed her off the cliff to shut her up?

It was going to take a process of elimination to figure out which of these potential suspects on her list might have had contact with Gwendolyn, provided, of course, her hunch was right on that front—and that the briefcase and books really were the key to Jared's murder. She did know for a fact that Gwendolyn was a customer of Nick and Ivy's at Time Travels, but Ivy was apparently out of town last weekend and Nick . . . well . . . given his lithe stature, she doubted he could have overpowered Jared and killed him. Besides, he did appear to be generally worried about losing Jared's funding and what that would mean to the future of his antique business.

In the Marine Drive vicinity, that left Sally Harrison from the candy store, Tara Wylie the hairdresser, Clay Diggens from the bait shop, the Thomas sisters at the B&B, and Matt Bellows from the tavern.

Addie glanced through her passenger-side window at the beauty salon door. Perhaps a few discreet questions were in order, and she might as well start here and work her way up the street. As she reached for the door handle, a blur of movement out of the corner of her eye caught her attention. Believing it to be a passing car, she paused. Then her chest constricted, and she struggled to catch her breath.

She couldn't believe what she was seeing. From the access road to Diggens Bait Shop and Boat Rentals, Gwendolyn Buchannan bustled across the street to a car waiting only two stores up from Addie. The chauffeur popped out and opened the rear door for his employer. Addie knew her eyes weren't playing tricks on her and causing her to see what she wanted to see. It *was* the grand dame of the historical association. One of Addie's questions had just been answered.

Addie waited until the black Lincoln pulled out and disappeared down the street. After counting one . . . two . . .

three, she drew in a few calming breaths and hustled down the access road to the shoreline and the small bait shop and booking office building.

Not seeing any activity and with no windows on this side of the building, she crossed her fingers and headed farther down the road to Clay's small private marina and pier. When she got closer to the water's edge, she could see right away that there was no line of sight down the beach due to the cruise ship pier and visitors' center. This also meant Picker hadn't wandered down the beach past here where Clay might have spotted her as there was no uninterrupted access to the beach given the marina and large cruise ship pier. Besides that, in the distance, Addie could barely make out the lighthouse towering above the trees in the park. If it had been Clay who tried to shut Picker up, he didn't see her on the rocky cliffs from here.

When she was kitty-corner from the bait shop and office building, she noted that unless someone was walking directly along the sea wall, there also wasn't a clear view of the street either. However, that still left the little matter of Gwendolyn being here recently. *Why?*

When she came around the corner of the building, she spotted Clay. His back was to her, and he reached up with a long-handled rod to pull the metal shutter down over the front window. Since he was in the process of closing for the day, it was going to make coming up with an excuse for her to be here even trickier. She'd have to think fast. But when she stepped onto the gravel pathway leading to the front door, the crunching sounds underfoot took away her opportunity to do that.

"I'm closed," he hollered as the shutter slammed down.

"Yes, I can see that, but . . ." *Think, Addie, think.* "I was just worried and wanted to make sure everything was alright here."

He pinned his cold, dark beady eyes on her. "What are you talking about?" He sniffed.

"It's just that I saw Gwendolyn Buchannan racing out of here, and she appeared to be upset about something. I only wanted to make sure everything was okay. That you were okay."

"Why wouldn't I be?"

"I'm not sure." Addie lowered her gaze as she tried to come up with something else. "I was just passing by, and it looked like something was wrong." She met his unyielding marbled gaze. "And being a concerned neighbor, I only wanted to make sure everything was okay here, that's all."

He spat. "A concerned neighbor or the town busybody?" His large liver-spotted hand gripped the metal rod tighter as he stepped toward her. "Like I said, I'm closed. Now, be off."

"Sure . . . no problem." *Now what?* "I see by the sign in your window that besides boat rentals you also do charter tours." She said hurriedly. "Is that Boston one listed a popular one?"

"What's it to you?"

"I just can't imagine that this time of year there would be much call for it. The weather and all that." Addie gulped as she took a step backward. With each step she backpedaled, the short hulking man took another toward her. "What about last week? Did you make a trip to Boston?"

"Last week?"

"Yes, did you happen to do a charter trip for say . . . Gwendolyn Buchannan, by any chance?"

"It's time for ya to leave. Now! I got stuff to do."

"Yes, yes, I imagine you do. Sorry to have kept you. It's only that I was thinking of taking my . . . umm . . . friend on a charter for her birthday and thought perhaps we could hire you and go to Boston to do a bit of shopping. And then it'd be nice to have you bring us back later in the day."

He glared down his short bull-like nose at her and spat.

"Okay." She winced. "I guess not."

"Look, girlie, I know who you are, so you tell that police chief friend of yours to back off, and the both of you stop stirring up trouble. Cause I know you coming here today is no more about your concern for me, just as much as I know who comes and goes from here, concerns you." He raised the rod crossways and shook it. "Now, be off with you!" he shouted and lurched toward her.

Addie power-walked out the drive to the road. When she was safely out of his clutches, she glanced back over her shoulder. He leaned on the rod, staring at her. She would have loved to wipe that smug smirk off his face, but knew, as he did, he had bested her. She was clearly unprepared for an interrogation and had failed miserably. However, the fact still remained that he knew Gwendolyn even though he wouldn't admit to it. Addie had seen her leaving here with her own eyes. His reluctance to acknowledge she had even been there was compelling to say the least.

Addie studied the roadside signage advertising that he had regular water access to Boston. Judging by his performance just now, he may well have been Gwendolyn's henchman in the retrieval of one or all the books Gwendolyn had arranged to pick up from the pawnshop. Until Jared and Kalea interfered in her plan.

Chapter 24

Addie stepped into the vibrantly decorated shop front. The air was heavy with the lingering acrid scents of perm chemicals and, if she wasn't mistaken, fresh paint. She pressed her tongue hard against the back of her front teeth to ward off an impending sneeze.

A trim stylist working at the chair closest to her glanced over. "Be with you in a minute, hon," she called as she flipped the black cape off her female client, spun the chair around, and held up a mirror for her to view the back of her cut. The client smiled. As she collected her purse from the stylist's counter and her coat from the rack by the door, the hairdresser came over to the desk.

"Hi, Tara, is it?" asked Addie.

The woman nodded and held out her hand in introduction. "Yes, Tara Wylie the owner of this," she waved her hand, "establishment, and you are?" She glanced down at the booking ledger in front of her. The woman's facial lines were etched like frost patterns on glass despite her obvious attempts to conceal them with makeup. She was actually far older than her rainbow-colored spiky hairstyle made her out to be.

"I don't have an appointment," Addie said, smiling apologetically.

"Oh . . . I see. Hmm . . ." She scanned the page. "I'm afraid I don't have any openings today. What was it you were looking for?"

"I was thinking of getting a trim, but," Addie gazed around, "it looks like you're pretty busy right now." From where she stood, it appeared every stylist chair was filled, and the staff was torn between running back and forth to the back hair-sinks and the stylist chairs.

"It's been like this all day."

"All day? Even around noon?"

"Nonstop since we opened at ten."

"So you haven't had a break all day?"

The hair stylist met Addie's puzzled gaze. "Let me put it this way, I'd kill for a cup of hot coffee right now."

Addie let out a short sympathetic laugh and glanced around again. "Is this usual?"

"No, I think ever since that baking competition was announced, everyone in town decided to get glammed up for the big event. I overheard one client say she had to look her best for the photo spread she was going to win along with the prize money."

"Speaking of that, could you tell me if a friend of mine was in today to get, as you called it, all glammed up?"

"What's your friend's name?"

"Gwendolyn Buchannan."

The woman scanned over the booking page. "No, not

today," she said and flipped back the pages. "Sorry, no one by that name's been in at all. Did she tell you she had an appointment?"

"I only know she's very keen on these sorts of community events, and I thought this was where she said she had an appointment, but I must have misunderstood."

"Never heard of her, but did you want me to fit you in? By the look of it, we'll be here at least until eight. You could come back later if it's urgent."

"No, that's fine. It's just my ends that need a trim so no rush. Tell you what. After the competition is over, I'll call for an appointment."

"Very good, I look forward to seeing you again."

Addie turned to leave and then turned back. "Can I ask if you've recently renovated?"

The stylist raised a questioning pencil-sketched brow.

"It's only that I detected a hint of fresh paint in the air, and the décor in here appears to be rather new."

"Yes, do you like it? Business has picked up so much that I needed to hire more staff and there was no room for them to work. I had to expand and sacrifice some of the storage room and staff lounge. Not that we get time to sit in there anymore, so I guess it was a good investment."

"It's very nice."

"Thank you. I'm glad you like it. Now then"—she slid a receipt to the customer she'd finished working on—"Mrs. Crayton, I have your bill ready. Do you have any questions about how to care for your new perm?"

It was clear to Addie as she stepped out onto the street that if she followed Marc's line of investigation—the motive for Jared's murder was because of one of his financial dealings going sideways—then Tara Wylie could come off her long list of suspects. Addie doubted the loan she had borrowed from Jared, apparently for a small store renovation, would have been enough to kill him over and, for that matter, try to kill Picker, too. Besides if Picker's attack was related to Jared's murder and the theft of the briefcase, Tara wasn't the culprit here. According to her, she hadn't left the store all day. Even if Addie followed her hunch about Gwendolyn and the stolen books and Jared's death being about a case of mistaken identity, Tara made it clear she didn't even know the name of Gwendolyn Buchannan. *Tara is a definite no.*

Addie wandered up Marine Drive to the next name on her suspect list. But as she made her way toward the candy store, most of the shopkeepers were in the process of hanging up their CLOSED signs. Could it really be five o'clock? She picked up her pace and arrived at her destination as a robust, fuzzy-haired bleach-blond stepped out of Sweet Treats Ice Cream and Candy Shop and locked the door behind her.

"Hi, Sally," she called.

"Hi, Addie, what brings you down here at closing time?"

"I left the bookstore a little early, hoping I'd get here in time, but I guess it wasn't early enough."

"I've already closed out the cash," she said, glancing through the glass door. "But I guess I could invoice you for whatever it is you're looking for?"

"No, that's fine. It's not urgent. It's not like I'm having one of those days when I'd kill for chocolate," said Addie with a short laugh.

"Are you sure?"

"Yeah, I'll pop in again another day."

"Okay, now if you'll excuse me, I have to get home to get in a quick bite before going to the community hall." Sally started to back away.

"Why, what's going on there tonight?"

Sally stopped and stared at Addie, a mystified look on her face. "It's the night the historical association is designating tables for the bake sale. Aren't you going to make sure you get the right sized table for your goodies and a prime location? You really do have to be there otherwise you could get stuck in the corner with one of those dinky little daycare tables."

"I had no idea that was tonight."

"Didn't you get the email?"

"Well, truth be told, I'm not entering the cooking competition."

"I'm not either. Too many good cooks in this town." She puffed out her ample chest. "However, there's no one who can top my handmade chocolate and candy assortments, so I'm pretty sure I'm going to need at least two tables for the sale to keep up with the demand. That's partially why I have to be there early tonight." She tapped her index finger to her temple. "Put that certain little bug in that society lady's ear."

"You mean Gwendolyn Buchannan?"

"Is she the one that struts around like she's the queen of England?" Sally asked, opening her car door.

"I guess. The tall matronly woman who wears pearls?"

"Yes, that's her. Boy, does she run a tight competition." Sally leaned on the hood of her gray car. "She wanted us to bring a list tonight of all the items we intend to sell through the two days of the sale."

"Really?"

"Yes, I've been a crazed woman all day, going through recipes and trying new ones to come up with a good assortment to sell so I could make up a list for her."

"So you weren't out of the shop much today?"

"This is the first breath of fresh air I've had since seven this morning, but I really gotta run. We'll get together and chat another day. How does that sound? Tootles." She waved and got into her car and pulled out into the road.

Well, that answered most of Addie's questions about Sally. She and Gwendolyn apparently didn't know each other, and she couldn't have been the person who attacked Picker on the cliff if what she told Addie was true. If she was going to work on Marc's theory, Addie would have to attend the table-designating meeting tonight and speak more with Sally to find out what her financial dealings with Jared involved. Addie turned to head back to her car, and a poster in Sally's store window caught her eye.

OPENING NEXT SPRING!
TWO NEW PERMANENT HIGH SEASON SWEET
TREATS ICE CREAM TRUCK LOCATIONS TO SERVE
YOU BETTER.
YOU'LL SOON SEE OUR TRUCKS AT THE VISITOR'S
CENTER AND BESIDE THE LIGHTHOUSE GIFT SHOP.
STAY POSTED FOR GRAND OPENING DATES!

And there was the reason for Sally's dealings with Jared. Besides, in Addie's mind, Sally really didn't seem like the type to kill anyone over the funding for ice cream trucks. Plus, the poster advertised the trucks arriving next spring. Apparently, they were not canceled or postponed, so clearly any financing Jared arranged for her wasn't a deal that had gone sideways either, which meant Sally Harrison could be crossed off her suspect list.

That left the Thomas sisters and Matt Bellows from the tavern. She glanced at the time on her phone. Right about now, though, both establishments would be starting their dinner rush, making a drop-in interrogation far worse than the last few had been. On the other hand, she had found out the answers to her basic questions, but she hadn't gotten any further in figuring out which of her suspects had motive *and* opportunity.

Clearly, it was time to call it a day. Pippi, along with her houseguest, would both need to be fed and watered. As she started to toss her phone in her purse, a text message from Serena popped up on the screen.

I just got an email to say if I wanted a table for the bake sale; I had to be at the community hall tonight at seven! Wanna be my wingman again? I'll buy dinner after!

Addie fingers flew across the small keypad.

Have I ever turned down a free dinner?

Her text alert pinged.

Perfect! I'll pick you up at six thirty!

Perfect was right. The Thomas sisters were bound to be there this evening, and a busy venue might just be the ideal environment to catch them unprepared and get a few answers out of them. She chuckled as she got into her Mini. She'd probably have more luck if Simon was at her side rather than Serena.

Addie, hanging her coat on the rack behind the door, was unable to ignore the excited yips of her furry friend. The little dog danced under foot for attention. Laughing, Addie scooped Pippi up into her arms but immediately turned her face away when threatened by fervent doggy kisses right on the mouth.

She glanced into the living room. The television in the

corner was on, but Kalea lay on the sofa. Her eyes were closed, and there wasn't even a twitch from her with the reunion commotion in the foyer. Addie kissed the back of Pippi's head and snuggled her close as she tiptoed across the room to switch the television set off. Kalea's eyes opened, and she jerked upright.

"Hi, I didn't hear you come in." She stretched and mumbled through a yawn, "Have you been home long?"

"No, I just got in."

"What time is it?" Kalea asked as she glanced around the room.

"It's five thirty. Have you been asleep long?"

"No," she said, pushing herself to the edge of the sofa and scouring her hands over her face. "I don't think so. I fed Pippi and let her out, thought about starting dinner but . . . I guess I never got that far."

"Have you eaten anything today?"

"Yeah, I grazed and had some of that leftover fruit salad."

"Good. Well . . . I have to go back out for a few hours, and I won't be here for dinner, but I can make you something before I leave if you want?"

"That's okay. I'm not really hungry, and when I am, I'm pretty sure I can boil an egg or something."

"Are you sure?" Addie asked, cuddling Pippi closer and kissing the back of her head. She knew she'd missed her friend these past few days, but up until now and after feeling the warmth of her little body nestled into her, she had no idea how much. Since Pippi wasn't squirming to return to Kalea's side, Addie hoped it was a sign that her cousin was doing better.

"If you're okay, then I'd better wash up and get changed before I have to leave." Addie glanced down at her furry friend. "Did you want to stay with Auntie Kalea?" When she made no move to be released, Addie knew Pippi had come back to her, and Kalea was through the worst of it.

Kalea handed Addie a sheet of fine linen stationary from the coffee table. "Before you go, can you read this and tell me what you think it means?"

Addie scanned the formal embossed letterhead printed across the top. "It's from the Granger and Forbes law firm in Boston. Where did you get this?"

"A courier company called today and wanted to know where to deliver it being as the dress shop was closed."

Addie glanced at the page. "Why are they contacting you?"

"You tell me. I read it and can't believe it, so I need you to tell me if you're reading the same thing as I was."

Addie sat down on the edge of the coffee table and tried to focus. Her head pounded and her mind raced with the thoughts of everything she had to do in the next hour, but this appeared to be important. She skimmed down the page, trying to understand the legalese, but none of it made sense until she got to the last paragraph. She gaped at Kalea.

"Well, what does it sound like to you?" Kalea edged forward on the sofa.

"Once you get through the legal mumbo jumbo, it sounds to me like they want you to be in Boston next week for the reading of the will and to discuss how you want to allocate or liquidate Jared's estate holdings."

"Why would that have anything to do with me?"

Addie swallowed—hard—and steadied her gaze on her cousin. "Because through all this legal jargon, it sounds like you're his sole beneficiary."

Chapter 25

"I'm not kidding, Serena. Kalea could end up being very, very rich, and I just can't believe that the only goal or dream she had for herself is going to really come true now."

"What's that?"

"As long as I've known her, which is my whole life, she dreamed of finding her Prince Charming and being taken care of. Growing up, she really had no goals or dreams of her own."

"But I think she's changed over the last couple of years, don't you." Serena glanced over at Addie. "Just look at her dress shop and the knack she has for design. She seems like she's finally found her calling and is well on her way to a brilliant and, I might add, lucrative career all on her own."

"Yeah, I suppose," said Addie, glancing out the passenger's side of Serena's Wrangler. "Plus, she was going to break up with him anyway, so maybe you're right. She has changed and . . . oh no!"

"What?"

"If Marc discovers she inherited Jared's estate, and you know he's going to, he's going to see that as her motive for murder."

"You're right," said Serena, pulling into a parking space along the side of the community hall. After putting the Wrangler in Park, she stared out the windshield and made no move to turn off the ignition.

"What are you thinking?"

"Having said what this is going to mean to her future, it now makes me think about what you're always telling me."

"What?"

"About how your father looked at evidence in a case."

"Do you mean when he used to say, how in any murder investigation, you have to look at who had the means, motive, and opportunity, and through your analysis, the clues and evidence will point to one suspect."

"Yes."

"I know. I've been wracking my brain to try to look at each suspect and make the link, but in this case, each point can be applied to more than one person. And more than one suspect had all three. The problem I'm having is establishing which one of them had the strongest motive."

"I would say that being the sole beneficiary of a financial tycoon's estate is a fairly good motive, wouldn't you?"

"It is, and Marc will certainly see it that way. But she

seemed genuinely shocked by the letter and had no idea this would happen."

"Maybe Jared mentioned something about it. Perhaps when she killed him, it was in hopes it would turn out this way."

"I hope you're wrong. I have to believe that the cousin I played with all through my childhood and roomed with in college wouldn't murder anyone, not even for an inheritance."

"I wonder what it's worth. If it's a large sum, then that's a lot of reasons to commit murder."

"I know, and it scares me to even think about." Addie opened the door. "But there's still other names on my suspect list, and a couple of them are going to be here tonight. Until everyone else can be excluded, I have to believe she's not guilty. Come on, let's get in there, so you don't miss out on getting a good table location."

Serena didn't move, and Addie retreated back inside, closing the door. "What's up?"

"I don't know if I want to do this?"

"What? Why not?"

"It's one thing to enter the cooking competition, but I don't know if I want to go through all the work of baking enough goodies to sell over the following two-day sale."

"But think of the advertising it will be for SerenaTEA. You make all that stuff for the tea shop every day for your British tea times. This is the perfect way to reach a wider audience."

"I know, I know, but I'm also rethinking the whole English tea shop idea, too."

"Whoa, since when?" Addie swiveled in her seat and pinned a gaze of disbelief on Serena. "I thought it was going well, and you enjoyed the switch up."

"It was. That's the thing. During tourist season, the visitors from the cruise ship and all those who came for the regatta and other festivals got such a kick out of it. It was a novelty, but now . . . well, the locals say they miss the old tea shop atmosphere, and to be honest, business has been sliding."

"I had no idea. I mean you just hired Vera on for the added help."

"Yeah, but that was so I could take a break and"—she rubbed her tummy—"I haven't been feeling well lately, either."

"Did you take the test?"

She shook her head.

"Serena."

"I know." She glanced toward the street. "I will, but I think I'm going to pass on this. Sorry to drag you here for nothing."

"No, not nothing. Come on. You can be my wingman then while I do a little digging, and you pretend you're interested in a table to give us an excuse to be here."

"Okay, I guess I could do that, and then *you're* going to buy dinner," she said with a short laugh as she hopped down from the Wrangler.

"Deal, let's go."

"Look!" Addie nudged Serena as they gained the top step into the large hall. "There's her ladyship now."

"Gwendolyn?"

"Yes, and number one on my suspect list," whispered Addie. "I'll tell you why later. Right now, I need you to find an excuse to talk to her."

"That's easy. We're late signing up, and I'm so distraught over the fact that I might have missed getting one of the prime table locations." She pressed the back of her hand to her forehead and faking a magnificent swoon.

Addie chuckled and elbowed her friend playfully. "Whatever works. I'll be there in a minute so she doesn't feel pounced on."

Serena gave her a cheeky grin and wove her way through the crowd toward Gwendolyn Buchannan.

Addie gave her friend a moment to get situated beside the grand lady and dashed over to the table, feigning a breathless puff. "I hope my delaying you didn't cause you to lose out on a good table selection?" She eagerly peered over Serena's shoulder and gazed at the table chart her friend held. She glanced up and met the pointed glower from Gwendolyn at her intrusion. Ignoring her, Addie pretended to scan the diagram of table arrangements. "Look, here are two that are together. You and my cousin could be beside each other for the weekend. That might be fun, don't you think?" Addie glanced at Serena, giving her subtle nudge in the side.

"Um, yeah . . . sure, fun." Serena peeked sideways at her from under a quizzical brow.

"Who might your cousin be?" asked Gwendolyn.

"Kalea Hudson from Hudson Creations on Main."

"I'm afraid I've never heard of her." Gwendolyn adjusted the fine gold-framed glasses perched on the end of her nose.

"Really?" replied Addie, looking at the woman incredulously. "She's a well-known local designer. Don't tell me that a woman as discerning as you has never been to her shop?"

"No, I can't say as I have."

"Kalea has created both day and evening dresses for half the women in this room."

"Sorry." Gwendolyn snatched the table chart from Serena's fingers. Impatience seemed to radiate from her. "Have you made your table selection from what's left, my dear?"

No! Addie couldn't let the subject change. She needed to keep the grand dame focused on the scene of the crime. If she was behind the book thefts and murder, something she had to say would surely give away her familiarity with Kalea or the shop.

"Sorry." Addie plucked the paper from Gwendolyn's hand and held it up in front of Serena's perplexed face. "We were too busy chatting, and I don't think we're done just yet, are we, Serena?"

Mystified, Serena shook her head and seized the table layout Addie waved in her face.

"I can't believe, Gwendolyn, that you aren't aware of my cousin's dress-making skills. After all, I heard that a number of the attendees to your Thanksgiving dinner will be wearing Kalea's designs."

"Really," she said, adjusting her glasses as she studied Addie closely, "and why would you think that?"

"Kalea has dropped a couple of her clients' names, and I must say your guest list sounds rather impressive. You certainly know the who's who of the most affluent and prominent people in Essex County, don't you?" She smiled innocently at the bewildered dowager woman.

Gwendolyn shifted uncomfortably and glanced around the room. "Name one woman here who says she's on my guest list for the evening because, I assure you, not one is. My annual dinner is a very private and exclusive affair." She harrumphed.

Oops. Addie's attempt at deception to get the woman

to spill her dirty little secrets appeared to be backfiring. *How was I supposed to know no one here was on the list?*

"What about Ivy Walker? Kalea said the dress she's designing for her is divine and sure to be the talk of the evening."

"Ivy Walker? The little waif from the antique shop?"

Addie nodded, feeling a sense of satisfaction at being able to pluck one legitimate name out of the air.

"I don't recall her being on the list of invitees."

"Really?" Hope slid from Addie. She was stunned. "I was under the impression she had been invited."

"Why would she think that?" The woman stiffened. "It's well known my Thanksgiving dinner party is strictly for ancestors I have traced to being related to Sarah Josepha Hale. By the look of Miss Walker, she's definitely of Southern European stock and not my great, great-aunt's northern European family line."

"Then why would she have a dress made for the occasion?"

"She did?"

"Yes, as I said, my cousin is the dressmaker."

"Then your cousin is mistaken because for anyone to receive an invitation they must first produce their family tree, proving, without a doubt, that they are who they claim to be. Now, if you'll excuse me, I have some tables to assign." Gwendolyn sauntered to a group of women scrutinizing the larger laminated table chart on an easel beside the registration table.

"That's interesting?" Addie said.

"What is?" asked Serena.

"Why would Nick tell me Ivy was attending Gwendolyn's dinner party, and why would she have a dress made if she weren't going? Something's not right."

"Maybe she's *hoping* for an invitation. She does follow Gwendolyn around like a lost puppy."

"I know, but it's most curious, don't you think?"

"Yes, but maybe crashing the party is worth it for the exposure it would give her to some very prominent people and future customers. She's probably depending on her business connection to the grand dame to ensure she won't be turned away at the door."

"That sounds pretty risky to me, and I'm all for doing what you can to increase business, especially since the economic downturn, however"—Addie focused on Gwendolyn—"I get the feeling Mrs. Buchannan wouldn't think twice about causing Ivy a lot of embarrassment at the door in front of the other guest, which would ultimately hurt Ivy's business."

"No, my guess is she maybe told Nick she wanted to be invited and is hoping she will be, so she went ahead and had the dress made in case."

"Perhaps." Serena shrugged. "Does it really matter?"

"No, and it was clear that Gwendolyn doesn't know Kalea or the dress shop, so that tells me if she is involved, she hired someone else to perform the theft and the reclamation of the books that were supposed to go to her."

"Do you really think she would have dirtied her own hands?" Serena gestured toward the regal woman holding court at the end of the table.

"No, but I was hoping for some sign of recognition at the name or an attempted cover-up about her awareness of Hudson's."

"Well, whoever she hired—provided you're right, of course, about that hunch—might not have told her about the briefcase ending up in the wrong hands or what happened when they went to retrieve whatever was inside for her."

"You might be right. If it was the pawnshop owner, he certainly wouldn't want to tell her how his young clerk messed up and gave the briefcase to the wrong person."

Addie glanced around the crowded room but saw no sign of the Thomas sisters or anyone else on her list that she hadn't spoken to yet. "I think we've accomplished all we can here tonight. Are you ready to eat?"

"You know what, I'm not feeling very well and don't feel like doing anything except going home. Do you mind if we skip dinner tonight. Maybe we can catch lunch tomorrow?"

"Are you okay, you look flushed?"

"I ate some samples that Millie Jefferson was giving out, and something didn't sit right."

"Sure, that's fine."

"I feel bad, though, because you must be starving."

"Don't worry about me. I'll fix something at home. You're far more important. Do you want me to take you to the emergency room? Maybe Simon can give you something to help settle your tummy."

"No, I think if I lay down, I'll feel better."

"Okay, I'll drive. I can drop you off and then pick you up in the morning. You shouldn't need your car before then, should you?"

"No, and Zach's there if I do. I can drive his, but really—" She heaved and slapped her hand over her mouth. "I don't think that's likely."

Chapter 26

The next morning, Addie stamped the slush from her boots on the welcome mat of Serena's early 1900s craftsman bungalow. Thankful for the covered front porch keeping the drizzling sleet off her head, she waited for her friend to answer the doorbell. When she finally did, Addie blinked.

"You're not even dressed yet?"

Serena glanced down at her blue fuzzy robe and then at Addie. "What time is it?"

"It's a quarter to nine."

"Oh."

"Oh? I have to be at the bookstore in fifteen minutes."

"Right." She stepped aside so Addie could enter. "To be honest, I forgot you had my Wrangler and were picking me up today. Sorry, just give me a minute to throw some clothes on."

"Aren't you going into SerenaTEA?"

"Yeah, but not till later. Vera's in this morning."

Addie studied her friend's washed-out complexion. "Are you feeling alright?"

"Yeah, I'm just tired." She made a feeble attempt at a reassuring smile that came off more like a half-lipped sneer. "Go in and sit down. I won't be long." She trudged down the hallway toward the bedroom.

Addie poked her head around a square, wooden pillar and peeked into the living room. A recent addition of an oriental area rug covered a large portion of the newly refinished hardwood floors. She glanced down at her dripping boots. "If you're not going to be long, I'll just wait here by the door," she hollered. There was no answer. "Serena? Did you hear me?"

Serena stepped out into the hallway from the bathroom, her toothbrush in her mouth, and nodded.

"Good," said Addie with a soft laugh. "When you didn't answer, I was afraid you'd gone back to bed."

Serena squished up her face in a mocking grimace and disappeared back through the door.

Addie shook her head and scoffed at her friend's antics. *She's something else, that's for sure.* Still chuckling, Addie surveyed what she could see of the house from the foyer. What she saw brought a smile of approval to her lips. It was no wonder her friend was exhausted. She and Zach had done a lot of work refinishing and decorating since Addie's last visit.

She glanced approvingly over the living room through to the attached dining room and decided Serena had missed her true calling. She should have been an interior decorator. Not that Gloria's house needed a lot of work when she sold it to the young couple. But, in all honesty, it had been well loved and a little neglected. The hard-wood floors were a good example of that. Now, they gleamed under a fresh sanding and re-varnishing and made the antiques Serena had chosen for the rooms pop. The love and warmth that wrapped around Addie as she scanned the rooms was the same feeling she had when she slid into the luxurious leather seats of the Tesla Simon drove in good weather. She enfolded her arms around herself and squeezed. Yes, it was like a hug from an old friend and made all that entered aware of the love that lived inside.

Addie dangled the Wrangler keys in front of Serena's face.

Serena waved them off. "You drive." She stopped be-side the passenger door. "I still need to wake up and clear my head."

"Okay, if you insist," said Addie, sluicing through the gutter slush to the driver's side. She couldn't help but be concerned. Something was really off with Serena lately. Of course, she hoped it was what she suspected, but if not . . . she glanced back at her friend and inwardly cringed. She prayed the abrupt change that had caused her to lose her usual upbeat sparkle was a temporary condition and the result of a teeny-tiny Serena or Zach beginning life inside her and not something ominous.

Serena silently stared out the passenger's window. Every time they hit a slushy rut in the road, she cradled her stom-ach.

"Wait, slow down," cried Serena. "Can we stop up there at the drive-through for the coffee shop first?"

Addie shot her a side-glance. "You don't drink coffee."

"I know, but I want one today."

"Hmm, something tells me we should be stopping at the drug store instead."

"Why?"

"To pick up one of those tests you don't want to take."

"That's ridiculous. Just because I feel like having a coffee to wake me up, you think I'm pregnant." She scoffed and stared out the window again.

"Not just because of that. I'm getting worried—"

"Look!" Serena cried. "There's Simon."

"Where?" Addie swiveled her head, trying to see where Serena was pointing. "It can't be. He's on night shift this week and"—she glanced at the clock on the dash—"at nine-thirty, he should be home, sleeping."

"Well, it looks to me like he's out shopping." She pointed again. "See, he just came out of Carman's Jewelers."

Addie lifted her foot off the accelerator, slowing the car, and peered out her window.

"Paige was right!" Addie swerved into a parking space on the far side of the street, giving her a clear line of sight to Simon and his truck.

"What was Paige right about?" Serena prodded, glancing from Simon to Addie.

"She thought he was giving me a ring this Christmas."

"That's great!"

"No, no, it's not."

"Why?"

"Just a minute." Addie fished her phone out of her pocket and thumbed out a text. "Let me text him first and say . . . *I know you must be sleeping, but I wanted to know if Picker woke up yet, and if she had any information about what happened. Let me know when you're awake. XXXX.* There, now let's see what he has to say to that." She hunched over the steering wheel to keep herself low in an attempt to avoid detection, but she kept her eyes glued on Simon as he walked around to the driver's side of his truck. He pulled his phone out of his pocket, glanced at it, and shoved it back in before stepping up into the cab and driving away.

"Look at that. He's going to ignore me."

"At least you didn't see him with another woman and that's not why he isn't answering."

"That might have been better. Then, at least, I'd know what he was up to." She glanced over at Serena. "This way I'm left guessing as to what he's hiding."

"Judging by the small gift bag he was carrying and the diamond sale sign in the window, I'd say Paige's hunch is right." Serena grinned impishly and then sing-songed, "You are going to get a ring for Christmas."

"There's no way." Addie shook her head and glanced over at the jewelry store and then straight ahead. Her mind reeled.

"Come on, you've known since you first met him that he's the one. That's why when Marc proposed, you couldn't say yes. What you felt for Simon haunted you. What's the issue now that you're finally going to get what you wanted?"

"It's just not the time."

"Why not?"

"Because I haven't even told him I love him."

"You haven't?"

"No."

"Why not? You do, don't you?"

"Yes."

"Then what's holding you back?"

"I just can't."

"Addie, what's going on?"

"It's just that"—she swallowed past the sudden lump in her throat—"the last time I told someone I loved them, they ended up dead."

"And you think telling someone you love them is going to kill them?"

She turned her tear-filled eyes to Serena. "No, it's only that the pain and grief I went through after was something I don't ever want to experience again."

"I get that," said Serena, squeezing her hand. "But what are you going to do Christmas morning when you open the box and find a ring and he's down on one knee?"

"I know, but . . ." Addie thoughts whirled.

"It better not be what you did to Marc."

"I know, I know . . . but what am I supposed to do?"

"I'd say you'd better figure out soon how you feel about him because seeing the pleased look on his face just now tells me he expects your answer to be *yes*."

Serena was right, of course. Addie couldn't keep ignoring the natural course that her relationship with Simon was bound to take after all this time. But was she ready for it. The evening Marc pulled the ring box out of his jacket pocket and got down on one knee rushed back through her mind. She could never forget the overwhelming sense of panic that overtook her. Would it be the same with Simon should he produce a ring Christmas Eve or Christmas morning?

Her mind reeled with what-if scenarios. No, she shook her head, this time it was different. She had made her choice. He was it, and he told her right from the beginning he would wait until she was ready. She guessed he saw something she didn't and figured the time was now. But was she really ready? Why hadn't she been able to utter those three little words yet? What was the real reason she was still holding back? Was it because of David and what she lost with his death, or was it something else? Yes, she needed to figure it out, and fast if what they had just seen was what everyone thought it would be come Christmas.

Addie hopped out of the Wrangler, leaving it running for Serena to take over and drive home. She lumbered toward Beyond the Page, her head swimming with *what-if* scenarios. She opened the door only to be met by the tinkling charm of the overhead bells and an unexpected onslaught of customers.

Guilt-ridden, she gave Paige, who was assisting a customer by the Civil War display, a sheepish smile and darted toward the sales counter. She threw her coat and purse on a box of books behind the desk, pasted a smile on her face, and cheerily greeted them. "Good morning, ladies, I trust you found everything you were looking for?" She glanced down at the pile of books in front of her and picked up the top one. "*Mary Had a Little Lamb*. Two copies, each?" She glanced from one middle-aged woman to the other.

"Grandchildren." The shorter, stockier one laughed. "It's a nursery rhyme I grew up with." She pointed to one of the *Godey's Lady's Book* posters on the wall. "And after reading that it was written by Sarah Josepha Hale, who was the editor of a magazine that turned into one of the most influential periodicals in the country for over forty years, well"—she puffed herself up—"I want my two young granddaughters to understand the role women played during the Civil War and after."

"Yes, something the history books don't always mention," chirped in the second woman. "That's why, even though my grandbaby is only a week old, I want her to know this book, too."

"A week old? Congratulations." Addie grinned and scanned the book. "The illustrations in this edition are vibrant, so I'm certain that no matter how young she is, she'll love the bright imagery."

"Yes, well, they say they're never too young to learn to love books and reading."

"I completely agree," said Addie, handing each woman their shopping bags. "I hope to see you both back here real soon as we're always adding to our inventory of children's books, especially the closer we get to Christmas."

"I'm sure we will be back soon. There is no better gift to give than books." The shorter woman grinned, and they left to the tune of tinkling bells.

The morning flew by, something for which Addie was grateful. She and Paige passed each other often, but there was no time for chitchat as they served the swarms of customers flowing through the door. It appeared that the theme of the cooking competition had lit a fire for anything Civil War related. Louisa May Alcott's classic story, *An Old-Fashioned Thanksgiving,* seemed to be the most popular of the day.

As the *cha-ching* of the cash register drowned out the tinkling door bells, Addie was relieved by distraction. It was a great excuse not to mention to Paige the jewelry store scene she and Serena had witnessed earlier. Addie wasn't quite ready for the I-told-you-so conversation.

When the clock struck noon, an eerie silence crept through the bookstore. Mystified, Addie glanced at Paige.

"It's time for SerenaTEA's English luncheon special," Paige said with a hearty laugh as she tidied up the sales counter.

"Does Serena know about this?"

"I guess so." Paige shrugged. "It's her shop."

"But she never said a word about it on our drive in this morning." Addie bit her lip in thought and then concern. "I wonder . . ." She dug her phone out of her jacket pocket, glanced at the stream of missed text messages, shook her head, and quickly typed out a text to Serena. After thinking better of it, she deleted it. Serena was already touchy, and if Addie were to question her memory anymore that day, who knows where that would lead.

"It looks like I have a few missed texts. Marc flagged his as urgent . . ." She scanned the message. "Yeesh, that was over two hours ago." She pulled a twenty out of her wallet and handed it to Paige. "Why don't you run next door and see what they're serving. If it looks good, grab something for the two of us, and let me know if Serena is there, okay?"

Paige took the twenty-dollar bill from Addie's fingers and exchanged it for a piece of paper. "Sure, but speaking of missed calls, before you got in, Nick Walker phoned and wanted me to tell you he had some botanical prints on old book pages that you might be interested in for the store."

"Those sound interesting. What do you think?"

"I think they would be a big seller. I can't believe how fast the bookmarks and bookends are selling."

"Okay, I'll call him and make arrangements to drop in later."

"Also, Catherine stopped by. Unfortunately, it was right before you texted and said you'd be late. If I'd known about the incoming rush, I would have asked her to stay until you got here."

"Did she say what she wanted? She hasn't changed her mind about coming to work, has she?"

"No, I don't think so. She just said she had something interesting to tell you, but she had a meeting at the library, so she said she'd be back later."

"Okay, thanks," Addie said, slipping the paper into her boyfriend-jacket pocket.

"I'm going to go," said Paige, waving the twenty in the air. "I don't know about you, but I sure worked up an appetite." She laughed and dashed to the back, grabbed her coat, and headed out the door to SerenaTEA.

Addie puffed out her cheeks and exhaled deeply. "Okay, Marc, what's so urgent?" She quickly typed. *I'm here, and it's not busy now. What's up?*

Chapter 27

Addie glanced up at the clock as she popped the last bite of her cucumber sandwich into her mouth and washed it down with a sip of cold coffee. "I'm not sure I can get used to the English tradition of putting salad garnishing and a dollop of cream cheese between two pieces of crustless bread, but it was good."

"They seemed to be a big hit while I was in there," said Paige, gathering up the sandwich wrappers and tossing them in the trash. "Those and the individual Cornish pasties and cottage pies that Vera cooked up. The place was packed, and there was a line waiting for a table."

"It's funny. Serena told me last night, since tourist season ended, her English tea house idea wasn't doing as well, but it sounds like it's doing just fine."

"I think the afternoon teatime has lost its sparkle for locals," said Paige, sipping on her take-out cup from Serena-

TEA. "But the new lunches Vera started are a hit because the traditional British food is such a novelty right now. No one else in town serves it."

"I hope it lasts, for Serena's sake. But I am concerned to hear she wasn't there."

"Yeah, Elli said it was weird. They called her to remind her, but there was no answer. Did she tell you she was going somewhere when she dropped you off?"

"Nope, not a word about an appointment, or anything," Addie said, not able to hide the concern in her voice. She dropped a pod into the coffeemaker. It was so unlike her friend to behave like this. Addie's gut wrenched, and panic overcame her. "What if she fell asleep at the wheel when she was driving back home this morning, and she was in an accident?"

"No." Paige shook her head adamantly. "Don't even go there. If something had happened, we would have heard by now."

Addie took a calming breath and clutched the edge of the counter. "You're right. Yes, we would have heard."

The door bells tinkled, and Addie glanced at the door to see Catherine's big hazel-brown eyes sparkling across the room at her. "Addie! Thank goodness you're here. I've just been busting at the seams all morning to tell you the news."

"Have a seat," Addie said, trying to switch gears and get her mind off Serena long enough to hear what her old friend was so excited about.

"Do you two remember Felix Vanguard from Serena's wedding?" Catherine perched on the edge of the stool beside Paige. "He's Zach's father's security man?"

"Yes," Addie and Paige replied in unison.

"He called me this morning . . . and . . . and he'll be in

town over Thanksgiving and wants to see *me*!" she cried with a squeal. "I can't believe it. You know it's just like they say. When one door closes, another one opens. Jonathan is gone, and who knows if he'll be back as he seemed so vague and distant, and suddenly up pops Felix."

Paige and Addie exchanged a look of disbelief.

"Just like that?" asked Addie. "After all these months, he called and said he was coming to see you for Thanksgiving."

"He said he would be in town over Thanksgiving and wanted to see me."

"Hmm." Addie tapped her fingers on the counter in thought. "I wonder what's bringing him to town."

"Who cares," said Paige. "He was a real silver fox and sure had an eye for our Catherine, didn't he?" She gave Catherine a good-natured poke in the ribs that made her squeal and jump. They succumbed to full-blown belly laughs—so much so, they barely heard the door bells.

The sound of a raspy voice clearing came from the doorway.

Addie whirled around. "Marc! Sorry, we didn't hear you come in."

"It appears I miss all the fun," he chuckled softly and removed his cap. His fingers fidgeted with the brim as he clutched it in front of him.

"Yeah, fun at my expense," said Catherine, trying to retain her ladylike stature as she swatted playfully at Paige, who was still choking on her giggles.

"Care to share?" His hopeful gaze flitted from one to the other. "I could really use a good laugh today too."

"It's nothing, really," said Addie, waving him off.

"Catherine has a new sweetie pie, and he's coming to see her soon," sang Paige laughingly as she jerked away from Catherine's reach.

"Anybody I know?" Marc asked.

"Remember Felix Vanguard?" said Addie.

"Yes." Marc dropped his gaze. "Yes, I do."

"You don't seem surprised," said Catherine, steadying her gaze on him. "Did he say something to you last summer on the yacht that I should know about? Because if he did say something to you"—she started to rise—"and you didn't tell me, I swear, Marc Chandler, grown man and chief of police or not, I will give you a good ear-boxing right here and now."

He thrust his hands up in the air, unable to stop a rumble from escaping his chest. "I swear Catherine, Felix did not say a word to me about you or coming to Greyborne Harbor for Thanksgiving *last* summer."

Addie searched his face. Something told her that was the truth, but he was hiding something else, and she was going to discover exactly what that was. He hadn't seemed surprised that Felix was coming to town, so what was up? Had Marc called him to consult on this case? After all, it could very well involve some rare missing manuscripts. She studied his squared jawline and saw no flinch. On the other hand, maybe Marc didn't know about the books that were stolen in Boston. He had been right about one thing in his text to her though. It was urgent they talked and now.

"Anyway, thanks for the laugh, ladies." He bowed his head in gratitude and glanced at Addie. "Can we talk?"

"Funny, I was just thinking the same thing."

"Look," said Catherine, "I have no plans for the rest of the day. You two go talk, and I'll stay up here and give Paige a hand."

"Are you sure?" asked Addie.

"Yes." She fluttered her hands in a shooing motion. "Now, go, we'll be fine. Won't we, Paige?"

Paige nodded and wiped the counter down with a sanitizer cloth. "It'll be fun." She eyed Catherine mischievously. "You can tell me more about exactly what *did* go on between you and Felix last summer at Serena's wedding."

"No . . . n . . . nothing," stammered Catherine. Her normal peachy complexion rose to a cherry flush. "Nothing that you don't already know about."

"I think the lady doth protest too much." Paige giggled and ducked out the way of Catherine's long reach across the counter.

"You two behave," said Addie, fighting to keep her own giggle in check. "You're no better together than two little kids taunting each other, and you know no good will come from that."

Catherine folded her arms across her chest, stared down her nose, and stuck out her bottom lip in a pout. "She started it, Mom."

This time Addie couldn't stop the laugh that burst from her chest. Breathless, all she could do was shake her head as she headed toward the back room. Behind her trailed the hearty whoops of Marc's laughter as he followed close on her heels.

When she reached the storage room and had managed to retain some composure, she glanced at him and let out a contented sigh. In that moment, she realized it had been a long time since she had heard him laugh from the gut like that.

"What?"

"Nothing," she said, a soft smile touching her lips. It was comforting to see the glimmer of the old Marc she had once cared for so deeply. Even though that fun-loving

side of him was hidden underneath all his personal tur-
moil and disappointments of the last few years, he was
still the same old Marc, when he let his walls down.

"Okay," he said skeptically and glanced at the covered
blackboard.

"Tell me something," she said and pinned her gaze on
him.

"If it's not police business, sure." He met her piercing
stare.

"Did you know Felix was coming to town *before*
Catherine told you just now?"

His gaze darted back to the board. "I hope you haven't
been doing on there what I suspect you have."

"Marc!" She stomped over to him and planted herself
directly in his line of sight. "You didn't answer my question?"

He shrugged and set his gaze over her shoulder.

She noticed the telltale tic of his jaw. "I'm right, aren't
I? Felix told you he was coming to Greyborne Harbor,
didn't he?"

"He might have mentioned it when he called me to ask
some professional advice," he said, toying absently with
his cap.

"He called *you* for professional advice? You didn't call
him?"

"Why would I call him?" Marc asked and finally met
her probing gaze.

"Because of the rare books stolen in Boston."

"What books and why would a theft in Boston concern
me here?"

"I can see we have some catching up to do!" Addie
grinned roguishly as she whipped the cover from the
blackboard.

Chapter 28

Addie pointed to the list of stolen book titles Barbara had sent her. "These books were all stolen the week before Jared was killed."

"Alright." He leaned against the small desk in the back room. "But what does that have to do with Jared?"

"Nothing directly. However, if you look at this case from the theory that I've pointed out here"—she tapped the chalk stick on the board—"where I have Gwendolyn Buchannan's name as a collector of Sarah Josepha Hale books and look at the last three titles, it all starts to make sense."

"So, your theory is that Mrs. Buchannan, an esteemed member of Massachusetts high society and the president of the Essex County Historical Association, pulled off a heist of rare books from a highly secured antiquarian bookstore in Boston. Then she hid these books in the false bottom of the briefcase Jared bought at the pawn-shop later?"

Addie eyed the board. "Sort of . . . yes. But I think she hired someone to pull off the theft and arranged to pick up the briefcase later. Kalea did tell me it was heavier than normal even when empty, and then there's the little fact that they never paid for it. The clerk told Jared, pointing to Kalea, that *she* had already paid. I think Gwendolyn was supposed to pick up the case, and the young man mistook Kalea for her when he discovered she was from Greyborne Harbor." Addie's glaze darted from the notes on the board to Marc. "So, yes, I am saying that Gwendolyn is most likely behind this."

"And you think she killed Jared to get the books back?"

"No, I think she hired someone to do her dirty work for her, and that someone could well be"—she tapped the chalk under *Clay Diggens—Diggens Bait Shop and Boat Rentals*—"because yesterday I saw her coming out of his marina driveway, and he advertises regular boat trips to Boston."

He stood up and stretched. "Well, Addie, it's an interesting theory, but, as you know, I have to follow the evidence. Right now"—he plucked the chalk stick from her fingers and circled Kalea's name—"*this* is the suspect who has all the evidence against her."

"But there's all this other evidence that needs to be considered still." She fixed her puzzled gaze on Marc's. "You can't dismiss it just because it doesn't fit into your nice, neat box."

"Addie, there is nothing nice and neat about any of this except that Kalea had means, motive, *and* opportunity." He gestured toward the board.

"So do all the other names on this list. Every one of them had the means, the clothes hanger, something that would have made a convenient weapon in the spur of the moment. Plus, they all had a motive because each one of them had questionable business dealings with Jared. As far as opportunity, any one of them could have been at the dress shop Monday morning, and because it was so early, they would have gone unnoticed."

Marc's voice reflected his impatience. "Look, we have interviewed every one of the names on your board, plus a few you've missed, and not one of them appears to have had enough of a motive to kill Jared. Yes, he ruffled feathers but not to the extent that would have led to plunging a dress hanger into him."

"Good." She looked at him, touting a sense of victory. "Since you've excluded that theory, can we operate under mine now?" She tapped *Gwendolyn* again. "I saw her, with my own eyes, coming out of Clay's boat shop. You need to interview him again."

Marc locked his gaze on hers. "Should I interrogate him about the four women from the state historical society, who disembarked from one of his excursion boats this morning? You know, the ones who were met by Mrs. Buchannan and then accompanied by her and a couple of other women from the local historical association over to Greyborne Point B&B?"

"What?"

"Yes, Addie." He leaned back against the desk. "Believe it or not, the police do know a few things that may have slipped past you. I'm guessing that when you saw her leaving Clay's, she was there arranging the boat excursion for the members of the Massachusetts Historical Society that will be participating as judges for the upcoming competition. At least, that's what the rumor was around the water cooler this morning."

Addie sank through the floorboards—not literally—but if she could have, she would have. "Hmm," was all she could manage as she slunk down onto a book crate.

Darn it! How could she have been so wrong? She was convinced the stolen books, Gwendolyn, and the briefcase were the key to the murder, and Clay had been her hired henchman, but now? She considered her notes on the board. If Marc had interviewed all Jared's business contacts and didn't find any viable leads and had now abandoned that theory, it only meant one thing—her cousin could well be guilty.

"Now can we talk about why I came by today?"

She nodded without looking up at him. She was so embarrassed by her arrogance in thinking she had it all figured out and cursed herself under her breath.

"Normally, I would never disclose this. However, since, as you reminded Jerry, she is your last living blood relative . . ."

So Jerry had tattled on her and repeated what she'd said to him. *Thanks a lot, buddy.*

"I wanted to inform you that I am about to make an arrest in the murder of Jared Munro."

Her head shot up. "I take it that means you're arresting Kalea."

His lips pressed into a tight line, and he nodded. "We have new evidence that reinforces a strong motive."

"Which is what?" she asked, rising to her feet.

"Her being the sole beneficiary of his estate."

"How did you find out about that?"

"You knew?"

"Yes," she said, "but both she and I only discovered

that when a courier brought a letter from a law office in Boston."

"She told you she had no idea about the inheritance before that?"

"Yes, she said it was news to her."

"Is that right?" He eyed her warily. "Well, once I make the arrest, then it will be up to the DA to determine what she knew and when, but even you have to admit, it is a strong motive to kill someone."

She glanced at the board. "But it's all too neat, wrapped up in a bright shiny package, don't you think?"

"I'm not following you."

"It's like what I suggested the first day. Maybe someone is trying to set her up for the murder."

"Not everything is a conspiracy."

"I know but think about it. *Someone* told you they were arguing Sunday night. *Someone* made it look like a botched robbery. *Someone* dumped the only missing item from that incident into the trash dumpster just down the alley from the dress shop, and now *someone* has made sure you knew she was receiving a large inheritance by his death." She spun around, meeting his darkening gaze. "I think if you investigate that *someone,* you'll find the true motive and the killer." She noticed small pearls of perspiration above his upper lip. "But it sounds like you've already made up your mind, so no matter what turns up, it's not going to sway you, is it?"

"It's not my mind I've made up. It's where the evidence leads."

"Yeah, yeah, yeah." Addie glared at the board and bit the side of her mouth to stop her flow of tears. "I bet Picker can identify who tossed the briefcase, and then you'd know it wasn't my cousin."

"What makes you think it wasn't her and Picker did see it."

"Because she hasn't left my house since Sunday, so she wouldn't have been the one to push Picker off the cliff to shut her up, would she?"

"Picker woke up and denies anyone else was on the cliff with her who might have given her a push. She said it was an accident, and she slipped."

Addie narrowed in on that clue she'd written on the board and hissed, "So much for that theory then."

Marc put his cap on and turned to leave. "But there is one thing, though."

"What's that?"

"Since I know nothing is going to deter you from trying to prove Kalea's innocence, I'll let you in on the curious thing. We *did* find a second set of footprints in the snow where Picker went over the edge."

"See, that proves she was pushed."

"Maybe, but due to the changeable weather conditions causing deterioration of the tracks, we have no way of determining who the footprints belong to. That means unless Picker tells us any different, we have to go on the evidence we do have." He paused at the doorway and without turning around, he said. "My advice is for your cousin to hire a good criminal lawyer and soon."

Addie shot glancing daggers at his back as he headed toward the front door, and then she reread her notes on the board. Did she worry from the beginning her cousin could possibly have killed Jared? Yes, it had been a niggle in the back of her mind, but did she still believe it? No. She had spent the better part of the week with her and seen firsthand her cousin's rebounding emotions to the incident. Plus, this was someone she had known her whole life. Someone that, in spite of her shortcomings and self-interested behavior, really wasn't capable of murder.

Marc was right about one thing, though. Nothing was going to deter her from trying to prove Kalea's innocence. She had to move fast.

"Catherine," she called, approaching the front counter. "I know we agreed you'd start next week but—"

"I take it Marc said something that you want to go and check out on your own."

"Yes, as a matter of fact, he did."

"Then go. Paige and I can handle the bookstore."

"Are you sure? I don't want to impose."

"Like I said earlier, I have nothing else planned for the rest of the afternoon, so go . . . shoo, do what you have to."

"Thanks." Addie kissed her friend's cheek, grabbed her coat, and headed out the back door to her Mini. She made a left at the end of the alley and headed down Birch toward Marine Drive. Words her father used to say echoed in her mind. *When things are as they appear, you have to look closer to find the one missing piece of evidence that completes the entire puzzle.*

Chapter 29

The high volume of afternoon traffic on Marine Drive took Addie by surprise as she passed through on her way to the lighthouse. She pulled into the entrance and managed to snag one of the few remaining parking spots beside the nautical museum located in the old lighthouse-keeper's cottage at the base. She hopped out onto the gravel parking pad but quickly veered off the path leading to the main door and slogged through the piles of drifted snow that had accumulated beside the white-washed lighthouse buildings.

As she rounded the corner of the lighthouse, a gust of blustery wind sucked at her breath. She put her head down and forged forward, cautious of not slipping on the rocky ground across the windswept cliff top. When nothing but a breathtaking view of the harbor and outlying islands lay before her, she mentally crossed her fingers, hoping her vertigo was in check, and peered over the cliff side.

Off to her right, about fifteen feet down, was a wide stony ledge. That's what must have saved Picker from certain death. Her head spun. She dropped to her knees and clutched at tufts of ground scrub as she studied the nearly one-hundred-foot drop down the side of the cliff to the crashing waves against the rocky base. She drew back, counted . . . eight . . . nine . . . ten to clear her wooziness, and then gingerly peered over the edge again. Below the stone overhang, a flutter of green on a jagged rock protrusion caught her eyes. She squinted and could just make out what appeared to be piece of a plastic garbage bag flapping in the brisk seaside winds.

Someone must have dumped a bag of garbage over the side, a problem the town had been seeing an increase in since the new dumping regulations came into play under Mayor Bryant. She'd bet ten to one that bag had landed on the ledge before the winds swept it off, and that's what Picker was trying to retrieve when she fell. *Or was pushed?*

Addie inspected the ground area around the cliff top. Whether Picker was pushed or just fell, Marc was right. There was nothing left to see. The week's weather had erased any evidence that might have led to what actually had occurred here in spite of what Picker claimed.

She shoved her key into the car door lock but stopped when she recalled Nick had left a message about some botanical prints he had at the antique store. She glanced down the lighthouse access road to Marine Drive and then at her Mini. After dropping her keys into her coat pocket, she clasped her jacket collar tight to her throat, and headed off on the three-block walk to Time Travels. After all, when she'd driven past, she noticed street-side parking was at a premium, so she decided she might as well leave her car parked where it was. Besides, even though the wind was nippy, the sun was shining. It would be refreshing to walk along the seawall for a bit before heading back to Beyond the Page.

Addie flinched when the warm air of the antique shop hit her wind-burned cheeks. She rubbed her icy hands together and paused in the doorway as her eyes adjusted to the indoor light.

"Addie, over here," Nick called from the sales counter.

She laughed and strolled toward him. "Ah, there you are, now that I can see again."

"Just let me finish with this customer, and I'll get the prints from the back for you."

"Thanks, that would be great." She smiled at the white-haired gentleman purchasing a box of vintage Christmas ornaments.

"My wife collects these." The man gestured to his prize. "I know these will get me out of the doghouse for at least a day or two," he said with a chuckle as he handed Nick his credit card.

"You, Fred?" Nick said, shaking his head. "I can't imagine Irene would ever be upset with you."

"You didn't hear her when I came home the other day from here with another piece for that model train set you got me started on." Fred roared with a barrel-chested laugh.

"Then, yes, you need to make peace because I'd hate to lose two of my favorite customers." Nick chuckled and handed Fred his bag.

The man tipped his head at Addie and, still sniggering,

sauntered out the door, setting the overhead bell into a frenzied dance.

Nick shook his head as he watched the man leave, and he smiled. "I wish all my customers were as good-natured as Fred and his wife and as avid of collectors as they are. It would sure help keep the books in the black."

"Really?" Addie glanced around the shop and noted a number of other customers browsing the displays. She dropped her voice. "Business appears good, or are they all tire-kickers and not buyers?"

"Ignore me," he said, waving his hand. "I was just thinking out loud. Ivy and I had words this morning, and I guess my mood hasn't shifted yet."

"That's too bad." She smiled weakly. "I know first-hand that working with family can be hard at times, but I'm sure your relationship is strong enough to weather those inevitable sibling disagreements."

"That's the problem. I'm not sure family ties, a topic she keeps rattling on about are enough this time."

"Oh?"

He leaned his palms on the desk and lowered his voice. "She's supposed to be heading to South Carolina next week for a couple of big estate auctions. Without Jared's financing, there's just not enough money in the bank to cover the costs of anything she bids on. Since I am the one running the operations of the store and doing the books, she seems to feel it's my fault. I can't make her see that the revolving credit line we had was what made us able to keep up with stocking new inventory and her ability to pay for the pieces her private collectors have on their wish lists. Sure, I have decent enough daily sales"— he waved his hand toward a couple by the china display—"but she said if we have a short fall, then it's *my* fault, that I must not be doing enough of what we agreed to when we decided to run our parents' business and . . . never mind. I shouldn't be saying any of this to you." He shook his head and glanced awkwardly at Addie. "You're a customer, and I have to remember that. Let me go and get the pieces you came in for." He started to turn away.

"Wait, Nick, I might be a customer, but I'm also a small business owner, and I do have some understanding of what you're going through."

"When Jared died, you lost your financial backer, too?"

"No, and I've never used Jared's services. I was lucky enough to get an inheritance to help offset lean times. However, I do know other owner operators and have heard how they handle money flow crunches like what you're experiencing now."

He shuffled back toward her. "Okay, I'm listening. Any ideas would help because I'm afraid that after fifty years in business, Time Travels won't make it through to Christmas. Despite my objections, Ivy took the money she needed for the buying trip out of the bank at noon." He thumped his hand on the counter. "And she knows full well that I still have the monthly bills to pay."

"Look, I have a friend who has run into a similar issue with revolving funds. Have you thought about reaching out to people who might be in a position to help with a short-term investment for a minimal return on their loan?"

"Like a private benefactor?"

"Yes, that's exactly what I mean."

"I wouldn't even know where to start with that. Any suggestions where I can find a rich patron?"

Addie glanced at the small wrapping counter behind the sales desk and noticed a framed *Godey's Lady's Book* print. "What about one of Ivy's private collectors like . . .

I don't know . . . Gwendolyn Buchannan? I know she's a regular customer, and she seems to be financially in a position where she could help. Plus, I'm sure she wouldn't want to see her supply line for all things *Godey's* or Sarah Josepha Hale go under."

"Gwendolyn?" Nick scoffed. "She couldn't care less. She'd just find another dealer."

"Really?"

"Oh yeah, and to be honest, I think Gwendolyn just barely tolerates Ivy. She certainly doesn't show her any preferential treatment. Which was why I was stunned when Ivy told me Gwendolyn had invited her to that big fancy dinner she's holding."

Addie recalled Gwendolyn's reaction when Addie mentioned something about Ivy being invited for Thanksgiving and glanced nervously at Nick. It was obvious he wasn't aware the invite had been bogus. Why would Ivy lie to him about it? Unless, of course, with the stress of money, she had hoped her brother would think she was closer to their important clients than she actually was. Then he'd relent and release the funds she needed for her buying trips based on the premise that she had to go to those auctions to keep people like Gwendolyn happy and as returning customers.

Addie eyed the print on the wrapping desk and could see from where she stood it was an actual page from a *Godey's* magazine, not a photocopy like the ones in her shop. "I take it that print is for Gwendolyn?"

Nick glanced over his shoulder. "Yeah, how did you ever guess?"

"One can hope it wasn't, and I could throw it in with my botanical prints."

He gestured to the print. "That, and how much it will

bring into the store is the main reason I tolerate Ivy's obsession with tracking down anything Gwendolyn Buchannan wants. She is willing to pay top dollar and then some for whatever Ivy finds her."

Addie replayed the clues she had on her board pointing to Gwendolyn. Just how far would the woman go to add to her collection? If losing Ivy as her agent wouldn't be a loss for her and she'd simply find someone else to work with, perhaps she already had. Maybe the new agent was the person who tracked down Jared to Kalea's dress shop and killed him to retrieve what Gwendolyn saw as belonging to her.

"But," he said, "my babbling on about my personal problems is keeping you. Let me go grab the prints from the storeroom, and you can decide if they might be something you're interested in for your shop."

"And you're certain that *Godey's* print can't be included?" Addie eyed him with a mischievous grin.

"I wish I could, but Ivy would have my head. Although, if you really need to hear a definitive *no* from her or think you have a compelling argument to plead your case against Gwendolyn's, then you'll find Ivy at the Lighthouse Museum. She went over to help them set up a new display of antique nautical odds and ends she came across at the sale last week in Boston."

"I just might do that. I've been told I'm like a dog with a bone sometimes." She softly laughed, thinking about Simon's words, as Nick disappeared around the corner into the back room.

Addie eyed the two paper shopping bags Nick was filling as he carefully wrapped up her treasures in tissue paper. Her heart still beat an excited tempo. When she saw the prints were a set of eight watercolor sketches of some of the flowers in Agatha Christie's secret poison plant garden at her family's holiday retreat on her Greenway Estate in Torquay, Devon, she knew she'd have to have the entire set. There was no way she was going to be selling them in her bookstore. Nope, this was a Christmas gift for herself.

She eyed the Victorian planter, the one Catherine had coveted, and that Nick had put on hold for her. She paid for it, but due to the size and weight, Nick convinced her to leave it, and he'd drop it off on his way home.

As she slipped the two shopping bags off the counter, her phone vibrated in her pocket. She set the bags back and fished out her phone to see a text from Simon.

I talked to Picker again. She finally admitted that just before she fell, she felt pressure in the middle of her back, like someone's hands pushing her forward, then nothing else. She swears she never saw who it was as she was too focused on getting down to the ledge to retrieve a green bag she could see. When she's less snarky, I'll try again later. This might be a long process to get info, but at least it's more than we had before. I'll call later. XXX

"Trust Doctor Dreamy Blue-Eyes." She smiled.

"Pardon?" Nick asked.

"Just a text from a friend," she said, shoving her phone away, and gripped the handles of the bags, sliding them off the counter. "Do you know a woman named Picker?"

"Picker?"

"Yes, she sells stuff around town that she finds."

"You mean the woman who lives out at the old grist mill?"

"Yes, that's her," said Addie. "So you know her then?"

"Not really. She's been in from time to time with something she wants us to buy."

"Anything good?"

"Occasionally, why do you ask?"

"She didn't happen to be by here this past week or maybe you saw her around Thursday?"

"No, can't say that I did," said Nick. "As a matter of fact, I don't remember the last time she came in. I think it's been a while."

"Would Ivy have seen her that day?"

"No, she was at a big auction in Salem on Thursday. That's where she got those prints you bought, and she didn't get back till almost dinnertime. Why?"

"Just wondering. Someone said they saw her around the other day, and I wondered if she stopped in here."

"No, but if she comes in, I'll tell her you're looking for her."

"That would be great. Thanks, Nick," she said with a wave as she headed for the door.

As Addie made her way back to her car in the lighthouse parking lot, her mind replayed Simon's text message. Picker was, in fact, pushed. It wasn't speculation anymore, but by why and by whom? Addie had already spoken with most of the names on her list of Jared's clients, and Marc didn't feel any of them had a strong enough motive to commit murder based on his investigation. Even so, to her, it appeared that someone was worried Picker could identify them from the alley on Monday morning if her hunch was right about Gwendolyn. Who had she recruited to do her dirty work? What and who was she missing off her suspect list? Perhaps a return to the scene of the latest crime would help clarify all the questions swirling around in her mind.

Chapter 30

Addie edged back from the cliff top. Picker had been lucky that a woman walking her dog up here by the lighthouse spotted her down on the rock after her dog began frantically barking and pawing at the bluff edge. But will I be as lucky? After all, if her vertigo kicked in again, there was no one around today to rescue her . . . or worse. So why risk it? She cringed at the sounds of the waves crashing below on the rocks and took another step backward.

"But the key must be here somewhere," she whispered to herself. "Why would someone want to silence Picker?"

Picker routinely checked the dumpsters around Main Street for cast-offs she could sell. She could have been in the alley when whoever killed Jared tossed out the briefcase Picker later found.

"There has to be someone I'm missing on my list.

Someone I haven't spoken with that could have seen Picker come to this exact spot and then given her a push."

Think, Addie, think. Of course, the Thomas sisters. Everyone else on Marine Drive she'd already discarded, but she hadn't spoken to either of them. Plus, the B&B was almost directly across the road, giving it a good line of sight to the lighthouse access road and the cliff.

Or it could have been one of the other suspects on the list of Jared's clients who didn't work on Marine Drive and had been following Picker. Like maybe Hal Washburn, Charles Wilson, or Adam and Evelyn Boyer. There were still a lot of names on that list. That was, of course, if she worked on Marc's theory that whoever killed Jared was after the documents in his briefcase and his murder had no connection to the books stolen in Boston. But, on the other hand, if she followed her gut feeling that the briefcase contained the stolen books, and Jared and Kalea coming into possession of it was a case of mistaken identity. That was in her mind, the true motive. Someone else not on the list might have been watching and waiting for the perfect time to silence the only person who could place them at the scene of the murder. She gasped. "The chauffeur!"

Why hadn't she thought of him before? It made perfect sense now. He was clearly loyal, which meant he would most likely do anything to help and protect his employer, and Addie knew first hand that his employer coveted at least three of the books on the stolen property list. "I have to tell Marc now!" Excitedly, she fished her phone out of her pocket. "He has to be the one. It only makes sense!"

"Did you say something?"

Addie jerked at the sound of a small voice behind her

and spun around, sending her phone careening into the air, but she managed to snag it before it went over the edge.

"Phew, that was close." She laughed nervously, shoved it into her pocket, and leapt back from the cliff top. "Hi, Ivy. I was just thinking out loud."

"Sorry I startled you," she replied with an apologetic wince. "Nick called and said you were heading over here to talk to me about the *Godey's* print or something. When I was leaving and saw you over here, I thought I'd better see what you wanted to know about it."

"Yes, yes, I did want to talk to you." Addie fought to regain control of her burst of adrenaline-induced breathing. "I wanted to ask you if it's for sale."

"Sadly, I already promised it to Gwendolyn Buchannan."

"And there's no way you'll consider another offer?"

"I'm afraid not. She's my biggest client, and what she wants, she gets. Besides, I've already told her about it."

"That's too bad. Since the theme of the cooking contest was announced, I've had a lot of inquiries for Sarah Josepha Hale works. Since you seem to be an expert at sniffing them out, well, let's just say I hoped you'd consider it."

"I wouldn't say I'm an expert, but I was lucky enough to have come across those bound *Godey's* volumes that I think you saw in the store."

"Nothing else since?" Addie glanced at the cliff edge and decided they should take this conversation elsewhere. The wind was picking up, and her heart was still pounding an overtime rhythm brought on by the phone incident. "That's too bad because one of the most popular fiction books in my shop this week has been the newer editions of *The Northwood: A Tale of New England*, the first book Hale wrote back in 1827. I was hoping you might have come across a first edition copy in your travels. I would love to get my hands on it."

"I can't say that I'm familiar with that one."

"That surprises me. Since Sarah Josepha Hale is considered the godmother of Thanksgiving and Gwendolyn's obsession with her work, you'd think that would be on the top of her wish list."

Ivy shook her head and shrugged. "She must already have a copy. Probably why she hasn't asked me to look for one."

"That could be," said Addie. "I guess I'll have to be happy with my newer editions." Addie began strolling toward the parking lot. "You know, the more I read, the more I realize what an interesting woman Hale was . . ." She paused and glanced back. Ivy had not followed her lead to go. "Is everything okay?" She stared questioningly at the woman, who remained motionless by the cliff edge.

"Yes, I was just thinking about what you said. Sarah being considered the godmother of Thanksgiving, and I felt a sense"—she swiped at the tears forming in her eyes as she gazed out over the harbor—"of pride I suppose."

"Pride? Why? However, she was a powerful influencer of women during her time, that's for sure."

"No," Ivy said with a sniff, "because . . . I'm related to her and . . . well . . . it just fills me with a sense of honor to know people today are still interested in her work and all she accomplished for women back then."

"I had no idea you were related to Sarah Hale."

"Yes," said Ivy excitedly as she stepped closer to Addie and farther away from the cliff edge. "I had my

DNA traced earlier this year, and it turns out that I'm a distant relative of hers."

"That's exciting!" said Addie, eyeing the woman's delicate facial features and stature. She was a far cry from the portraits she had seen of Sarah Josepha Hale, who appeared every bit like her father, Captain Gordon Buell. She could not see a trace of the famous Scottish and Rhineland lineage.

"Oh," said Ivy, a flush brightening her alabaster skin. "I know what you're thinking. How can someone who looks like me be related to such a majestic woman."

"No, not at all."

"To be honest, when I got the results, I couldn't believe it myself, so I did a little digging around in my family tree and discovered an adventure-seeking cousin of Sarah's had spent some time in Spain during the nineteenth century, and, well . . . Let's just say he made an everlasting impression on a great, great, great-aunt of mine, and four generations later, here is the result." Her hands motioned a sweep down her petite-framed body.

"Does Gwendolyn know about this family link? It must have blown her away to discover the woman she idolizes is related to you, too?"

"Yes, she does. That's why I'm going to her Thanksgiving dinner party."

"Is it?" Addie eyed her skeptically, recalling what Gwendolyn had said.

Ivy dropped her gaze. "Even though I wasn't invited, and I'm guessing by the look on your face, you already knew that, didn't you?"

Addie bit her lip and nodded.

"Yeah, she discarded the claim, saying those commercial ancestry tests are hooey and aren't definitive proof."

"That must have hurt you, but you're still going to the party anyway. I mean that is why you had my cousin design you a dress, isn't it?"

"Your cousin?"

"Yes, Kalea Hudson, she has the shop on Main Street."

"Kalea? Sorry. I wasn't aware you were related to her. Yes, I am, because I'm taking a few gifts with me that I know Gwendolyn *won't* be able to resist. If that isn't enough to prove to her that I am a legitimate member of her family"—Ivy bit back the tears threatening to reform in her eyes and puffed out her chest—"what I'm going to give her will show her I'm just as good as she is, and I belong at her party. Heavens knows I've done everything else that woman demanded of me. All so I could please her and be accepted into the family."

"Can I make a guess as to what you're going to take with you to get through the door?"

"Sure, but I don't think you'd ever believe it."

"It wouldn't happen to be a first edition of *Mary Had a Little Lamb*, would it?" Addie gulped in expectation of what Ivy was about to reveal.

"Yes, how did you know?" squealed Ivy. "Gwendolyn is going to be thrilled to discover I finally got my hands on it for her. She's wanted that book for as long as I've known her."

"Yes, I imagine she has," said Addie, eyeing her as she took a step back. In spite of the chilling winds, beads of perspiration prickled at the back of Addie's neck, and she drew in a deep slow breath. It all made sense now. It was Ivy. She was the one working with Gwendolyn, the one who was supposed to pick up the briefcase last Sunday in Boston. She'd been there, at least earlier in the week. Who was to say she didn't go back or stay longer after the auction than she admitted to? She proved by lying to her brother about the dinner invitation that she was willing to lie to get what she wanted.

"I hope it all works out the way you want it to." Addie hoped her tone was as lighthearted as she planned. She eyed their proximity to the cliff.

"It will," Ivy said matter-of-factly, and a smug look crossed her face. "I think, for once and for all, I will have proved my loyalty to the family, and she'll finally accept me."

"Yes, I'm sure, but I should be going now." Addie glanced at the cliff side as she edged around Ivy to put more space between them. "I only stopped out here because a friend had an accident on Thursday, and I was excited to check out the luck she had by landing on the ledge and not . . . but never mind. Nick told me you were in Salem that day and didn't get home until later, so I doubt you would have heard about all the commotion up here." Addie widened her circling and kept her gaze steadfast on Ivy. "Unless, of course, you got back earlier in the day to see the lights and sirens."

"Yeah, I wondered what was going on, but I never bothered to check it out."

"You weren't concerned? I mean you donated items to the museum. Didn't you wonder why at about noonish there was such a commotion around the lighthouse? The lighthouse could have been robbed or something."

"No." Ivy's gaze narrowed. "I really didn't."

"So you did return from Salem earlier than you told your brother?"

"That's none of your business, is it? It's bad enough that I have to account for my every move with my brother. Why should I tell you anything?" She recoiled and took a step backward. "It sounds to me as though you're accusing me of pushing that old woman!" She edged back farther.

"I didn't say anything about an old woman." Addie's gaze flitted to the looming cliff edge as Ivy nudged closer to it. "Stop!"

"Why? Are you going to tell on me for lying to Nick again? Is that what this really is all about? You've got the hots for him, right? I've seen the way you look at him. What is it, Addie? You want to get your claws into him and force me out of the business so you can get your hands on my client list. Admit it! You'd do anything to find out where I get the *Godey's* books and prints, wouldn't you? Then you'll steal Gwendolyn away from *me*. Well, you can't have her. She's *my* family, not yours!" Ivy's face contorted with rage as she danced another step backward.

"Ivy! Watch your step!"

"Watch my step?" she cried. "Why would I do that now when I'm so close to being accepted by Gwendolyn? Don't you see? When I give her the gifts on Thanksgiving, she'll have to see me as worthy, won't she?" Her arms thrashed wildly in the air as she teetered on the edge.

"I meant literally *watch your step*!" Addie lunged at the woman and seized one arm just as Ivy slid over the side.

Addie dropped spread-eagle to the ground, struggling not to be pulled over by the flailing woman. "Stop squirming or we'll both be done for," Addie screamed as she fought to get a tighter grip. Her feet splayed out behind. She scrambled for a foothold, and one boot toe lodged against a rock embedded in the ground. Her grip on Ivy's arm slipped. Addie flung out her free hand and grabbed Ivy farther down her arm, exposing a white gauze wrapping. A vision of the mysterious blood on Jared's shirt sleeve rushed through her mind. Her hand cramped, and her fingers slipped, barely maintaining the grip she had on Ivy's wrist.

"Help," Addie screamed as she fought to hang on to the woman flailing like a fish on a hook above the crashing waves below.

"Help us," Ivy wailed as she twisted and turned under Addie's grasp.

Horror surged through Addie when her toe slid over the rock anchor. Inch by inch, Ivy's weight tugged Addie closer to the brink as she struggled to keep hold of the thrashing woman. *Let her go or you'll die too!* Addie's mind screamed. Despite being hauled closer to the edge and going over herself, she grunted and dug her toes into the ground. *I can't do that.*

"Oomph!" A heavy weight crashed down on her back, knocking the breath out of her.

"Let her go *now,* Addie!" Marc's voice commanded as he seized Ivy by her arms and hoisted her up and over the cliff edge to solid ground.

At the same time, hands grabbed Addie's legs and dragged her across the wet ground.

She screamed with the flurry of activity and floundered onto her back and stared in disbelief into Jerry's anxious face.

"Are you okay?" he asked.

She glanced over her shoulder and focused her gaze on a tuft of wild grass on the edge of the cliff just feet from where her head lay now. Tears spilled from her eyes as Jerry helped her sit up and draped his police issue parka over her shoulders. She nestled her head into his chest and sobbed into his shirt. Jerry's arm clasped her shoulders. He held her tight and gently rocked her until the flow of adrenaline-induced tears stopped.

"It was never about the money." Addie hoarsely choked and stared up at him. "None of it." She sniffled and wiped the icy pearls of tears from her cheeks. "She killed Jared just to gain acceptance into a family that she was desperate to be part of and darn near killed me too."

"It's over now. The chief has her," he soothingly whispered. "But right now, I think you're in shock, so let's get you into a warm cruiser, and you can tell us exactly what happened here."

She managed to shift onto her knees and, with Jerry's help, made it to her feet. Her legs buckled, and she wobbled. Jerry's arm tightened around her, steadying her. She nodded in gratitude, clasped his jacket collar tight to her throat, and leaned into him as he guided her to the parking lot.

Chapter 31

Addie's fingers tightened around the cup of hot coffee in front of her, and she stared blankly at the floor under Marc's desk.

"Are you okay?" he asked, sliding into the chair beside hers.

Her face contorted, and a sob escaped her throat. "Oh Marc, if you hadn't come when you did . . . I'd be . . . I couldn't hold onto her anymore. I was—"

"Shhh . . . it's okay." He wrapped his arm around her shaking shoulders and pulled her into his side. "You did well. You both survived."

"But, but . . ." She looked up into his eyes, unable to stop her tears. "I wanted to let her go . . . I didn't want to save her. My hands cramped, and I wanted to let go."

"But you didn't, did you?"

She shook her head.

"Addie, you're a good person, and no matter what you thought, I know as long as you had the strength in you, you would have done anything to have saved the both of you."

"But if you and Jerry hadn't come along when you did . . . it would have been a different story, wouldn't it?" She sniffled and blew her nose with the tissue Marc offered her. "How did you know to go to the lighthouse anyway?"

Marc sat back, but his hand lingered and stroked feathery circles on her shoulder. Addie glanced at his hand and shifted uncomfortably in her chair. She didn't miss the tightening in his jaw or the blush on his cheeks.

"Umm, sorry." He cleared his throat, and removed his hand, resting it on the back of her chair. "Yeah, we went to the antique store to take Ivy in for questioning, and Nick told us that's where she was."

"But how did you figure out it was her? I didn't until we were talking on the cliff."

"When you showed me the list of rare books that had been stolen in Boston, we made some inquiries with the Boston Police Department. It seems they had a certain pawnshop owner and his brother, a seasoned professional criminal, under surveillance for some time. When we shared what we had and compared notes on the two cases, they decided there was enough evidence and moved on it."

"And the pawnshop owner confessed?"

"Eventually, yes, at least to being the middleman. Apparently, a woman he's met through prior transactions arranged to pick up the briefcase containing a couple of not so valuable books from him that Sunday. He said it was weird because the books weren't worth much, but

she was desperate to get her hands on them, one in particular—"

"*Mary Had a Little Lamb?*"

"Yes, and she paid him well, so he didn't ask any questions."

"He named Ivy as the mysterious woman?"

"No, he wouldn't divulge her name. He said it would
implicate him in too many other charges over the past
two years for items he had procured for her, and then he
clammed up."

"Then how did you figure out it was Ivy?"

"Picker finally admitted to Simon who she saw toss
the briefcase into the dumpster."

"So Picker was there in the alley that morning?"

"Yes, she told us that she always checks the dumpsters
around Main Street early Monday mornings before the
disposal trucks come and empty them. She told Simon
she was farther up the alley when she heard a car alarm
go off. She crept closer to see what was going on, and
that's when she spotted Ivy."

"Yeah, she'd know her from a few deals she'd done
with the antique store."

Marc nodded. "Anyway, Picker said she found it odd
that the alarm was going off and Ivy was just standing by
the back door of the dress shop. She said a man came out
in to the alley, probably to check on his car because of the
alarm and the flashing lights, and then Ivy slipped into
the shop behind him."

"That's why there was no sign of a break-in."

"Exactly."

"What did Picker do then?"

"Nothing," said Marc, shaking his head. "As you
know, Picker's a pretty private person and treats people

the same, kind of a live-and-let-live attitude. She said she went about her business, checking the dumpsters, and never thought about it again until about fifteen minutes later when Ivy ran out the back door. Picker said she was inside the dumpster one store down from the furniture store and saw Ivy searching the briefcase. She took something out of it and shoved it in her jacket pocket then threw the case into a dumpster. Picker didn't realize then that Ivy had spotted her peeking over the rim of the dumpster, but when Ivy showed up on the cliff Thursday and confronted her, Picker realized she had been seen."

"Did Picker say why she was on the cliff?"

"Yeah, she saw a green garbage bag down on the rock ledge and was trying to figure out how to get it without breaking her neck."

"And that's when Ivy gave her a shove?"

Marc nodded. "Picker told Simon that when she didn't die then, she was afraid Ivy would come back and try to kill her again, so she was afraid to say anything to us before."

"And she well could have. Ivy was desperate to get her hands on that *Mary Had a Little Lamb* book."

"I know. When we interviewed her, she kept telling us to let Gwendolyn Buchannan know she finally got it for her."

"What else did she say? Did she say why she killed Jared?"

"Yes, sort of. She said when she went to the pawnshop later to get the briefcase, as you suspected"—he glanced sideways at her—"the young clerk told her he'd already given it to the woman from Greyborne Harbor."

"So it *was* a case of mistaken identity."

His ears turned red. "Yes, Miss Smarty-Pants, it was."

If she wasn't feeling so drained, she would have stuck her tongue out at him, but even that would take more effort than she had right now. The adrenaline of her experience was wearing off.

Soberly, Marc continued laying out the case. "The kid described the woman he'd given the case to, and as soon as he told Ivy she had a fondness for the vintage dresses, she knew it was Kalea. Ivy, as a client of Kalea's, had been to the dress shop, I guess. Anyway, apparently when she set off the alarm on the car, thinking it was Kalea's car, she thought when Kalea came out to check on it, that she'd be able to convince Kalea to hand over the case and tell her about the mistake."

"But it was Jared that came out."

"Right. She said she was as shocked as he was. But given that Jared was apparently even more startled to find someone inside the shop when he went back in, she had no problem keeping him off guard at first and managed to locate the briefcase. Then she tried to convince him to sell it back to her. He refused. They argued. She tried to make it past him out the back door with the case but he stopped her. She grabbed the closest thing at hand, a broken clothes hanger from the box on the shelf beside her, and threatened him with it. They fought over it. She got a scrape on her arm in the kerfuffle, but managed to swing her arm around bringing the briefcase down on the side of his head. He lurched forward, unfortunately, he fell directly onto the broken hanger she still brandished and . . ."

"So, the cut she got on her arm was the other blood smear on his shirt sleeve."

Marc nodded. "Yup, and she has a rather jagged cut on the inside of her lower arm to prove it."

"What about tossing the store? Did she say why she did that? Was she looking for something else?"

"No, when Jared collapsed on the floor, she panicked. She hadn't gone there expecting to kill anyone. She thought she'd be confronting Kalea and be able to convince her of the mistake, and she'd just hand the briefcase over. She said she didn't know what to do and in the spur of the moment she decided to make it look like an attempted robbery."

Addie shook her head.

"What?" asked Marc.

"It's just that if she had taken the books out of the briefcase and left it there. We would have never put the stolen books and it together, right? I mean we didn't know until later that it had a false bottom and would never have connected the book theft in Boston to the pawnshop and eventually back to a Greyborne Harbor connection, would we?"

"We?" He glanced at her, a half smile on his lips. "If you recall it was you who put all those clues together."

"Well, I helped just a wee bit, maybe," Addie said with a chuckle.

"But I did say to her pretty much the same thing," said Marc, "and she told me, she was frantic and didn't know what to do. She knew if Jared was downstairs then Kalea must still be upstairs and she was afraid your cousin would walk in at any moment. She felt she had to take something and fast to pull off her ruse, and the briefcase seemed logical at the time."

"That makes sense, but you know what I've never understood, and I never asked Kalea about—I guess because I was scared of her answer—was how she never heard any of this going on downstairs and why didn't she go down and check it out?"

"I asked her before about that and it seems she was having trouble settling down after her and Jared's argument, so she took something to help her sleep."

"Very deeply by the sound of it."

"So it appears, but forget about all that for a minute. How are you now? Any calmer?"

"Yes, I think so. At least, I've stop shaking," she said with a light laugh, holding her hand out. "See. But what I don't get"—she dropped her hand to her lap—"is Ivy knows Kalea. She's a customer, so why didn't she just wait until the shop opened and ask Kalea about the case then?"

"Good question. Maybe when she discovered the error made by the clerk in giving it to the wrong person, she panicked, thinking the longer Kalea had it the more chance there would be in her discovering the secret compartment and the books." He shrugged. "But I will pass that along to the DA, and he can question her about it."

"Her defense lawyer might try to use that as a call to her state of mind," said Addie. "Gathering by what she was saying about family and Gwendolyn finally going to accept her, I don't think it's too stable right now, do you? He might try to use that to plead temporary insanity."

"Addie!" Simon cried as he bolted through the door. "I heard what happened. Are you okay?" he asked, rushing toward her.

"Simon!" She twisted around in her seat and clutched on to him as he wrapped his arms around her.

"I was just sick when I heard what happened," he whispered hoarsely. "I don't know what I would have done if

I'd lost you today." His arms tightened around her, pressing her close to his chest.

"I'm fine, really I am. But I must say, for a few moments, I really was afraid I'd never see you again either."

Marc slithered his arm out from between them and rose to his feet.

"But how did you know?"

"Marc called me."

She glanced over Simon's shoulder into Marc's forlorn eyes and mouthed *thank you*.

He nodded.

She didn't miss the slight quiver in Marc's Adam's apple when his cheerless gaze darted from her to Simon.

"I love you so much," Simon murmured as the back of his hand tenderly stroked her cheek.

Marc's jaw ticked, and Addie stiffened at the fleeting glance and thinly veiled smile Marc gave before quietly slipping out, closing the door behind him. She glanced at Simon trying to shake off the haunted look in Marc's eyes as he left them alone.

"What's wrong," he asked.

"Nothing," she murmured inching her lips closer to his. "Just kiss me."

Chapter 32

"Has anyone seen Pippi?" Addie asked, rising to her feet from the sofa where she'd been seated between Nick and Bill, and glanced nervously around the living room.

"The last time I saw her, Emma was chasing her into the dining room, trying to put her dolly's clothes on her," said Paige matter-of-factly from one of the wingback chairs flanking the fireplace. "And my motto as a mother is if I don't hear a crash or crying, then I don't worry." She chuckled softly as she flipped through an antique auction catalogue.

"Poor Pippi." Addie stifled a laugh. "I think I'll go refill the coffee carafe and see if she needs rescuing by now."

"I wouldn't worry about Pippi." Paige handed the catalogue across the table to Nick. "When she's had enough, she'll let Emma know the game is over and come running." She glanced at Nick. "Are you going to that auction? There's a few things in there that might be good for the bookstore."

"If you're going for coffee"—Nick glanced up at Addie and gestured toward his empty cup on the table— "I could go for a refill." He refocused on Paige. "Yes, next week. I've hired someone to work with me in the shop that way he can cover while I go on the occasional buying trip. Since Ivy will be going to the prison psychiatric ward and won't . . ." He swallowed and drew in a deep breath. "Just make a list of what you're interested in, note what your highest bid limit is, and we'll see what happens from there."

"Bill, are you ready for more coffee?" asked Addie, eager to deflect some of the attention of what she knew must be a heartbreaking situation for Nick to face about his sister.

"Nah, I'm good for now, thanks." Bill waved her off and played his chess piece. "Check-mate." He grinned across the board at Logan who was seated on the other side of the ottoman between them on the other wingback chair.

"Logan," said Addie, eyeing him teasingly, "after your second loss of the afternoon to Bill, you look like you could use another coffee."

"I could, thanks." He steadied his gaze on Bill before resetting the board. "I want to be black this next game."

"Do you really think that will help your game?" Freda retorted teasingly from where she'd been watching over the back of Logan's chair.

Addie gazed around the room and smiled. She knew it had been a longshot inviting Picker and Nick for dinner

with her closest friends. But after she found out they'd
both be completely alone for the holiday, how could she
not? Martha even went to great lengths so Picker wouldn't
feel out of place. She looked like a different person from
her new cropped haircut to wearing one of Martha's oversized blouses cinched at the waist with a navy belt and
paired with complementary navy trousers. The transfor-
mation from the person Addie met a few weeks ago was
absolutely astounding. "I should see how everything's
going in the kitchen. Be back in a minute."

"My guess is," said Paige teasingly, "they'll stop you
at the door, refill the pot, and send you off before you can
do any damage in there." She laughed as she glanced out
the window. "Where are Kalea, Serena, and Zach? It
smells like dinner will be ready soon, so shouldn't they
be here by now?"

"I haven't heard from my cousin since yesterday, and
she swore she'd be here in time. As for Serena, who
knows. She's been so off in la-la land lately, she most
likely forgot today was even Thanksgiving," Addie said
with a laugh as she grabbed the empty coffee carafe from
the warmer on the coffee table and headed down the hallway toward the kitchen. She paused at the dining room
entrance when she heard Emma's small voice.

"See, Pippi, it fits. Now stop wiggling while I get your
jammies snapped up."

Pippi's small head peered out from beneath the bottom
hem of the tablecloth. Addie's hand shot to her mouth to
stop the laugh bubbling up from her chest at the sight of
Pippi sporting a frilly baby bonnet.

"You come back here," squealed Emma gleefully.
"We're not finished," she cried, tugging Pippi back under
the table.

Addie, chuckling, shook her head and stuck her nose into the kitchen. "Mmm, it smells delightful in here, and I know a few people in the living room who are ready to eat soon." She strolled over to the island and set the coffee carafe down beside an assortment of the foil-covered dishes her guests had brought. She made a beeline for the oven, tipped the door open, and drew in a deep whiff.

"Unless you're going to baste it, keep the door closed, or we won't be eating until midnight," Catherine teased her and thrust a glass turkey baster into Addie's hand.

"Okay, okay, but I am much more competent than you think, and I can help out more in here than doing just this." Addie filled the tube and squirted it over the slowly browning turkey skin. A chorus of laughter broke out behind her, and her searching gaze flitted from Catherine to Simon to Felix and paused on Martha. "I am really."

Martha *harrumphed* and turned back to the mashed potatoes she was scraping into a serving bowl. Catherine giggled and resumed setting out other serving bowls to be filled, and Simon's shoulders shook so hard he nearly tipped over. His snickers echoed through the room.

"I trust you are, my dear," said Felix, his gunmetal-blue eyes sparkling as he toyed with a dish towel he was polishing the wine glasses with. "However, as you can see, we have it all under control in here."

"But you're all guests, and this doesn't seem right. I mean everyone brought the side dishes and the only thing I've supplied for our dinner was buying the turkey. Then you wouldn't even let me cook it." Addie scanned each of their faces, looking for sympathy or moral support from her friends that never came.

"What doesn't seem right is that your guests in the front room don't have their hostess present. Now scoot.

Refill the coffee and go back and do what you do so well. Be the perfect hostess." Catherine, with a gleam in her eyes, shooed her away.

"But I can cook. Really, I can."

Deathly silence fell over the room only to be broken by a banging on the front door.

"See," choked out Simon. "Your services are required out front. I suggest you go see who's here."

Addie spun on her heel and marched down the hall. "I *can* cook you know," she called back over her shoulder.

Once again echoes of laughter followed her.

She flung the door open and was greeted by a squall of snowflakes whirling into the foyer. "Kalea! You made it!" She seized the handle of her cousin's suitcase, tugged her and it through the door, and slammed it shut, keeping out the blustery weather raging outside.

"No thanks to my driver who nearly put us in the ditch on the interstate at least a dozen times," she said, brushing the snow from her cashmere coat.

"Your driver?" Addie pulled back the curtain on the side window and peeked out, catching a glimpse of two red taillights through the flurry of snow. "You should have invited him to stay for dinner. It is Thanksgiving after all."

"He's fine," Kalea said, waving off her concern. "He has a niece or something in the area, and he's going there for dinner."

"Okay, good. I hate to see anyone alone for the holidays."

"Here, give my sleeve a tug. This coat is so fitted . . ."

"Is this new?" Addie assisted her cousin with removing her coat and hung it on the coat rack behind the door.

"Yes," said Kalea, finger-fluffing her hair by the

gilded mirror over the side table. "I got it at the most marvelous couture shop in Boston."

"It's very nice," Addie said, smoothing her hand over the soft fabric and turned to her cousin. "Well, come in, come in. I can't wait to hear what's been going on this past week. You were so cryptic and secretive in your texts."

"I'd love to, but I really have to get upstairs and pack."

"You mean unpack."

"No, I mean *pack*. Tomorrow I have a company coming to pack up my apartment. I just couldn't bear to do it myself." She gave her reflection in the mirror a satisfied nod and faced Addie, who stared blankly at her.

"I'm moving into Jared's—*my*—penthouse condo in Boston. Isn't that fantastic?" She excitedly clapped her hands and giggled.

"What about your dress shop?"

"You won't believe everything I have to tell you." Kalea grasped the handle of her suitcase and rolled it toward the stairs. "But first let me get sorted out upstairs."

"No," Addie said, crossing her arms. "First, you will have Thanksgiving dinner and tell me what's going on. After what I went through to clear you of a murder charge, I think you, at least, owe me that much."

Kalea hesitated. "You're right," she said, leaving the bag at the bottom of the stairs. "I guess there's no rush tonight. I'm just so excited about what's transpired this week. I got carried away with wanting it all done now. You're also right about owing you more than a rushed explanation. You nearly died proving who the real killer was."

"I'm not tallying any scores, but yes. You do owe me something, and, yes, it was a rough one." Addie shivered.

"Who knew that someone could be so desperate to gain acceptance and approval that she'd actually steal and kill to be part of a family circle?"

Kalea's gaze dropped. "I felt that way after my mom died." She met Addie's gaze. "That was part of the reason I eventually came to find you."

"It was?"

"Yeah, I wouldn't have killed though, but I was desperate for a family connection."

"Aw, come here." Addie held out her arms and hugged her cousin tight. "I was, too, so I guess that's why I put up with all your nonsense for as long as I did." Addie smiled weakly as she brushed away a tear. "We're all the family we have left."

Kalea swiped at her own tears. "Oh no! Look what you've gone and done now." She stared at her reflection in the mirror. "My mascara's running."

"You're as beautiful as ever. Come on, let's go in, and you can tell us all your big news."

Kalea shored herself up, fluffed her hair, and followed Addie into the living room.

"Hi, Miss Kalea." Bill waved and resumed moving his chess piece on the board.

Kalea glanced around the room and leaned into Addie. Dropping her voice, she whispered through lips that barely moved, "This is quite the collection of guests you have here." She smiled a strained greeting at Nick.

"There's always room at my table for anyone who needs to be part of a family." Addie grinned and scanned the faces of her friends, old and new. "Now, can I get you a coffee while we wait for the others to finish performing their magic in the kitchen?"

"No, I'm good, thanks," Kalea said, dropping into the only empty seat in the room, on the sofa between Nick and Bill.

"Okay, I'll go get the carafe and be right back." Addie spun around on her heel and thudded into Simon.

"Whoa," he cried, dancing backward, propelling the carafe upward out of the way.

Addie patted her thudding chest and laughed. "You should see the look on your face."

"I didn't want to see the look on your face when a pot of hot coffee went flying." He chuckled and set it down on the warmer on the coffee table. "I thought I'd save you a trip back for it, but I see now, I should have just let it be."

"That was thoughtful of you, thank you."

"I'm thinking your gesture had more to do with keeping her out of the kitchen, right?" chirped Paige, a sly grin on her face.

"Right," said Simon, "and I drew the short straw for which one of us was going to bring it out for her to stop her from going back in there." He disappeared through the double-wide doorway, the sounds of his laughter trailing behind him.

Paige tsked as she refilled her cup. "I told you that your help wouldn't be appreciated in there."

"I can cook, you know."

Kalea and Paige glanced over at each other and simultaneously rolled their eyes.

Addie sputtered and opened her mouth to protest but was interrupted by a rapping at the front door.

"It's Serena and Zach," cried Paige, peering out the window. "I think everyone's here now, so I hope that means dinner will be ready soon because I'm starving."

Addie opened the door and stepped aside to allow her last guests entry into the foyer. She quickly closed the door to keep out the swirling blast of cold and snow.

"It smells soooo good in here," said Zach, stomping the snow off his boots.

"Here, let me take your jackets." Addie hung their jackets on the last peg. "I was getting worried. Is everything okay?" She glanced at Serena.

"Yes, fine. I had the historical society magazine photo shoot all day."

"That was today? But it's a holiday!"

"I know," said Serena, removing her boots and placing them on a rubber shoe mat behind the door. "Gwendolyn wanted the photographers to do it on a day the tea shop was closed so they could "stage" the set." She hooked her fingers in air quotes. "We both know that what Gwendolyn wants, Gwendolyn gets. But to be honest, it's been a long day, and I could really use a nap right about now."

"Hang in there," Addie said, placing her hand reassuringly on Serena's arm. "Dinner shouldn't be much longer and then . . ." She glanced at Zach and Serena's empty hands. "Didn't you bring your award-winning, traditional, spiced-pumpkin pudding dish for us to try tonight?"

Zach grimaced and glanced sheepishly from Serena to Addie. "That's another reason why we're running late." His voice faltered.

Addie glanced at Serena.

Serena drew in a deep breath. "Let's just say that on our way to the car, there was a slippery sidewalk—and a whole tray of mini pumpkins filled with pudding that got splattered on it." She gazed up at Zach, giving him a weak, supportive smile.

"Aw." Addie's hand flew to her chest. "Well, don't

worry. We have plenty of food, including a dessert or two that your main rivals in the competition brought. I'm just glad it was the pumpkins and not you that ended up splattered across the sidewalk." Addie gestured to the living room door. "Come in. Most of us are in the living room, and the rest are finishing up in the kitchen."

"Yeah," piped in Paige with a chuckle, "but only those who can cook are allowed back there. So Miss *First Place*, Make it - Bake it competition winner, you might like to join the group in the kitchen."

"If I can have your attention," Simon hollered from the doorway and glanced at Serena and Zach. "Since everyone is here now, we can take our seats in the dining room, if you please." He stood back, motioning a sweep with his hand.

"I hope we weren't holding you up," Serena said as she passed him.

"Not at all, but perfect timing as the turkey just came out."

Addie stood on the other side of the double-wide doors and waited for her guests to file down the hallway and enter the dining room. As Paige passed through, Simon whispered something to her, and she conspicuously hung back, feigning straightening the antique catalogues on the table. Addie hesitated and waited for her assistant.

"You go ahead," Paige said. "I'll just tidy up here for a moment."

Addie glanced over at Simon, who merely shrugged.

"Yes," he said, meeting Addie's bewildered gaze. "You go ahead. I have to get back to the kitchen to help serve the food."

"Okay." Addie glanced skeptically from a not-so-innocent-looking Paige to an equally as guilt-ridden Simon and trudged toward the dining room.

Chapter 33

At the dining room door, Addie paused and glanced back just as Simon produced a small blue box from his blazer pocket, flipped it open, and held it out to Paige as the two stood in the living room doorway. The look in her assistant's eyes flashed from wide-eyed incomprehension to one of smiling approval. Simon grinned, flicked the box closed, shoved it back into his pocket, and whispered something to Paige that Addie couldn't make out.

Addie darted around the door frame just as Simon turned and strolled past, grinning like a cat savoring his latest hunt, but when Paige came around the corner into the dining room, Addie grabbed her blouse sleeve. "What was that all about?"

"Addie, you scared the bejeezus out of me!"

"What was in the box Simon showed you?"

Paige glanced away and tugged her arm free.

"Paige!" Addie whispered. "You have to tell me."

"I can't. He swore me to secrecy."

Addie glanced over at the table where her guests were chatting and settling in for dinner. "I mean it, Paige. If it's what I think it is, I have a right to know."

Paige grimaced, gnashing her teeth together. "It's not," she said quickly, "so don't get your hopes up."

Addie's chest deflated as though someone had punched her in the stomach, and she wasn't sure she'd be able to catch her breath. "It's not a ring?"

Paige shook her head. "No, it is your Christmas present though, and I think you're going to like them," Paige said, sounding hopeful. "It's—"

"No." Addie waved her hand. "Don't tell me. I'll look forward to *that* surprise. This one"—she took a deep breath—"I'm not sure about . . . just give me a minute . . ."

"Did you really want a ring for Christmas?" Paige whispered, staring up at her. "I mean, really? You said before that you haven't even told him you love him yet."

What Addie really wanted to blurt out was . . . *"Yes, of course I wanted a ring for Christmas. I really do love him and want to marry him."*

What Addie said instead was . . . "I know I haven't said those three little words, but he knows how I feel about him."

"If that's the case"—Paige leaned closer, her eyes on the table—"then perhaps he also knows you're not ready yet. Are you?"

"I don't know. I thought I was . . . well, ever since Serena and I saw him coming out of the jewelry store, but that's when I thought he must be ready, too, but I guess if he's not, then . . ."

"My suggestion is the two of you sit down and talk about how you see your future. That's the only way you're going to get on the same page with any of this, right?"

"You're right, but I can't think about it right now." Addie stretched out her rigid shoulders and glanced over at her guests.

"Are you coming, Mommy?" Emma asked from her seat beside Martha.

"Let's go eat." Addie cemented a smile on her face as she took her seat at the end of the long table and wished she felt as cheerful as her friends appeared to be.

She wasn't sure why Paige's news had such an impact on her as she manufactured a level of merriment with her guests and friends, but it did. However, Paige was right. She and Simon would have to have a real heart-to-heart. It was time they figured out if they had a future together. As hard as it was going to be, she was going to have to let him know she had finally come to terms with the fact that he wouldn't die if she told him how she felt, and that she was ready to make a commitment that a ring would bring with it. Talking about her feelings hadn't been easy since David, but it was time.

She flicked out her napkin with a little more force than intended, bringing a curious glance from Simon, who was seated at the far end of the table. She smiled weakly at him, dropped her gaze and placed it ladylike across her lap wishing it was a leap year. According to an old Irish legend, women were allowed to propose to men every four years. Yes, a leap year was exactly what she needed, or . . . a spine and the courage to just blurt out a proposal herself.

At least then, she wouldn't have to bear her soul to him in an actual conversation about *feelings*. She could simply ask him to marry her without dredging up her painful memories—which, of course, also meant he was right not to give her a ring now. If she couldn't talk about it and still changed the subject any time he tried to, clearly, she wasn't ready to completely move forward. She took a sip from her water glass. Yes, her not receiving a ring this Christmas was for the best. It seemed he knew it better than she did.

On the other hand . . . she gazed down the long table toward him. If she could only catch his eye, in spite of all the excited chatter going on around him, because as they say—the eyes are the window to the soul—and maybe if he looked into hers now, then he'd know for sure what she felt in her heart, and that a ring this Christmas would be perfect.

Unfortunately for Addie, at the precise moment, she was mentally wrestling with her mixed emotions. Felix shuffled through the door closest to the kitchen, carrying a serving platter containing the most perfectly roasted turkey Addie had ever seen. He was greeted by excited oohs and aahs as he set it on the table in front of Simon, who was already prepped with a large knife and fork and ready to commence with surgeon-like precision carving of the massive bird.

"If I could have a moment before we get started." Felix tapped a fork on his water goblet as his silver-haired head bobbed back and forth commanding attention from one guest to the other. "I would like to make an announcement and propose a toast." He raised his glass and glanced at Serena. He lowered his hand. "Is your brother not joining us this evening?"

"No." She glanced fleetingly, almost apologetically, at Addie and then back at Felix. "He decided it best to work this evening so more of his officers could have the night off to be with their friends and family."

"Good for him, and I'm happy that his officers get to spend the evening with their loved ones as it should be." He winked at Catherine and raised his glass once more. "First, I will begin by saying that I am truly honored to be here this evening in such delightful company." He grinned down at a blushing Catherine. "Secondly, may this gathering be the start of my bright future here in Greyborne Harbor."

Stunned, Addie stared at him. What did he mean? She could tell by the silence around the table that she wasn't the only one confused.

"Are you moving here?" asked Catherine, her tone as bewildered as the expression on her face.

"Yes." He glanced at Zach and then down at her. "I recently have left Zach's father's employment, and, with the help of Hollingsworth Realty, I've purchased a fine home up on the hill not far from here."

"Well . . . I'll be." A grin crept across Catherine's face. "That is something to celebrate, isn't it?" She glanced disbelievingly at Addie and then raised her glass.

"Wait!" cried Kalea, jumping to her feet. "Since we're toasting big changes in people's lives, I'd like to announce mine."

All eyes were on her in anticipation.

"With the blessings of the board of directors, I've accepted a purchase offer on Jared's investment firm, and the group that's going to buy it wants to take Hudson's Creations coast to coast. They love my designs and ideas for expansion and will help finance the entire venture. So I'm hiring someone to run the store here while I work with my new financial advisor in Boston to get the chain up and running."

Martha sputtered something incoherent.

"What's the matter, Grandma?" asked Emma, her little voice quivering on the verge of tears. "Does that mean I can't get a puppy of my very own for Christmas?" She sniffled.

Martha didn't say a word as she lowered the glass that she'd held high for the toasts. Her faded-blue eyes reddened as she stared despondently across the table at Kalea.

Addie's grasp tightened around the water glass she held high, and she glanced at her empty wine glass, wishing it was filled. "But what about the dress I ordered?"

Kalea glanced at Paige then at Addie. "No worries. I found the perfect fabric in Boston and have completed the design. It will ready by Christmas," she winked.

Addie nodded her gratitude and slunk back in her chair. However, between discovering there would be no ring from Simon this Christmas, Catherine finally finding a man who wasn't running around half the world saving it—from who knows what—and now Kalea's news, she really didn't know if she could take any more surprises or shocks tonight. Instinctively, she reached under the table, searching for Pippi's cold wet nose on her hand . . . and there it was. She sighed with the knowledge that at least one thing hadn't changed in her life.

Serena quietly rose to her feet amidst the celebratory congratulations for Felix and Kalea's news and pinged a spoon on her water glass. "Since we're making announcements"—she glanced down at Zach urging him to stand up—which Addie noticed as she filled her wine glass, he did begrudgingly—she knew he detested being the center of any attention—"Zach and I also have an announcement to make."

The room fell eerily silent. Even Emma ceased her tear-filled pleas to her grandmother as to why she should be allowed to get a puppy just like Pippi. Though Addie had noticed that little Emma's appeals had seemed to fall on deaf ears since Kalea's announcement, and even now with Serena fully commanding the floor. Martha's attention had never wavered from blankly staring across the table. Perhaps it was the realization that the person she had befriended and then treated better than her own daughters was going to be leaving town that caused the tears to form in the corners of Martha's eyes. But judging by the radiant smile on Serena's face, Addie couldn't think about that now.

"You're not . . ." Addie shot to her feet, bumping against the table and knocking over her wine glass as she gaped at Serena's tummy.

"Happy Thanksgiving everyone," squealed Serena raising her water glass. "We're pregnant!"

Addie exchanged a knowing look with Paige and then scanned the other grinning faces around the table. The announcement seemed to have taken everyone else by surprise. Except of course Simon, and there her gaze paused. She'd finally caught his eye. He held his glass high in honor of the news, and nodded at Addie. Overwhelmed by all the unexpected announcements of the evening and the surge of jumbled emotions coursing through her, she picked up her water goblet with an unsteady hand and returned his gesture of a toast. Holding his gaze, she willed him to look deep into her eyes, in the hope he would see her true feelings for him behind the mask she knew she too often wore.